Trans-Light-Element

"The Finnish Connection"

by

Michael Irvin Bosley

Michael Irvin Bosley

Trans-Light-Element

"The Finnish Connection"

Promised Harbour Publications

ISBN-13: 978-0-692-99762-8

Library of Congress Control Number: 2017963655

Printed in the United States of America

Trans-Light-Element

the Adventure Series

is dedicated to the memory
of my parents,

Talmadge Oliver Bosley & Doris Olivia Houser

Their devotion was the hallmark
of our childhood years.

This episode, entitled,

"The Finnish Connection"

is dedicated to my Finnish Friends
whose brave ancestors forged a great nation
from a cold land of harsh realities. It is a pleasing poetic
coincidence this episode is finally released for publication
in the Year 2017, the 100th anniversary of Finland's
National Independence.

Never ending gratitude and credit goes to my eternal
companion and best friend

Edna Bosley

Our children, grandchildren, extended family and many
friends have contributed inspiration, suggestions, and ideas
often unwittingly – nevertheless valuable and significant.

Front Cover Image Photo

Historic wilderness winter cache on a pole; on display at Seurasaari Island Open Air Museum, Helsinki, Finland. The Author captured this photograph during a return visit to Finland in June 2017.

Author Introduction

Michael Irvin Bosley was born in Wyoming, grew up in Texas, and gained a deep abiding love and appreciation for the Finnish people while living in Finland as a young man between the age of 20 and 22. Mike is a 9th generation descendant of Walter Bosley who was born in Staffordshire, England about 1660 and came to Baltimore about 1690. Mike loves genealogy and is working to discover more historical data about his ancestors.

Mike also loves science. He has a Bachelor of Science in Computer Information Systems and a Master of Science in Space Systems Operations. Twenty plus years with the Air Force instilled essential life lessons. Retired from active duty, he continues to work as a professional consultant and technical advisor, writer, and publisher.

Mike is devoted to his wife, Edna, and their five grown children, and several grandchildren. His personal hobbies include photography, astronomy, gardening, craft shop, model trains, a keen pursuit of history, science, and a quest for the unknown. He enjoys visiting national parks, monuments, museums, old sailing ships and other places with nautical themes. He appreciates a good movie as well as a good book. To him, adventure is a by-product of learning – education is a gift to be shared and enlarged upon daily.

Table of Contents

Introduction

In Episode One, entitled *"The Open Door"*, Benjamin Reuel is instrumental in saving his father from an accidental encounter with a unified energy field vortex. In the process of trying to unravel the mysterious effects of Dr. Reuel's experiment, they discover a new universal substance which Ben names "Trans-Light-Element" (T-L-E, for short). Meanwhile, international corporate spies have pinpointed the epicenter of the unified field event and marked the Reuel family residence as a target of espionage. As if that were not enough, Ben's little brother, Joseph, has been diagnosed with a rare form of cancer. Mark Leppänen, who is a member of the Finnish Council of State, and an old friend of Dr. Reuel's, pays an unexpected visit and offers the Reuel family a safe haven in Finland where they can continue vital research in seclusion.

With help from Trevor Nibley, another old friend whom Dr. Reuel has engaged to protect his family and secure his research – the Reuel Family speeds across the Arctic Circle in a brand new Nibley Corporation prototype high altitude hydrogen powered jet to their secret sanctuary in Finland where they have also engaged a renowned cancer treatment specialist to help find a cure for young Joseph.

Ben and his father must race against time to solve the mysteries of T-L-E before conspiring enemies steal the secret unified field containment ratio and turn the world upside down. Join the Reuel family as their new Finnish friends help them get acquainted with the land and culture of Finland in this second Trans-Light-Element adventure – entitled,

"The Finnish Connection"

Helsinki Senate Building from Upinski Cathedral

Upinski Cathedral

Images photographed by and belong to the Author

Michael Irvin Bosley

Chapter 1
Wake Up!

Ben struggled to catch up to his sister. He and Vanessa were running to catch a bus on a busy city street in Helsinki, Finland. Just as Vanessa reached the bus stop ahead of him, a hand reached out from behind a recessed doorway to a flower shop and grabbed Ben's arm. Ben looked down at the hand pinching his elbow in a vice like grip. With sudden alarm, he looked up into the startling cold eyes of Carl Ungman!

Ben struggled to get away as he watched Vanessa board the bus and sit down unaware of the drama unfolding behind her. She did not even look out the window as the bus went on without him. Ungman waved a pistol in his other hand to motion Ben through the doorway into the shop.

Inside, Ben walked by rows of fresh flowers but all he could smell was ozone from torsion generators at full power. Looking around the flower shop, Ben searched in vain for his father's Unified Field Array.

Ungman prodded Ben impatiently through the back door into the alley. As Ben looked frantically up and down the alley, he found, to his dismay, they were alone.

Ungman demanded, "Where is your father? Where are his secret formulas?"

Ben laughed and said, "You will never get them."

Ungman cracked a scary smile and reached over to pull a breaker switch on the side of the building. The smell of ozone intensified and the side of the building became a chaotic churning mass. It seemed the very foundation of all existence was being ripped apart by the violent power of the three primary universal energy fields now forced upon each other; not able to achieve unity without his father's precise containment ratio, bucking in and out of phase like a wild bronco violently tossing all unwanted riders.

Ben watched as Ungman picked up a garbage can from the behind the flower shop and tossed it through the vortex in the brick wall. Then turning back to face Ben, Ungman said, "We know how to get this far – what we don't know is how you stabilized the vortex. Give me the containment ratio, or you will be next!"

Ben turned and ran down the alley as fast as he could, but somehow Ungman was faster. He felt a rough grasp on his shoulders dragging him back. Ben struggled with all his might to get away – but Ungman pushed him perilously towards the churning TLE wall.

From the distance, Ben heard a voice calling him, "Ben, wake up! We are here! The plane has landed."

Chapter 2
Where is My Watch?

Ben awoke with a start. He could not say how long he had been sleeping. His haunting dream riveted his fear even as direct memory of details began to recede from his conscious thoughts. Ben glanced over at his brother, Joseph, who was staring back at him from his seat across the aisle. Vanessa was on the other side of Joseph – still sound asleep. Then he recalled hearing Joseph's voice in his dream… "Ben, wake-up! The plane is landing."

Ben felt the small Hydrogen Heavy airframe rumble and heard the screech of wheels touching the runway. Raising his window cover, he eagerly took in his first view of Finland. Bright morning sunlight reflected off the runway as the plane vibrated across the tarmac. Vanessa awoke and raised her window cover. Ben could hear Mom and Dad talking from their seats two rows in front… but it was too low to understand their words.

Ben checked his watch. It was still on Denver time, – 6:57 pm. The trip across Canada and the North Atlantic had only taken 7 hours. He marveled at the speed of the new Nibley corporate passenger aircraft. Routine direct flights still took 11 hours and 57 minutes. He told himself, "I can't wait to ride the new trans-continental Hydrogen Heavy Sub-Orbital. Just think – any place on the planet within a half hour!"

Joseph asked, "Ben, when will we be at the Leppänen's?"

Ben answered, "I don't know. We will have to ask Dad."

Glancing outside through the window on his side of the plane, Ben said, "It looks pretty green outside. From the position of the sun, I would guess it is about 6am. Let me think. It is 7 pm in Denver. Helsinki is 9 hours ahead; so, that would make it already Sunday morning, and – Wow! It is only 4 am in the morning here – but the sun is already up!" Ben reset his watch.

Vanessa replied, "That is because we are at 60 degrees North Latitude – approaching the longest day of the year – the summer solstice. The sun rose here this morning at 3:13 am. Just a few hundred kilometers north of here is Lapland, the land of the Midnight Sun."

Ben asked, "Where did you learn that?"

Vanessa answered, "…from this book the Flight Attendant gave me; 'Finland, Jewell of the Baltic'… I finished it an hour before we landed."

Ben asked, "Can I read it?"

Vanessa gave him the book, "Sure. Only don't crinkle the dust cover or mess up the pages – and don't lose it." Her stern big sister glare captured Ben's gaze.

"Oh, I won't. Does it talk about where we are going to be living?"

"Not specifically, but it gives a general description of Finland and a short history."

Ben thumbed through the publication with fascination. It was full of maps, charts and glossy photographs. He slid it carefully inside his back pack, zipping the side flap closed.

The Flight Attendant's voice sounded overhead, "The plane has come to a rest. You may remove your seatbelts and disembark."

The clicking sound of un-latching seatbelts releasing eager passengers filled the plane for a few seconds. Ben stood up and shouldered his pack before removing Joseph's out of the overhead bin. He waited as Vanessa unbuckled Joseph and followed him into the aisle to pull her own backpack from the overhead bin. Ben followed them both up the aisle behind their parents.

The Nibley corporate flight crew was busy preparing the plane for the return trip home. Gamiel remarked to Rachel, "This crew gets a short stay in Helsinki today to catch up on their rest – and right back in the air tonight in time to be home Monday morning."

The Reuel Family stopped at the exit to thank the flight crew who had all worked an extra unplanned shift to make this flight possible. Rachel took the hand of the Chief Flight Attendant, and said, "You don't know how much this means to us! Thank you! Thank you!"

Joseph grabbed his mother's leg and hugged it. Mrs. Reuel smiled down at her son, relieved they were all safe on the ground again – feeling remotely hidden from the evil clutches of their enemies.

Soon they would meet Dr. Mäkkinen and begin Joseph's treatments. Looking into her youngest son's eyes, Rachel Reuel reflected on how relieved she would feel once again to get Joseph well and her family back home. For now, however, she was determined to enjoy this enforced family get-away. "…some vacation," she mused to herself.

Portable boarding stairs rolled up to the exit hatch as the flight attendant opened the door. Rachel led her children out of the plane onto the top of the stairway.

Gamiel followed his family out the exit, carrying Rachel's luggage as well as his own backpack. The Reuel Family had traveled very light this trip. He reflected upon the unexpected changes that had occurred in his family in just one short week. He thought to himself, "A lot can happen in a week."

As Gamiel joined his family standing just outside the passenger exit, he saw a black Mercedes Limousine, flying the Finnish national and ministerial flags, pulling up at the base of the stairs. A familiar tall blonde haired man in a dark blue suit emerged from the passenger compartment. Gamiel waved at his friend, Mark Leppänen, who waved back.

Mark greeted them eagerly, "Hyvä päivä! Toivottaa tervetulleeksi Suomeen!"

Joseph looked at Vanessa, and asked, "What did he say?"

Vanessa smirked and replied, "You think because I read one book about Finland I can understand that?"

Gamiel answered, "Mark just said, 'Good day! Welcome to Finland!' Everyone wave and say, 'Kiitos! Hyvä päivä!'"

The Reuel Family waved as they clambered quickly down the stairs. The sounds that came out of their mouths did not sound anything like the Finnish words Gamiel spoke. Mark smiled with fond amusement at their willingness to try.

The Reuels loaded their luggage in the trunk and began loading themselves into the spacious passenger compartment – two seats facing each other.

Gamiel stopped outside beside Mark and shook his hand, and said, "We can never repay you for your help."

Ben stood behind his Dad, surprised to see a diplomat blush.

Mark said, "Gamiel, there is no debt between friends."

It was Gamiel's turn to choke up as he quickly turned to enter the car. Ben followed and buckled up.

Mark got in last and motioned to the driver in the front seat to proceed.

Conversation was excited. The new sights and sounds, Mark's presence in the car, the strange language – all combined to immerse the Reuel Family into a completely Finnish environment.

Mark said, "You must come to our Feast of St John the Baptist in three weeks. It is when our people celebrate the birth of John, the Forerunner of Christ. It also coincides with an ancient pagan summer solstice ritual regarding the longest day of the year. Swedish speakers still call it Midsummer. In Suomi (Finnish), we call it 'Juhannus Päivä' (Yu' hah noose Pie - Vä <short 'a' as in Cat>). The entire country turns out to go to lakeside cabins or back home to parents; or just go somewhere to get in touch with nature. Even those who must remain in the towns and cities enjoy relative peace and quiet because everyone else is gone. I usually have all of my relatives and my wife's relatives over to our bonfire by the lake on my property."

Ben looked out on the silent streets of Helsinki, Finland, just waking up to a Sunday morning, finding it hard to imagine how busy they could be. He wondered whether it would be more fun to join the noisy crowds by the bonfires or just walk the quiet city streets.

Mark continued with a twinkle in his eyes, "Over the centuries, Juhannus Päivä has become a national holiday with traditional festivities marked by music, dancing, food, and a ceremonial bonfire ignited by a ceremonial torch carried in the hands of the honorary bride and groom just married earlier that day and pre-selected to preside over the festival."

Vanessa was enthralled by the enchantment. Joseph simply took everything in as he watched the scenery pass by the window where he sat.

Mark added, "Midsummer, or Juhannus Päivä, is also our national Flag Day. The flag remains at full staff all through what is called the "white night" until it is taken down at 9 pm the following day."

Mrs. Reuel said, "How fascinating. We very much look forward to participating in your celebration."

Gamiel was pleased with Rachel's forward engaging mode. That meant the family would be getting settled down soon – and he wouldn't have to worry about a homesick spouse.

The talented chauffer handled the large government limo with enviable skill as it cruised from the airport along a thoroughfare with street signs in both Swedish and Finnish. Ben tried to pronounce the Finnish name - 'Lahdenväylä'.

Mark pulled a paper map from the back pocket of the driver's seat. "See, we are now here, and we are going here. We will proceed north on the Lahti Freeway to a point north east of Lahti, then turn northwest towards my home near the small village of 'Asikkala' <Ah' C Kah Lah> situated on this narrow neck of land between two lakes. Asikkala was founded in 1848. It is a small little village about 25 km from Lahti, 125 km from Helsinki, variable tree covered terrain altitude between 78 and 160 meters above sea level. A key point of interest while you are visiting will be the Vääksy <Vack Sue> canal."

All members of the Reuel family leaned over to view the map together as Mark pointed to the names on the map, and said, "These are Finnish names. The letter 'ä' with the two little dots above it is different from the letter 'a' – and, it is pronounced like your short 'a' in the word – '**cat**' just like in my name – Lepp' ä nen.

Ben felt a keen interest in the Finnish language. He listened to every word as Mark continued, "See the Finnish word for lake is 'järvi'. South of the narrow isthmus of Asikkala – you see the word 'Vesijärvi' <Vessie Yärvi> and north of Asikkala you see the word 'Päijännejärvi' <PieYAnnie Yärvi>."

Pointing to a word on the map just north of 'Asikkala', Mark said, "This part of lake 'Päijänne' is called 'Asikkalanselkä' <Ah' C Kah lawn – sell' kä>. When we talk in Finnish, the accent always falls on the first syllable of every word. If you think you hear two accents in a single word – it is because some of our words are actually two or more little words combined – like A'sikkalan-sel'kä. The Finnish word 'selkä' means 'back' but when used in this context it also means 'open', and, refers to the open back waters of Lake Päijänne adjacent to the village of Asikkala."

Rachel asked, "I see a lot of lakes on this map. How many lakes do you have in Finland?

Mark answered, "Finland has been referred to as the land of a thousand lakes. However, our latest count tabulates 55,000 lakes at least 200 meters wide; and 188 thousand bodies of standing water larger than 500 square meters."

Rachel nodded, and said, "Wow."

Mark added, "Lake Päijänne is the second largest lake in Finland. It is also the deepest – 95.3 m or 313 ft. Water from Päijännejärvi naturally drains through the Kymi River into the Gulf of Finland."

Vanessa asked, "Have you lived here long?"

Mark said, "I was born in Asikkala not long after my father purchased our family estate on the shores of Lake Päijänne and moved my mother there. I have known no other home."

Rachel said, "We are very grateful to you for inviting us to your home under such imposing circumstances."

Mark quickly answered, "Mrs. Reuel, you and your family are no imposition whatsoever! We are excited about having you as our guests."

Gamiel looked out the window and swallowed to keep from choking up.

Vanessa noted her father's reaction and listened attentively to Mark, entranced by his manners and accent. Finland had captured her heart and fired her imagination. Initial resentment towards her father melted before the love she could see existed between Gamiel and Mark.

Gamiel asked, "Mark, has Trevor been in touch with you?"

"Yes. In the time you were rocketing over the top of the planet to our fair land, Nibley Security has been tracking your friend, Carl Ungman. He was sighted two hours ago traveling under false papers boarding a flight for Munich. That is his base of operations."

Ben asked, "What does he do?"

Mark answered, "He is an international corporate spy. He has connections with German nationals who are conducting similar experiments as your father."

Gamiel asked, "So, who is paying for his services?"

Mark said, "Funding for his operation comes from a loose confederation of scientists and businessmen who are shareholders in a London Corporation with strong ties to several American investors."

Vanessa chimed in, "Do we know who these American investors are? What is the name of the London company?"

Mark looked at her with an amused smile, and said, "I don't remember the names of the American investors, but, the company does business as Imperial Planet, Inc."

Gamiel asked, "Do they have an office in Finland?"

Mark answered, "We have identified two businessmen in Finland with ties to this company. We are watching them very closely."

Gamiel asked with concern, "Is it possible they know we are here?"

Mark shrugged his shoulders, and said, "I don't see how they could. Trevor did not file a flight plan – his hydrogen powered plane flies so high, he virtually owns the skies at that altitude. The President granted the Nibley corporate jet diplomatic privilege so it could make an unscheduled landing."

Gamiel nodded and dismissed immediate concerns. His thoughts moved to Joseph's medical needs, "When do we meet Dr. Mäkkinen?"

"Tomorrow afternoon at 2 pm; his offices are in Lahti."

Mrs. Reuel asked, "How long before we arrive at your home this morning?"

Mark answered, "A little more than an hour from here."

Vanessa said, "Great – that will give us time to get a shower and rest. I am beat."

Mark laughed, and said, "Jet lag is never a fun experience for me, either. I like my rest – and sleeping on a plane has never worked for me."

Rachel said, "I look forward to stretching out in bed and catching up on lost sleep, too."

Mark said, "Your rooms are all ready, and Gamiel, the Sauna will be hot tonight."

Gamiel sighed, and said, "Sauna. I can't wait."

Joseph asked, "Daddy, what is a Saw Uhn Ah?"

Mark laughed at Joseph's correct pronunciation of the much abused Finnish word.

Gamiel explained, "Well, it is a hot room full of steam where you sit and get all sweaty until all the dirty oil in your skin can get washed away. Then you run outside and jump in the cold water to cool down really fast so the pores of your skin can close before any dirt can get back in. It relaxes your tired muscles and makes you feel great!"

Vanessa said, "It sounds a little adventurous to me. I like to cool down slowly. Doesn't that shock your heart?"

Mark laughed again, and said, "Just wait until you have had your first Sauna. You will wonder why your father has not already installed one for you in your home."

Time passed in casual conversation. An hour later, after driving through what Vanessa decided was the most enchanting urbanized country-side she had ever seen, their limo pulled up to a large gate in a stone fence.

The fence line stretched out of sight into the woods in both directions. The chauffer punched the security code that opened the gate and the car passed quietly through onto a wooded estate with a long winding road.

It took another 5 minutes meandering through the woods over sharply rising hills and back around again before Joseph spotted the house.

"Look, Ben, a big house!"

A mansion it was indeed. The Reuel Family was enthralled. Vanessa said, "I thought we were going to live in a country cottage on the lake."

Mark smiled at Gamiel. Gamiel answered, "Just wait. The lake is behind the estate. There is a great little cottage on its shores – with a wood burning Sauna."

Joseph laughed and repeated the sound of the word in his throat, "Saw Uhn Ah." Vanessa hugged her little brother.

Vanessa noted the local time was 6 a.m. as their limo pulled up under the circular drive pavilion covering the front entry way to the mansion. She found herself catching her breath at the beauty of the grounds, gardens and grassy areas manicured to perfection.

Gamiel searched the seat around him and asked, "Has anyone seen my watch?"

Rachel replied, "Did you leave it on the plane?"

"No, I took it off in the car to give my wrist a rest – and, I thought I laid it on the seat right here beside me."

Mark said, "It may have slipped between the seat cushions. I will have my valet search the car for you after it is parked."

Gamiel gave Mark a grateful look, and said, "My father gave me that watch. It is an old time piece manufactured in Geneva, Switzerland; 14 karat gold case with anti-magnetic insert and diamond movements. It keeps near perfect time; loses less than a hundredth of a second per day. It is a family heirloom."

Mark smiled reassuringly and said, "Don't worry Gamiel. We will find your watch."

Everyone got out of the car. Service personnel came out of nowhere; picking up luggage, escorting the Reuel Family to their rooms. Gamiel searched each of the house servants with his eyes, concern clearly showing.

Mark noticed the look and said, "Don't worry Gamiel. This is my personal staff. Each one has a government clearance. All they know about you is that you are my guests."

Gamiel relaxed, and said, "You are right. I am still too keyed up."

Mark spoke to all the Reuels, "Please make yourselves at home. Take a nap if you wish. All your rooms are adjacent. House Security will be around every so often just to make sure you are OK. The buffet will be kept fresh until you are ready."

Vanessa followed Rachel through the 10 foot high double door, each about 5 feet wide, hand hewn oak, between 3 & 4 inches thick, ornate time worn carvings preserved in old fashioned dark red stain.

Ben and Joseph strolled behind them into the grand reception hall.

Joseph asked, "Ben, what are all these statues for?"

Ben laughed and said, "I don't know. Some people like this kind of art. I guess Mr. Leppänen does, too."

The two brothers gazed together upon the interior scenery in amazement. To them, museum decorations were unexpected in a private dwelling.

Large neo-classic Greek pillars held up the high dome ceiling of the rotunda that covered the reception hall. Early morning sunlight streamed through crystal sky-lights to reveal curious old paintings and classic artifacts of a by-gone age.

Ben estimated the diameter of the circular hallway must have been at least 60 feet. This was clearly the central feature of the Leppänen home, intended to make a lasting impression on guests.

All the guest rooms were situated off the grand reception hall on the ground floor. Ben and Joseph shared the same room. The maid smiled at Ben as he ushered Joseph into their room. Ben said, "Let's get a shower and go get something to eat."

Joseph said, "Yeah, Vanessa says their food is weird."

With a tired sigh, Rachel entered the room reserved for her and Gamiel. Gamiel remained in the reception hall, locked in deep conversation with Mark. The servants carried Rachel's luggage into their room. Gamiel made sure everyone's luggage followed the right person into their rooms.

Vanessa stopped in the center of the hallway, looking up, entranced by the dazzling skylight and gorgeous drapes framing the windows on the outside walls. It was like stepping into a Baroque fairy tale. She wondered when it was built – and what dramas had played out under this enchanting roof.

Just as she was turning to go into her room, she saw a very young man who resembled Mr. Leppänen emerge from a grand door half-way around the circular hall. There was a hint of books on shelves stretching to the ceiling visible through the half open door. Then she noticed the new stranger had a phone in his hand.

His soft voice spoke in perfect English with the same accent as Mark. "Father, this urgent call just came in from the President – encrypted, Top Secret."

Juhannus Bonfire, Seurasaari, Helsinki 2017

Image photographed by and belongs to the Author

Chapter 3

Alexi

Mark introduced his son, "Gamiel, this is my oldest son, Alexi. Alexi, this is Dr. Gamiel Reuel and his daughter, Vanessa. The Reuels will be our house guests this summer. Gamiel, please excuse me, I was expecting this call."

Alexi smiled broadly and looked directly at Vanessa with those same alluring eyes his father once unwittingly used to sweep her off her feet. He took her hand in greeting, saying, "My pleasure."

Vanessa was unable to contain the spontaneous blush that covered her face. Gamiel witnessed the exchange and could not contain his own smile of amusement.

Mark took the phone to a private corner with a chair and table lighted by an ornate 19th century lamp. The only other items on the table top were a writing tablet and a pen. He began writing on the tablet as he spoke in Finnish.

Alexi turned and shook Gamiel's hand, saying, "Dr. Reuel, it is indeed an honor. My father has mentioned you often. He regards you highly."

Now, it was Gamiel's turn to blush; barely able to contain it with a smile and a firm handshake. Gamiel was surprised at the strength of Alexi's hands and forearms and noted his fine athletic build.

Gamiel asked, "Alexi, do you play Soccer and Ski as well as your father?"

Alexi's countenance took on a mischievous expression peculiar to Finns as he answered, "Even better."

Gamiel smiled even broader as he recognized the same competitive sportsman his father had been years ago. Alexi was nearly the spitting image of his father – with some special refinements obviously endowed from his mother.

Gamiel asked, "Is your mother here?"

Alexi said, "She is visiting her sister in Lahti this evening."

Gamiel said, "I knew your father before he married; therefore, I never met your mother. I look forward to our families becoming better acquainted. Vanessa just graduated 10th in her senior class. She hasn't decided what University she wants to attend."

Alexi looked at Vanessa and said, "I will be attending University of Helsinki next semester."

Vanessa gazed at the library doorway and asked, "Do you spend a lot of time in that room?"

Now it was Alexi's turn to blush. He answered, "Actually, I was just returning a book. My father is a collector and curator of old books. He is very strict about not leaving books lying around. He says that is how they get lost or damaged. Would you like to see the library?"

Vanessa blushed again and looked at her father.

Gamiel waved her along with a smile.

Vanessa's look said thank you. The two young adults walked casually to the library, engaged in conversation as if they had known each other for years. Gamiel turned his gaze back to his friend, Mark.

Rapid Finnish comments reached Gamiel's ears; Gamiel translating almost as quickly as Mark spoke, "…thank you President Salmo. I am sure the Reuel's will be grateful for your help. Yes… I will be sure and tell Dr. Reuel, myself. …No, we just arrived.

Yes, I will ask him. Thank you very much. We will, sir. OK. Goodbye."

Gamiel was surprised at how much he could still understand of Mark's side of the conversation. Mark terminated the call and softly laid the cordless phone upon the table.

Standing quickly he came over and said, "I apologize for keeping you – you must be dead on your feet by now."

"Not at all… I was surprised at how well I could still follow your Finnish."

"So, you do still have the gift?"

Gamiel waved off his friend's honorific and said, "A gift, perhaps, but one thing is certain; I spent too many hours in the Helsinki University Library under your grueling tutelage to just forget it. What did President Salmo want you to ask me?"

Mark looked perplexed, and said, "He expresses his regret over not being able to have your distinguished family attend a formal public state dinner with him so he can welcome you to Finland as you deserve."

Gamiel smiled and asked, "How did my family become so distinguished? I am just a small college professor; besides, no one is supposed to know I am here – least of all, why."

Mark was quick to explain, "President Salmo only knows I have asked for special diplomatic privileges for you and your family. He also knows you are a friend of Trevor's."

"And what has Trevor been doing in Finland?"

"You didn't know?"

"Please, don't keep me in suspense."

"Last year, Trevor was visiting Nibley Enterprises Finnish Office in Turku the same day President Salmo was in town on official business. Nibley

Security spotted a sniper on the Nibley Building roof and apprehended him. He was carrying a Pakistani passport with written instructions for shooting the President!"

"No!"

"Not only that, but the other documents he had on his person led to the arrest of one high ranking Finnish government official and several other foreigners who were here on education and work visas. The trial is next month, in fact. Trevor may be called to appear and testify.

Gamiel rubbed his chin and commented, "I wonder why Trevor never mentioned it?"

Mark went on, "A public scandal was barely avoided. A terrorist cell was uncovered. A few other Finns have been implicated, but they insist they knew nothing and have hired expensive lawyers. Some of our outspoken political parties have begun calling for tighter immigration controls. As you know, Finland practically has an open border policy when it comes to accepting people from other countries. Most come here because we have free tuition; and, because we have one of the strongest economies in Europe with good employment."

Gamiel commented, "Finland is a generous country. I am surprised more people have not flocked to your doors looking for opportunity. I know I would."

Mark replied, "There are many in Finland who are beginning to express concerns that our country will soon be overrun."

Gamiel asked, "And what of your own safety, my friend?"

Mark recognized his expression and quickly followed, "Do not worry, Gamiel. Everyone on my staff is loyal to me as well as our country."

Gamiel looked his friend deep in the eyes, and said, "We both know all it takes is one whose loyalty comes with a price."

Mark nodded, and replied, "Finns still enjoy the highest standard of public integrity in the world. If I cannot trust my own countrymen – especially my friends, then none of this is worth the trouble – wouldn't you agree, Gamiel?"

Gamiel stared at a new side of his old friend in awe. After a moment's reflection, he nodded and asked, "So, President Salmo knows me as a friend of Trevor's?"

"Yes. He also remembers you as a young attaché from the U.S. Embassy when you were here before. You may recall we escorted him and his family during the international conference?"

Gamiel retrieved a memory he had not touched for some time. A smile of recognition covered his face. "Yes, it comes back to me now. He had three little girls; his wife was a special envoy to the U. S. Ambassador and he was serving on a cabinet post.

A look of cloudy consternation crossed Mark's face.

Gamiel asked, "What's wrong?"

Mark continued, "He has invited himself to my private bonfire celebration of the Feast of St John."

"What's wrong with that?

"I don't want his Security Staff all over my grounds. To be frank, I can't control them. Depending on how far along you get with your new laboratory by then, it could spell trouble."

"I see what you mean. What do you plan to do?"

"Arrange for them to take a holiday so my people can have the opportunity to demonstrate their skills, maybe get a little more recognition."

Gamiel laughed and asked, "Can you really do that?"

"Well, we members of the Council of State do have some pull."

Gamiel laughed and walked a ways with his old friend towards the center of the rotunda. He looked up admiring the early morning sun splashing around the reception hall; warm inviting patches of bright light contrasting with shadowy nooks and crannies. At that moment, a wave of exhaustion flooded over his mind and body. How he wanted a nap. He looked at the open library doors wistfully wishing Vanessa would return.

Mark smiled and said, "Alexi doesn't normally befriend young ladies he has just met. Your Vanessa seems to have captured his fascination."

Gamiel grinned and said, "Your Alexi has captured Vanessa's heart."

Mark looked surprised, "So fast?"

"Tell me you have not heard of love at first sight?"

Mark laughed, "You think so?"

Gamiel's expression tightened into more somber lines as he said, "I know so."

A moment of silence passed between them.

Mark said, "I guess we fathers need to stay in touch with developments."

Gamiel smiled and relaxed, taking a closer look at one of the neo-classic pillars holding up the rotunda, he asked, "Mark, how long has this house been standing?"

"Three hundred years. I added the skylight."

Gamiel released a long breath through pursed lips to convey his admiration, and said "You have kept it in immaculate condition. Who were the original owners?"

"It first belonged to a Swedish Count and his children. When the Russian Emperor Alexander the First wrested Finland from Sweden in 1808, this house was forcefully transferred to a Russian family; the Swedish Count took his family back to Sweden."

Gamiel asked, in amusement, "How did it fall into your possession?"

"After World War II, the Finnish government kept it until my father bought it from them in 1950. My father restored it to its original splendor. I am just the fortunate heir. It has been my sanctuary from the world."

Gamiel smiled as he once more glanced at the library doors hoping Vanessa and Alexi would return soon. Pointing to the library, he asked, "Did your father build that library, or you?"

"It was my father's dream to have a home library. He loved books. In time, his love became mine, too. He built the library and started collecting books. I helped him when I was young. The library had nearly a thousand books when he passed on."

Gamiel said, "Quite an accomplishment."

Mark said, "Yes, well I decided to continue in my father's footsteps; however, I took it a step further. As you already know, I began to collect and restore old books back when you were here years ago."

Gamiel nodded.

Mark continued, "I installed a book restoration workshop in the basement just below the library. At first, I had a lot to learn, but I kept at it until it became 2nd nature to me. This was the basis of my continuing learning and research – eventually becoming the foundation of my doctoral dissertation."

Gamiel smiled, and uttered through his tired cloudy thoughts, "A most admirable undertaking, indeed."

Mark confessed, "Even today, I enlist the help of my children when I find a little bit of time. Together, we continue to locate and collect very old books; priceless literary treasures – which by the way, now include 20 original copies of the Kalevala!"

"No! Twenty?"

"Yes!

Mark Leppänen's face was bright with an intensity Gamiel remembered from years past. Mark's energy arrested Gamiel's tiredness temporarily. He asked, "What does the title, Kalevala, mean?"

Mark answered, "Loosely interpreted, it means "The Land of Kaleva" or "Kalevia"

Gamiel admitted, "Although I have been aware of this book, I have to confess, I never read it. What is it?"

Mark replied energetically, "Kalevala" was a collection of oral traditions and poetry regarded by Finns as the national epic of old Karelia and Finland."

Gamiel said, "I did not know that. Who was the author?"

"Elias Lönnrot, a physician, botanist, linguist, and poet who lived from 9 April 1802 to 19 March 1884. He was a literary collector, too."

"Oh?"

"Yes. Elias collected an oral anthology of ancient Baltic cultures. His activities spanned fifteen years and eleven field trips to remote towns and villages of what is now eastern Finland and western Russia."

Gamiel nodded and commented, "That was an incredible effort. I wonder what inspired him."

Mark answered, "He possessed a great love of his people and their history. His example has been an inspiration to me."

Gamiel nodded, and asked, "Was his work well received in his day?"

Mark answered, "It was this old book that helped inspire Finland's emerging national consciousness. Some believe it became our unifying cultural reference that helped inspire our declaration of independence from Russia in 1917."

Gamiel asked, "But it was published in 1835. That means it took a couple of generations to catch on?"

Mark replied, "Elias published two versions. I have copies of both. The first version (called The Old Kalevala) was published in 1835. The second was published in 1849. That work contains 22,795 verses, divided into fifty songs. And, yes, by the time we declared independence, we had a generation of Finns who were very much grounded in this epic."

Gamiel marveled over Mark's command of dates, details and history. He asked, "How do you do that?"

Mark answered, "What?"

"Remember all these dates and details."

Mark blushed, and said, "Gamiel, I don't know. I suppose it is a gift, but when you spend as much time thinking about these things as I do, some of it has to stick. Surely, you have experienced something like this in your own work?"

Gamiel nodded, "Yes, I suppose you are right."

Mark said, "What I know for certain is I love Finland and I enjoy restoring priceless literary works."

Both men looked at the library, both feeling perhaps they should walk over and encourage their children to cut their visit short.

Gamiel smiled at his friend and shook his head, with the comment, "Thank you again my friend. It has been a long week, and a very long day."

Mark smiled and put his arm on his friend's shoulder, with a reply, "I am very glad to have you back, Gamiel. I did not realize how much I missed you."

Gamiel said, "Tell me more about your book collections. What else have you found?"

Mark answered, "I have also located, purchased, and personally restored 13 copies of Bishop Michael Agricola's original Finnish Bible!"

Gamiel stared in amazement. He asked, "When was that published?"

Mark continued, "His work took about 11 years, but his final version was published in 1548. It has been cited as the true beginning of our written language."

Mark laughed and added, "Like most Uralic languages our modern Finnish does not have grammatical articles that translate your word 'the'. Bishop Agricola tried to institute them in his writings but it never caught on."

Gamiel smiled.

Mark added, "It was once believed only a hundred copies from his original 500 remained. I have been able to raise the confirmed count to 137. I have the names and addresses of every single owner."

Gamiel shook his head, and said, "The Lord has blessed you, indeed."

Mark looked down momentarily, then back at Gamiel, then said, "You are very tired, my friend. Let me go and get your daughter so you can rest."

Gamiel smiled, and said, "Let them visit a little bit longer. Vanessa needs this. She resented my taking her away from her friends. Now, I think she is having a change of heart. Tell me something."

Mark looked closer at Gamiel and asked, "What?"

"Your New Testament was printed in the mid 1500's. Kalevala was published in the mid

1800's. Was it Kalevala or your Finnish Bible that inspired the Finnish people on to Independence?"

Mark mused a moment, then answered, "While our Finnish Bible stems from a time when Sweden still ruled the land, in my mind, it also marks a long turning point in Finnish national history contrasting the ancient oral legends Lönnrot later preserved in "Kalevala" with a new modern national acceptance of Christianity."

Gamiel smiled and quietly remarked, "Perhaps, then, both were part of the same forge if you will of this new nationalist pride. It seems as one looks back through time the hand of God is clearly visible in your national epic. I even wonder if you Finns are not descended from one of the Ten Lost Tribes of Israel."

Mark smiled at that, amused and inspired by an unexpected observation from his Jewish friend.

Gamiel added, "When our new Trans-Light-Element research lab is operational, you will be thrilled by how it can help you locate old historical documents. It opens possibilities beyond your wildest imagination. Why, we could..."

At that moment, Alexi and Vanessa came out of the library on the run.

"Vanessa, what's wrong?" asked Gamiel.

Alexi handed Gamiel a sealed envelope, exclaiming, "This just landed in my arms out of thin air! It is addressed to you – from a Mr. Trevor Nibley."

Forging of the Sampo *(classic scene from the Kalevala Mark has praised to Gamiel)*

Artist - Axél Waldemar Gallén   Finnish Painter
DoB 26Apr1865 Pori, Grand Duchy of Finland, died 7Mar1931
Stockholm, Sweden
Public Domain in country of origin and areas where copyright term is the author's life plus 80 years or less. Public Domain in the United States (published or registered with U.S. Copyright Office) before January 1, 1923

Chapter 4
Tying Up Loose Ends

Detective Grand closed up his case files and locked the cabinet. Locking his desk, he reached across the back of his desk chair to retrieve his suit jacket, hat, and umbrella. Exiting his private office directly into the hallway, he took the elevator from the 5th floor to the main lobby.

In the lobby, he noticed the bulletin board on the opposite wall was being updated. Responding to an unexplainable prompting, he walked across the lobby to observe the postings. One caught his eye as he drew in a sharp breath. The photograph of escaped prisoner Carl Ungman was being sponsored by the FBI – with a reward for information leading to his capture.

Detective Grand took the poster with him out the door to the taxi stand. A taxi pulled up, and he opened the door and slipped into the back seat. Giving the driver a card, he said, "Please take me to that address."

The taxi driver moved quickly into the stream of traffic nodding gratefully as his passenger engaged the seat belt. The driver recognized Detective Grand – and refrained from interrupting his thoughts with chit chat.

David 'Tracker' Grand let the rhythms of the road settle his nerves as he processed the chaos that often flooded his thoughts. Allowing the passing cars and road signs to set the tempo, he focused on the Carl Ungman poster in front of him.

A police veteran with twenty years on the force, 'Tracker' Grand knew his town like the back of his hand. Known by his comrades on the thin blue line for his tenacity as well as his compassion, he had established a reputation as a professional public servant worthy of the trust so many placed in him.

He made it his business to keep track of the pulse beat of crime as it ebbed and flowed through his community like a pack of wolves looking for an opportunity to pillage the lives of unsuspecting victims. It had been too many years now for him to question why people became criminals. He no longer wondered why human beings perpetrated horrible things upon other human beings. He only knew they did – and spotting the perpetrators had become second nature to him. He only wished he were half as good at predicting when and where they would strike.

Carl Ungman had showed up on his radar before. Carl was different. He rarely did bad things to people – and had in some cases actually helped people. It was not like him to get caught. In fact, this was the first time Carl had ever been caught. Something clicked in 'Tracker' Grand's mind. It occurred to him that Carl had taken an uncharacteristic risk by making a personal appearance at the Reuel residence. He had underestimated his target, to be sure – but there was something more.

It had to be something huge to induce Ungman to expose himself in this manner. What was so lucrative at the Reuel residence?

Reflecting upon his interview this morning with Dr. Reuel and son, the Detective wondered where they were now. It was late enough in the day; he hoped they might be back home.

On the other hand, Detective Grand knew if it was his own wife and children at risk he would have his family on the first flight to a secret island in the Pacific.

Pulling his smart phone from his vest, Detective Grand called up the map of the residence address of Dr. Gamiel Ben Reuel. The GPS indicated they were almost there. His phone had a special police app that also reported real time traffic as well as the location of other cell phones that were powered up. He clicked for a report of the owners of the signals at the Reuel residence. No member of the Reuel Family showed up.

However, inside the home, three signals indicated a private unnamed corporation. That told the Detective this was a special task force using tools to block inquisitive police probes. So, who was at the Reuel residence? Was it Homeland Defense? Or, was it a private security contractor with a high level clearance? He would know one way or the other very soon.

The Taxi pulled up in front of the Reuel home and the Detective got out. He handed the driver his business card and credit card and said, "Wait right here. I won't be long."

The doorbell was answered in a few seconds by a comely well groomed young man wearing business casual, shined shoes, and a very powerful physique. Judging by the loose fitting sports jacket, Detective Grand suspected a shoulder holster.

Handing the young man his card, he asked, "May I speak with Dr. Reuel?"

The young man took the card and said politely, "Please come in Detective. May I take your jacket?"

Stepping inside, the veteran policeman politely declined to remove his jacket.

The young man smiled and asked, "Would you have a seat in the living room? I will be right back with my boss."

Detective Grand said, "Thank You" and sat down.

In seconds the young man returned with a much older distinguished looking gentleman who carried a military bearing in his comfortable golf attire.

Detective Grand stood up and offered his hand, saying, "Pleasure to meet you, my name is David Grand, Chief Investigating Officer for the City. I need to talk with Dr. Reuel. Do you know where he is?"

"Detective Grand, my name is Trevor Nibley. I am a close friend of Dr. Reuel's. He has asked me to keep his residence secure in his absence. I am very sorry you missed him. Perhaps you could share your message with me, and I can pass it on?"

"Mr. Nibley, I thank you for your offer, but, I am sure you must realize I cannot discuss Dr. Reuel's case with anyone else without his express permission."

The young man smiled and excused himself.

Trevor Nibley said, "Please, have a seat while I explain a few things I have been granted permission to discuss."

Both men took a seat in one of the chairs in the Reuel family living room. Trevor began to relate a brief synopsis of carefully guarded comments.

"Detective Grand, …"

The Detective held up his hand, and said, "Please, call me David."

Trevor smiled, and said, "Thank you, David. Call me Trevor. Dr. Reuel shared a few facts with me from his interview with you this morning. You must understand he has taken reasonable precautions to protect his family. You can see by my presence here that also includes protecting his home in his absence."

The Detective reflected then asked, "I suppose that means you will not tell me where he is – and therefore I cannot speak with him today?"

Trevor shook his head, saying, "Not today – and possibly not this year. However, we do hope to have things wrapped up in a couple of months such that the Reuels will be able to come back home."

"Now see here, Mr. Nibley, I am only trying to help. I may have information that will protect Dr. Reuel's family. How do I know you are even authorized to be here?"

Trevor smiled, and said, "Well, sir, I would submit that if we are here illegally, we probably would not have invited you in at all – nor cooperated in anyway outside of a search warrant."

"This is true, but I would at least expect you to offer me proof you are who you say you are – and Dr. Reuel is not tied up somewhere in the basement?"

Trevor presented his guest with his card, and a copy of the Power of Attorney signed by Gamiel. The policeman scrutinized both with a practiced eye, handing the legal document back – but retaining Trevor's card, which simply read,

Trevor Nibley, President & CEO
Nibley Corporation
Nibley Enterprises, Nibley Security
101 Nibley Blvd
Ogden, Utah 84403
nibley1@nibleyinc.com

Looking up, his gaze captured Trevor looking directly into his eyes. There were two seconds of recognition between them that seemed to freeze eternity. Both somehow subconsciously knew innately they could trust the other.

Detective Grand relaxed a little and breathed in measured droughts – a habit he had formed years before – finding it helped him stay calm under stressful situations. He broke the silence, recognizing in Trevor the practiced salesman / interrogator.

"Trevor, I have been aware of Carl Ungman as a criminal operative for some time. He rarely comes into my jurisdiction – but, the reason I am here today – is because I believe whatever motivated him to take an extreme risk and expose himself as he did last night – means he will not give up. He may even return here very soon. Or, he could already be pursuing the Reuel family – wherever they might have gone?"

Trevor smiled at the Detective's voice inflexion in his last phrase. It was a question – suggesting a need to know. Trevor answered, "We have been tracking Mr. Ungman and we know where he is. I can say with confidence he does not know where Dr. Reuel and his family have gone, and probably won't find them for several days, at least. If I have anything to do with it, he will never find them. I will be happy to cooperate with you – and share all our intelligence on the whereabouts of Carl Ungman."

David Grand smiled, and said, "That will be most helpful. There is one other concern I have. If I may be so bold, what is going on here at the Reuel residence that has enticed Ungman to come and get arrested? That is not his style. The stakes must be astronomically high for him to take such a risk?"

Trevor assessed the Detective's deductive reasoning with admiration, and said, "David, this universe is full of mysteries we do not yet understand. I have made it my life's work to seek understanding of truth wherever I find it. You are correct in your conclusions – and yes, Carl Ungman is seeking the ultimate scepter of power. He thinks Dr. Reuel may possess it. I can tell you, no man can possess the power Carl is seeking – because it will only possess him who seeks it. Dr. Reuel may have made some discovery in his personal research that Carl wants to steal. But I am not at liberty to divulge this intellectual property – neither the context – nor the fact of its existence. For that, you must wait until you have a chance to ask Dr. Reuel himself."

David Grand let his mind expand to comprehend the full portent of what Trevor was telling him. He was about to ask another question, when Trevor continued.

"What do you say we work together to keep Gamiel and his family safe? I will share what I know about Carl's activities. You let me know if anyone else appears on your radar. I can tell you this. Carl is not alone. He has friends in high places. He also has others – competitors – who want to beat him to the finish line. I not only have to worry about Carl, but possibly as many as three hundred other organized espionage cells all after the same unholy grail. I can tip you on their identities, as well. I like to cooperate with the police in my work. I hope you and I can cooperate."

Detective Grand stood up and said, "I have a cab waiting longer than I intended. Please let Dr. Reuel know he and his family are in our prayers."

Trevor escorted David to the front door. David turned as he was exiting the doorway, and added, "I appreciate your candor, Trevor. I think we can cooperate on many levels. However, keep this in mind. My public professional obligations cannot allow me to function as a party to your private business pursuits."

Trevor noted David's fixed gaze, as his guest continued, "However well-meaning you may be, and despite the fact that you are operating with a lawful charter – I am government – you are a private citizen.

I can make no promise to help you – and in some cases – may need to consider you under suspicion – as well as Dr. Reuel."

Detective Grand reached in his vest pocket and removed a business card – handing it to Trevor. "Please call me anytime."

Trevor watched as this complex public servant made his way to the taxi, and then made sure the taxi drove away. He concluded David was a man to be respected – perhaps even loved – and feared.

Trevor made a mental note to add David to the Nibley Security persons of interest watch list. Then, he cast his thoughts upon the more sensitive Trans-Light-Element mysteries his team was scrambling night and day to solve. Turning with urgent haste to get back to work, Trevor closed the front door.

Chapter 5
Finnish Food and Jet Lag

Gamiel read Trevor's letter twice before returning it to the envelope and putting it away in his dinner jacket pocket. The short nap he had taken earlier had cleared his mind and rejuvenated his spirits. He would have to draft a reply tomorrow. For now, the food on the table was too delicious to ignore any longer.

Mark and his son, Alexi, were more than amused by the delight around the buffet attending the various selections by the Reuel family as they explored newly discovered Finnish foods. They had never imagined Americans getting so excited about ordinary food.

Gamiel was heard to exclaim, "Ah hah! Karjalan Piirakat! My favorite!"

Ben asked, "Dad, what are Car Ya Lawn Pea-Rockets?"

Everyone laughed.

Gamiel held up a sample, and answered, "These are like single wrap thick-shell rye bread burritos cut in-half so they resemble leather moccasins or flat bottom canoes with rounded bow and stern on both ends containing buttered semi-sweet rice pudding." Gamiel inserted one of the pastries he was describing into his mouth and bit off half with a delightful smile on his face.

Ben loaded his plate with two 'Pea-Rockets' and several other delicious items and returned to the table. His family's conversation was the most care free he could remember in a long time. It felt so good to get away from Unified Field and Trans-Light-Element and Carl Ungman.

Glancing over at Vanessa; Ben caught her sneaking a look towards Alexi. Ben was amused until he caught Alexi staring at him. Ben smiled back and held up a 'pea-rocket', saying, "Delicious."

Joseph was visiting with Mark quite famously. He reached for his beverage glass and asked, "What is this? It tastes like lemons."

Mark answered, "This is Sima, a traditional Finnish beverage made with lemon slices, white and brown sugar, dark syrup, yeast, and raisins. We shave the yellow peel from the lemons and set it aside. Then we shave the white off the lemon and throw it away and slice the lemons very thin. Then we boil water and turn off the heat. While it is cooling, we stir in the shaved yellow peels along with sugar and syrup until the sugar dissolves. We cover the kettle and let the contents cool down until it reaches 25° C (75° F). Anyone have any questions, so far?"

Everyone shook their heads, and Mark continued, "After Sima water cools to just the right temperature, we remove the lid, add lemon slices and yeast then replace the lid and leave it alone overnight. First thing in the morning, we drop one raisin and one teaspoon of white sugar in bottom of clean washed beverage bottles. Then we pour all the Sima into bottles through a strain (that removes the lumpy lemon parts.) Then we seal the bottle caps and wait for raisins to rise to the top. Depending on the ambient temperature, we might have to wait from 3 to 7 days. That's when you know it is ready to drink. It is best served chilled."

Joseph looked wide eyed at his mother who commented, "That was quiet a recipe, Mark. Perhaps you could show us how you do it sometime?"

Mark smiled and said, "Any time."

Rachel asked, "Mark, what is your wife's name?"

Mark smiled as he answered, "Kaila."

"When will she be joining us?

Mark added, "She will return from her sister's sometime this afternoon. Her sister's mother-in-law was in a car accident yesterday and they are preparing a meal to take to the family while she is recovering. We are concerned she may not pull through."

"Oh, I am so sorry." Rachel looked at Gamiel whose countenance reflected renewed concern for his friend. She was impressed by the fact that Mark could take in visitors from America at the same time his own family was experiencing distress of their own."

Ben watched with interest, taking in the non-verbal indicators that spoke louder than words.

Gamiel said, "Now we are adding our burdens to yours. We want to help, if we can, Mark."

Mark smiled and said, "You already have my friend. Your presence is like a breath of fresh air."

Ben was about to make a comment of his own, when his gaze was drawn behind Mark to a lovely young Finnish girl entering the dining room from the reception hall.

She said, "Terve Isä! Mitä kuuluu?" <Tare-vay Eessää!> <Mee-tä Coo-luu?> <translated Greetings Father! What is heard? (meaning… what's going on?)>

Gamiel stood, looking at Ben, who also stood up, followed by young Joseph following their example.

Mark stood up the same time and said, "Hyvää kuuluu. <translated Good is heard. – meaning things are fine.> Koira, these guests are my friends. I would like to introduce Dr. Gamiel Reuel from Colorado in the United States; his wife, Rachel; daughter, Vanessa; and sons, Ben and Joseph. Gamiel, this is my only daughter."

Koira turned and took each of their hands, and said in very clear English, "Oh, very nice to meet each of you."

Ben could tell she was not as practiced as her father and older brother – however; he guessed she was probably 15 going on 16 – and decided when he could speak Finnish as good as she spoke English he might be in a position to correct.

Ben blushed as she shook his hand.

Joseph laughed and said, "Koira, I like your name."

Koira sat down, and the men took their seats as the meal continued; both families becoming instant fast friends – and perhaps more. Conversation was lively, edifying, and sometimes entertaining – eliciting more than one laugh from all.

Ben noticed how Joseph was laughing with the rest and, despite his condition, seemed completely absorbed and engaged – not distant as he had been.

After the meal, the Reuels helped clear the table and clean up over Mark's exclamations they really didn't need to do it. Everyone was still smiling when the Reuels excused themselves to get some more rest. Jet lag was something only time and rest would cure.

Mark conferred with his house security supervisor and made sure everything was in order before retiring himself. "Pekka – please make sure no one disturbs the Reuels today. They have had many stressful days and need rest. I will be napping in my study if you need me. I did not sleep last night, either."

Pekka nodded with understanding and went to prep his security staff for compliance with his employer's wishes.

The Finnish sun was still high in the western sky when Kaila Leppänen returned home. She entered the study and started to wake her husband, but decided not. She went into the kitchen where she took her lunch – then went to the family den where she read and studied quietly.

Alexi came into the den and greeted his mother. They spoke in Finnish about their new house guests. Kaila noticed a different light dancing in her son's eyes as he spoke of Vanessa.

Alexi settled down to reading quietly to himself. At length, he laid the book in his lap and asked, "Mother, are we going to our worship services today?"

Kaila answered, "Yes. We should be back before they have finished their nap."

It was 1:40 pm local when Mark, Kaila, Alexi, and Koira ventured quietly out the door in their Sunday best to attend church.

Ben awoke and looked out the window as they were getting into what looked like the family car – not the Mercedes. He wondered where they were going, but decided it was not his business. He fell back asleep. Time passed in a dream about Finnish food, riding in the Mercedes, and what it might be like to experience a Finnish Sauna.

Two hours later, Gamiel awoke to the silence in the house. He got up and stepped to the door. Opening it a crack, as he gazed into the reception hall he spotted house security making their rounds.

Closing the door, he sat down at the desk and pulled out Trevor's letter. It was a typical business form – obviously personally drafted by Trevor himself. Gamiel smiled. No extra people involved where it wasn't necessary; as few risks as possible. Trevor was still running a Navy Seal Team, just like the old days. The embossed corporate letterhead set the tone for what followed.

Michael Irvin Bosley

Nibley Security, Inc.

10 PM, Saturday

Doctor Gamiel Ben Reuel, President
Reuel Research Laboratories, Inc.
T-L-E Space Port, Inc.
Asikkala, Finland Field Office

Dear Gamiel,

In the past 12 hours since you left this morning, much has transpired. You will be pleased to know our Legal Department has completed all necessary filings <on a Saturday, I might add> to register your new Corporations – Reuel Research Laboratories and T-L-E Spaceport. It cost me a small fortune to expedite these matters – but we both agreed immediate action would save us court costs in the future. You may rest assured your work as well as your laboratory assets are now legally protected.

Attachments to this letter contain your certified copies of pertinent legal documents including a copy of limited exclusive rights to T-L-E you signed to me for research and development purposes. Please file them away safely. I have back-up copies in my personal safe. All copyrights, trademarks, and patents have been formally registered. Your general Unified Field and Trans-Light-Element Theories and other related research publications have Library of Congress Catalogue Numbers and will appear in the very next edition of two top international scientific journals.

Your idea about publishing a general treatise that does not disclose proprietary specifications was brilliant! It will leave no doubt about who owns the process while avoiding unsafe disclosures.

One of the first commercial applications of your T-L-E Door, as you have seen for yourself – is package delivery – anywhere, instantly. This letter is the first commercial package delivery. The fact that you have this letter demonstrates the T-L-E Door is working – at least in one direction.

All day today, my top research analyst has been putting his team through several drills. Please note the results of our first test day:

1. T-L-E Door pulls three dimensional coordinates into the T-L-E Vortex Wall – no matter how far away. We stopped at Pluto because we have no way to measure the space-time warp differentials – no way to calculate margins of error – no way to calibrate our instruments. We must return to this after we accrue sufficient test data with local T-L-E Doors.

2. T-L-E Door is not visible from the other side of a stabilized T-L-E vortex. We started pitching pennies through the Door into a bowl on Rachel's kitchen table. One of the staff stood in the kitchen and watched pennies fall out of thin air. He tried putting his hand right where he thought the pennies appeared and discovered he either caught them as they came through – or they appeared right behind his hand. His hand was never actually in the vortex. That means we probably will not endanger anyone by parking a T-L-E Door inside their bodies – but this requires more study. I want to see if the Door will focus down to microscopic space – I have some ideas I want to discuss along this line later.

3. We could not reach through the door to retrieve the pennies. The research technician tried inserting his hand through the door and the result seemed to be like pushing a curtain ahead of you.

4. We did toss an insect, a fish into a fish bowl, and finally a rabbit through the door onto the patio outside the Lab. It would seem a certain critical velocity is needed to convince the T-L-E 'curtain' this mass is coming all the way through the vortex. The team is compiling a mass-to-velocity ratio table even as I speak. We will start testing launching strategies for sending larger items through the one-way T-L-E door on Monday morning. I hope this doesn't mean we will need a hundred foot run-way to 'shoot' the generators through. That could get a little tricky.

5. Since we cannot detect the 'door' from the outside, there seems to be no way of coming back through our one-way opening. I believe it will become a two-way opening if we calibrate two open doors on the same exact coordinate with inverted values. <More on this later...>

I have called in extra construction crews to speed up the new T-L-E Space Port Facility we are building under the City's Open Space park grounds behind your house. I think we can be done inside of the month. Let me know when you are able to start receiving light equipment transfers. Their smaller mass and weight will mean we won't need to "throw" them through the vortex too fast. Also, if you get any ideas about how we can just 'push' things through the door gently, that will be a big help. Enjoy your 'vacation' but don't relax too much. We have lot of work to do.

Sincerely,

//Signed//
Trevor Nibley

P.S. Almost forgot – my first installment for permission to use T-L-E was deposited this afternoon into your new secure corporate bank account. Your new corporate bank card is enclosed.

Chapter 6
Timo and Niina

Ben read the letter from Trevor special delivery via T-L-E. The Reuels had all awakened from their naps. He and Joseph had joined his parents inside their large suite. Joseph was sitting next to his mother as she wrote a letter to her mother.

Ben asked, "Mom, are you going to mail that from Finland?"

"No. Your father promised to send this through the first T-L-E door from Finland. Trevor will put a domestic postage stamp on it and drop it in the mailbox in front of their house in Colorado."

"Oh! Why can't Dad just have T-L-E drop it directly in Grandmother's mail box?"

Gamiel was going through his back pack looking for his laptop power cord and internet connector. He chimed in, "Well we thought of that and decided that would be the same as putting it in the mail box without a postmark ourselves. Technically that is still illegal. We could just drop it on Grandma Carlson's dining table, but then she would be pestering us about how we got it there. We don't want to mail it from Finland from obvious reasons."

Ben nodded and went back to reading Trevor's letter. He exclaimed, "Wow, the door actually works! Living creatures can pass through unharmed!"

"Ben, please. Not so loud. We don't want to disclose these things to the servants – and until Mark tells me, we should not discuss this with his family members, either."

"Sorry Dad. I forgot. This is just too exciting. When do we start building the lab here? Where will we build it?"

"Mark thinks he wants us to put it in his basement. I don't want to endanger his house. I think we should probably start in that old barn the other side of his lakeside cottage. That way, if something crazy happens, there is less chance of spoiling this beautiful historic residence."

Ben nodded as he re-read the results from the first day of the T-L-E Door tests. His thoughts began sub-consciously working on some of the problems. He wondered if the research team was missing something obvious. Looking up, he snapped his fingers and asked, "Dad, what happens to my T-L-E marble every time the vortex opens? We never had a chance to follow-up on that variable."

Gamiel put his hand to his chin in his sudden inspiration pose. That is a good question, Ben. As soon as I can get online I will send Trevor an encrypted email with your question.

Ben looked out the window to see the Leppänen family returning and asked, "What church do they attend?"

"I am not sure," answered Gamiel. "Let them tell us when they are ready."

Ben was curious, but cautious. He did not want to offend his hosts.

Vanessa came into the parental suite – freshly showered, wearing a new dress and a new hair-do.

Ben teased her, "Wow, Vanessa. What is the occasion?"

"Quiet – Lab Boy – or I will make you pay for many moons."

Ben could tell she was teasing back, but sensed cold sincerity in her threat. He decided to leave it alone, but he guessed she was intent on impressing their hosts, one in particular.

Vanessa asked, "Mom, do you think this dress is loose enough? I think I am gaining weight."

Ben smirked. Rachel gave her son the 'look' while answering her daughter's question, "You are not gaining weight. The dress is fine – nice, and modest – just loose enough. Were you planning on going somewhere?"

"Well, Alexi and Koira had mentioned something about going to Lahti after they got back from church."

Gamiel looked at Vanessa with renewed concern, and said, "Let me visit with Mark about this. It is his family's safety we must consider, too."

Just at that moment, the sound of voices greeted them from the grand hall way, "Hello, is anyone home?"

Gamiel opened the door to see the entire Leppänen family standing outside in the hall. He gestured them to come into the large guest suite.

Ben put the letter he was reading in the desk drawer out of sight.

Rachel put down her writing and stood up, saying, "Kaila, it is a pleasure to meet you. We have really enjoyed your enchanting home… and your charming children."

Gamiel was surprised and pleased with his wife's diplomatic poise. He seriously wondered if she had missed her calling.

Ben noticed for the first time how Alexi stood the same height as his father, Mark, with remarkably similar features. He also noticed Vanessa was stunningly radiant. What a change! Alexi was more composed but could not keep his eyes off Vanessa.

Kaila took in the entire seen with the comprehension of a mother, and smiled at Rachel's complement. Her reply in English was clear and understandable, but the Finnish accent was unmistakable. "Thank you, Rachel. My husband has had nothing but high praise for all of you. I am delighted to have you in our home. We are planning a Sauna and cook-out at the Lake-side cottage tonight; just a family gathering… with my sister and her family. Would you join us?"

Rachel sensed the authority of the Finnish matriarch in her kitchen and searched Gamiel for a cultural clue. Gamiel looked at her and nodded his prompting to accept the offer.

Rachel replied, "We would love to join you. What is the attire?"

"Casual wear, except for when you go into the Sauna – we have swim attire you may change into then. Afterwards, we will meet under the gazebo next to the cottage for supper."

Ben noticed Mark was unusually quiet.

Alexi asked, "Mrs. Reuel, would it be permissible for Vanessa and Ben to go with Koira and me to visit some of our friends in Lahti?"

Ben looked at his father, as Gamiel searched Mark's gaze for comment.

Mark saw the unspoken question, and replied, "As long as you children do not get out of the car in public places and, Alexi, remember what I said – these are family friends visiting on vacation from the United States – no discussions about diplomatic immunity or why they are here. Is that clear?"

Alexi nodded his head, and said, "We understand Father."

Mark continued, and you must be back by 7 pm sharp – that is when the Sauna will be hot and I don't want to waste wood keeping it hot any longer than one hour. We will be sitting down to supper at 8 sharp. Don't miss Sauna."

"Yes, Father."

Ben looked at Joseph and could tell he wanted to come, too, but decided not to bring up the subject and get his hopes dashed.

Mrs. Reuel looked concerned and asked, "Vanessa, you do understand our situation? You and Ben both – please be careful."

Gamiel looked directly at Mark, and said, "This could be more difficult than it seems. Alexi's friends will ask normal questions one might be expected to answer."

Mark replied, "These are close friends of the family – they attend church with us, their children are similar ages. I expect no problems."

Vanessa replied, "We'll be discreet. Don't worry, Mom. Everything will be fine."

Joseph got up from the couch and gave his sister a big hug.

Vanessa hugged her baby brother back and said, "We will be right back, Joe. This is just a quick trip to see Alexi's friends."

Mrs. Reuel took Joseph's hand as his older siblings made their way out the door.

Ben said, "Dad, I put the letter in the desk drawer."

Gamiel nodded with a smile, saying, "Thank you, Ben."

Alexi drove, the girls sat in the back, Ben in the front. Conversation was open and exciting. The sights were all so new; both Ben and Vanessa were completely lost in the enchanting lake side scenery between Asikkala and Lahti.

Alexi drove straight to his friend's house and pulled into their drive way. It was painted in bright blue with yellow trim and completely enclosed with shrubbery bushes and small trees. They got out and walked around to the front door. Koira pressed the front doorbell button. Ben noticed a shoe-scrub rug and a scraper bar on the front door-step. He guessed it was quite useful during wet muddy seasons.

The door opened; Ben was struck by the contrasting dark hair of the young person who greeted them. "Päivä. Mitä teille kuuluu?"

Alexi returned the greeting, "Hyvää kiitos, entä sinulle?

Ben listened, trying to catch on, but it was too fast. The young person at the door replied back to Alexi, "Hyvää onkin!" Ben looked at Alexi for a translation.

Alexi blurted out, "Hey, Timo, these are our friends, Ben and Vanessa from the United States. We wanted you to meet them. Are your parents home?"

"Oh, sure. Come in, please." Timo motioned as if he were afraid his guests might not be able to understand his English. He called down the hall, "Äiti! Tule tänne, ole hyvä."

Alexi translated, "Timo said, Mother! Come here, please."

Timo turned his head to look back as he was walking and said, "Sorry, we speak English, but sometimes we don't understand. Alexi, when did they come?"

Alexi answered, "They just landed in Helsinki this morning.

"I guess that's why we did not see them at church.

Alexi said, "They are not of our faith."

Timo smiled and said, "Oh. Sorry. I thought…" His voice trailed off.

Timo's mother came down the hall from the kitchen, "Oh, hello, Alexi, Koira, what charming friends you have." She extended her hand to Ben and Vanessa in turn.

Alexi said, "Mrs. Seppälä, this is Ben and Vanessa, our friends from the United States. We wanted to introduce them to Timo and Niina. Is that OK?"

"Yes, of course. Timo, take your guests out to the back patio. Niina is there helping her brother memorize a presentation for next Sunday."

Ben and Vanessa followed their hosts through the clean Finnish home into the back yard.

Timo called, "Niina, hei, Tämä on Alexin ja Koiran ystävät. (Translated - These are Alexi's and Koira's friends.) We need to speak English."

Niina stood up from her chair and said, "Oh, my English is not that good. Please excuse me. Will you be in Finland long?"

Alexi answered, "They are on vacation for the whole summer!"

Ben wanted to tell them about Joseph, but decided to wait.

Timo asked, "Alexi, are you still planning the day trip to Helsinki?"

Alexi answered, "Yes, and now we are hoping Ben and Vanessa may go with us, too."

Vanessa said, "We would love it. When is it?"

Ben was reserved. He wanted to see Finland, but was concerned about Ungman. Recent memory of his close brush with this intense desperate soul struck fear he was glad his sister did not know. He knew Ungman would stop at nothing to locate them.

Koira spoke up, "If our parents agree, perhaps we might go next week, before everyone starts preparations for 'Juhannus Päivä'."

Timo rubbed his chin like Gamiel. Ben was amused, and wondered where he got that from. Timo looked at Vanessa, and said, "Maybe this week, we could also show you around Lahti."

Niina asked Ben, "What are your favorite sports?"

Ben blushed as he said, "Soccer and Baseball."

Niina responded, "Hieno! (He'-N-Oh!) Timo and Alexi play football, that is what we call soccer here in Finland, on the city youth league. Maybe you could play with them at Juhannus Päivä tournament?"

Alexi said, "That would be fun. Timo, would you call our coach tomorrow and see if he can write Ben onto our tournament roster. Would you like that, Ben?"

"Sure." Ben never passed up a good soccer game, even if they did call it football. He asked, "Do you have little league? Joseph was supposed to start this summer."

Niina said, "Yes! This is my youngest brother, Aki. He has been playing since he was four. How old is Joseph?"

Vanessa answered, "He is 4 years old, and will be 5 in October."

Aki stood up and shook Ben's and Vanessa's hand.

Vanessa said, "Very nice to meet you, Aki. What are you memorizing?"

Aki looked at his sister, questioningly who translated Vanessa's greeting and question. He answered in Finnish, "I can't say it in English, do you want to hear it?

Niina translated for him.

Vanessa smiled, and said, "I would love to hear it in Finnish."

Niina translated what Vanessa said and added, "Go ahead Aki. I will translate it for you."

Aki opened his mouth and said, "Me uskomme Jumalaan, iankaikkiseen Isään, ja hänen Poikaansa, Jeesukseen Kristukseen, ja Pyhään Henkeen."

Alexi said, in Finnish, "Very good, Aki. Soon, you will have all of them memorized!"

Niina said, "Translated, that is - We believe in God, the Eternal Father, and in His Son, Jesus Christ, and in the Holy Ghost."

Vanessa smiled, and gave Aki a big hug, and said, "That was wonderful. Keep it up."

Niina translated her words for Aki.

Timo asked, "Hey, Alexi, are we still planning to go out on your parents' lake barge?

Ben heard the phone ring in the house.

Timo said, "I better go see if that is for me," and went back inside.

Vanessa asked Niina, "Alexi tells me he will be attending University of Helsinki this year. Are you planning to attend?"

Niina looked at Alexi, and said, "I plan to attend next year. Timo is thinking about trade school. He wants to work with his hands learn how to make cars."

Vanessa asked, "Is vocational school a good way to go here?"

Niina said, "Oh yes, vocational crafts are very much recognized in our public school system."

Alexi said, "Recent new laws make it easier to enroll in vocational programs. You can also get higher college education as well at the same time."

Timo came back out onto the patio with the house cordless, and handed it to Alexi. "It is your father."

Alexi took the phone, "Hello?" The conversation continued in Finnish. Alexi's expression changed to reflect deep concern. Ben and Vanessa listened carefully, but simply could not follow the language.

Alexi handed the phone back to Timo, and said, "We have to go. Thanks Timo. We will call you tomorrow. I will ask Father about using his barge. We could have a great time on the lake. Are you still holding your Detective Club meetings?"

Timo answered, "Yes. Could we hold our next meeting on your barge?"

Alexi answered, "That would be perfect. Sorry we have to leave so quickly."

Everyone said goodbye, Ben and Vanessa followed their hosts back to the car. Once they buckled in, Vanessa asked, "Alexi what is wrong."

Alexi said, "My Aunt's Mother-in-Law was just rushed into intensive care. She is having a stroke – hemorrhaging of the brain. My parents need to go to the hospital. They want us back before they leave."

Chapter 7
First Sauna

Alexi parked the car in the circle drive by the front door of the Leppänen lakeside estate. Everyone got out and rushed inside. Alexi went to find his father. Koira went with Ben and Vanessa to their parents' room.

They found Gamiel on the phone. Mrs. Reuel was engaged in a personal conversation with a woman who looked a lot like Mrs. Leppänen. Joseph was playing on the floor with another young boy close to his age.

When he saw Ben, Joseph ran up to him with a toy dump truck in his hand, and said, "I am playing with my new friend, Seppo; that lady is his mother – she is nice but very sad. Seppo doesn't talk English, but I am learning Finnish; this is his toy dump-truck. He calls it a Lelu Kippiauto." (pronounced (Lay'-Loo Keep'-Pea-Ah-U-Toe)

Ben said, "That is neat. You really are learning to speak Finnish." Ben was glad Joseph had a playmate his age.

Ben asked, "Koira, is this your Aunt?"

"Yes, my Aunt Laila Laaksonen and my cousin, Seppo," answered Koira.

Ben listened to his mother talking to Koira's Aunt. Mrs. Reuel was saying, "… Laila, Gamiel and I want to go with you and your sister to the hospital. Ben and Vanessa can help watch Seppo."

Mrs. Laaksonen was in tears as she said, "Thank you."

Ben tuned-in to his father's phone conversation. Gamiel was looking out the window with his right hand on his hip, left hand to his ear with the phone, saying, "...I realize its 8:30 on a Sunday morning there, but we need to try. At this point the patient has nothing to lose. No, we won't perform anything intrusive. How soon can you fire up the generators? That's right, reset the calibrations for microscopic and see if the T-L-E door will open to coordinates inside objects - without disturbing the real space-time matter. If it does, then this may work."

Ben edged a little closer to hear more clearly.

Gamiel smiled and nodded at him, continuing, "Oh, by the way, while you are practicing your T-L-E peeping calibrations see if you can find my watch. Yeah, it's the very same, the one my father gave me, <pause>... yes, the one you threw overboard and had to dive to save. Yep. <pause> I don't know! Mark and I have searched the car, the path to our room, and I have looked through all our bags. <pause> OK. Thanks. I will call you from the hospital. Later."

Ben asked, "Who was that?"

"Trevor."

"Oh!"

"I can see you have questions, but we have to go now. We need you and Vanessa to help watch the young boys – and each other. OK?"

"Sure."

"I'll explain everything when I get back."

At that moment, Mark walked into the room with Alexi and Mrs. Leppänen. He said, "Gamiel, it's all set, we need to go quickly."

The young people followed and watched their parents climb into the car and ride quickly out of the circle driveway back onto the country lane leading to the gate at the main road.

Ben looked at Alexi, and asked, "Why are all the grown-ups going to the hospital?"

Alexi answered, "My Aunt Laila wanted Mother and Father to comfort her husband. Uncle Jarmo is devastated about his mother's condition. I guess your mother and father just wanted to support our parents. Your parents are good people."

Koira sat down on the floor and asked Joseph, "What are you boys doing?"

Joseph said, "We are driving a dump truck and a bulldozer around the lake."

Seppo said something in Finnish. Koira answered back in Finnish.

Alexi said, "Father said it will probably be late when they return, so we should go ahead and get supper when it is ready. He also put me in charge of the Sauna. Does everyone want to try it?"

Everyone exclaimed, "Yes!"

Joseph laughed and said, "Saw Uhn Ah."

The small crowd of six scrambled out the Great Hall doorway into the backyard, Alexi leading the way. Ben felt the soft give of the packed sawdust trail that lead from the large back patio to the lakeside cottage. This trail was lined on both sides with small granite stones cut square and laid tightly end-to-end through a lush field of green grass and occasional thick moss.

When they got to the Sauna, which was a room attached to the end of the lakeside cottage, Alexi showed the boys through the door into the Men's dressing room. Vanessa and Koira went into the Ladies' dressing room.

Alexi explained, "Here is the clean towel cabinet, here is where we throw our wet towels and swim wear when we are done. Here is where you will find new swim wear provided for our guests. Pick one that is your size and put it on. You can put your clothes and shoes in these lockers, but no need to lock them.

After you get changed, follow me into the Sauna, and I will explain the safety rules once everyone is inside. Be sure to get a personal body brush and a rag."

Ben could not help marveling at Alexi's grasp of the English language. He wished he could speak Finnish that well. He helped Joseph get changed while Alexi helped Seppo. Then they all went into the Sauna.

The first thing Ben sensed was the high temperature inside the enclosed room. It had a door from each dressing room and a third door to the outside dock beside the lake. In the middle of the room was a large pile of ceramic heating stones roughly cut into an assortment of shapes ranging in diameters between the size of basketballs and baseballs. Ben could feel the radiating heat pouring off the rock pile.

Along the walls were high benches made of the same soft native Finnish pine as the walls and window sills. The windows were closed. Ben guessed the only time they ever got opened was when it became necessary to air out the Sauna. In front of the rock pile was a large water bucket with a dipping ladle. A round thermometer with a calibrated wire coil needle gage hung from the wall above the outside door. It read 62° Celsius.

The girls came inside and sat on the bench opposite the boys. Alexi checked the fire once again. Then he sat next to Ben where he could reach the water bucket and dipped a ladle of water onto the rocks. Steam dispersed immediately, taking the dry edge out of the air.

Alexi said, "The first rule of the Sauna is to keep the air moist. This bucket of water is called in Finnish, "löyly" <lewr-lew> meaning steam. The temperature in an average Sauna in Finland ranges between 60 to 100° C (140 to 212° F), but we usually try to keep it between 70–80° C (158–176° F) so it is above the dew point even with the löyly water vapors. That way, there is no visible steam condensation like there is in a Turkish sauna."

"2nd Rule; do not touch the rocks. They fill a deep fire bucket. The bottom of the bucket is sitting in the wood fire of the ´kiuas´ meaning sauna stove, underneath the Sauna. The rocks collect and hold the heat." Alexi demonstrated just how hot the rocks were by throwing a tissue on a dry spot. It quickly turned brown, then black before bursting into a brief flame.

He continued, "When I pour "löyly" water on the rocks in the ´kiuas´, it never makes it to the bottom of the bucket before the heat completely vaporizes it. This is a safe Sauna because all the smoke and fumes from the fire are vented directly outside from under the Sauna – no smoke ever comes in this room."

"3rd Rule; if you feel yourself getting faint or dizzy, leave the Sauna and go cool down gradually in the shower – then get a good drink of water because you are dehydrating."

"Rule number 4: No running or jumping inside the Sauna!"

"Now - how to use the Sauna... Sit and enjoy the warmth; relax, visit with friends, forget the pressures of the outside world. It is against our customs to bring the cares of the world into the Sauna. Everyone is supposed to be friendly and relaxed. In many public and private Sauna's no clothing is worn – even in mixed company. But our family has made a conscious decision to not impose that on our guests. When it is just our family – and just the guys or just the gals, then no clothing is worn. Today, we all wear swimsuits."

The young people luxuriated in the seeping warmth slowly raising skin and body temperature. Koira picked up one of the birch leaf branches and began using it to slap her skin lightly. Vanessa gave it a try, too. Alexi gave a branch to Ben.

Ben asked, "What is this for?"

"It helps the blood circulate better at the surface of your skin; your skin radiates heat more efficiently, stimulates the pores to release more toxins. Your skin is designed to clean your body inside out." Alexi began beating himself vigorously to make his point.

Koira said, "In a Sauna, you want to sweat a lot. That helps the cleansing process. We soap down with a soft brush then rinse off with these extra buckets of water. Don't worry; there are drains underneath the wood grate floor. While you are in the heat and steam, listen to what your body is telling you. If you get too warm, just leave and cool down slowly under a lukewarm shower."

Alexi continued sharing, "My father designed a lakeside swimming pool outside the Sauna. We use the natural waters of the lake to refill the pool when it gets low. We pump lake water into holding tanks through a rock and sand filter which is continually flushed clean by the currents of the lake. This water is drawn through ultraviolet lights to reduce bacteria count; then forced through large carbon filters into another set of underground holding tanks. We fill the pool from those holding tanks. The pool is completely isolated from the lake; built of concrete, the bottom and side surfaces are coated with a soft cushion of foam rubber. If you accidentally hit your head, it absorbs the impact – and does not scratch. The pool water is continually circulated through a secondary filter."

Koira joined in the explanation, "When we need to empty the pool <like when temperatures drop below freezing>, we pump the pool water into a third set of holding tanks and cover the pool. The water in the third set of tanks is re-filtered back into the second set of tanks as we refill the pool again."

Vanessa asked, "So the deck around the pool is not by the lake?"

Alexi answered, "The concrete wall of the lakeside of the pool separates the pool waters from the lake waters. The lakeside of the pool deck meets the boat dock that extends from shore out over the lake water against the poolside. The dock wraps around the pool in a semi-circle meeting the lake shore around the lake side of the pool. At the other end of the pool you will notice a boat house. Next to the boat house is the Gazebo where we will be having supper tonight. You will see everything when we leave the Sauna to jump in the pool."

Ben noted the thermometer had climbed to 76° Centigrade. It continued to rise as both steam and conversation filled the air. They all took turns washing each other's back with a brush after soaping themselves down and dumping the water over their bodies. It felt good to sit in the steamy air.

At length, Joseph said, "Ben, I am getting too hot."

Alexi said, "OK, follow me out the door where we will jump in the pool." He opened the outside door, stepped outside; walked quickly to the pool and jumped in.

Seppo needed no encouragement. He had done this before. He leaped almost the same time as Alexi. Joseph followed Seppo without hesitation. Koira jumped in next; followed by Ben. Vanessa stayed at the poolside, unsure.

Alexi called to her, saying, "Vanessa, it is just like going swimming; jump in."

Vanessa said, "Oh well, I guess you guys do this all the time. I don't know what I'm worried about." She threw caution to the very light breeze that was making small puffy waves on the lake and jumped in the pool with everyone else.

The early evening lake waters were about 40° F. The pool was 65° F, having been heated by the internal circulation pipes wrapped around the Sauna fire box. The Sauna had been about 176° F. In the few seconds Vanessa had stood on the dock cooling down, her internal body heat may have reduced down to 140° F. Following her jump into the pool, the instant contrast of sudden immersion was shocking; her pores closed instantly. As her body cooled down from the outside, her bones radiated heat into her body, loosening up tired tense muscles – creating the sensation that her bones were melting.

Ben said, "Vanessa, this is amazing. I have never felt so relaxed all at once in my life. No wonder the Finns do this. Let's ask Dad to build one of these when we get back home. Alexi, do you feel the same when you cool down in the shower?"

Alexi said, "Almost, but nothing matches the feeling of jumping through a hole in the ice on the lake in the dead of winter."

Vanessa said, "I think I would draw the line there. It gives me shivers just thinking about it."

Ben said, "All mental big-sister... just your frame of mind."

Koira laughed. Vanessa stuck out her tongue at her younger brother.

After a while, Seppo asked in Finnish, "Alexi, can we go back in the Sauna, now?"

"Yes, it is time; before we get too chilled."

Alexi climbed up the ladder on the inside pool wall, helping Seppo. Vanessa helped Joseph. Ben and Koira followed.

Ben asked, "So, you just keep going back inside the Sauna, get hot again, just so you can run back out and cool down?"

Koira answered, "As often as you want, within reason, of course. We usually do it twice; and, if we have time and feel the need, we go back in a third time. The idea is to steam and sweat your body clean, soap down and rinse off, then heat up again to make sure you sweat out any residue that may still be in your pores."

After another round of jumping into the pool, the Sauna bathing process was completed. The girls went through their door as the guys exited theirs. Everyone undressed and finished washing and rinsing off in the showers, dried off and got dressed for supper.

It was 8:45 pm when Ben checked his watch as they were finally sitting down to supper under the Gazebo in the rays of the late Finnish evening Summer Sun. He wondered what had happened to his Dad's watch. He could remember seeing it on the car seat between them. It did not make sense that it should disappear like that unless one of the servants kept it.

The people serving the food were kind and thorough. Supper passed in grateful consumption and happy enjoyment of new found friends. Ben decided he wanted to learn to speak Finnish. Besides being able to talk with his new friends, it would be fun to understand what the servants were saying. They finished eating and went back inside the house.

Ben noted the sun set at exactly 9:23 pm. He mentally calculated changes he would have to make in his Stonehenge Mural to build one just like it in

Asikkala, Finland. As he followed Joseph to their room, he checked his watch again and wondered what was happening at the hospital.

Finnish Sauna

Image was photographed by and belongs to the Author

Chapter 8
Medical Miracle

Gamiel sat in the white sterile surroundings of the Intensive Care Unit. The hospital room wasn't large, but there was enough room for the two beds and the curtain between them. He was grateful for the quiet corner the architects had designed for the benches where he sat watching Laila and her husband, Jarmo, Laaksonen standing with immediate and extended family members gathered around Grandmother Laaksonen.

Rachel was standing with Kaila fully attentive and taking in all the English explanations that were offered amidst the avalanche of Finnish conversation. Even Gamiel had given up trying to keep up with all that was being said. It had been too many years and would still require a few months before his Finnish was fully fluent. Gamiel was surprised at how Mark and Kaila's family had completely accepted Rachel even though she was a complete stranger barely in-country 15 hours. Part of this acceptance was largely due to Rachel's gracious heart and warm personality. He reflected on what a treasure his wife was to him.

Mark came back in the room, and sat down beside Gamiel. He said, "I called Pekka. He told me the kids were having a great time in the Sauna and would be getting supper shortly."

Gamiel smiled. This was the first time his children experienced the true Finnish Sauna and he was not there to see it. He determined to not miss any more 'firsts'.

Mark, as if sensing his thoughts, commented, "I am sorry our family crisis is intruding so heavily upon your family affairs, Gamiel. It was too gracious of you and Rachel to come down this evening. You both must be very tired."

Gamiel put his arm around his friend's shoulder, and said, "My friend, of all the treasures of this earth, and all times that are more important than another, there is no treasure nor moment in time that is more precious to me than the welfare of my friends."

Mark looked Gamiel in the eye, and revealed a tear of gratitude. "Thank you, my friend."

At that moment, the cell in Mark's pocket rang. He took the call and answered in Finnish. "Terve, hei. Oh, yes, I am going secure now." Mark put the phone in encrypted mode and handed it to Gamiel, saying, "Gamiel, this is Trevor."

Gamiel took the phone. "Hello Trevor. What you got?"

The voice on the cell was familiar to Gamiel. It had been a central theme most of his adult life. Gamiel wondered what it was that brought certain men together to accomplish great things that decided the fate of nations. Here they both were again involved in something that could save a life – and, in a larger sense, if the Unified Field Door and T-L-E performed as expected, people of all nations could be blessed beyond their wildest imaginations.

Trevor said, "Gamiel, I took the liberty of flying my personal physician to Denver while I was testing these new T-L-E Door calibrations. I want you to talk with Dr. Garrett while I finish my preparations."

"Hello?"

Gamiel took the phone into a quiet side chamber and closed the door, "Hello, Dr. Garrett, my name is Gamiel Reuel. Trevor is my most trusted associate. You are in my lab where we have built a very fascinating device Trevor can explain later– if he has not already – but, right now we are going to do something that has never been done before."

From the other side of the world, came the new voice into Gamiel's ear, "Yes, I understand, Dr. Reuel, Trevor has told me everything. If it is true, I am privileged to be a part of it. What have you told the patient, their family members, and the Attending Physician?"

Gamiel expected this. He answered, "At the moment, nothing; reason being, the patient is expiring and the Attending Physician has given her no hope of recovery. I believe we can at least try to see what the T-L-E Door will open to our view. Hopefully, you can find a way to save her. The patient's son has given his permission."

"Dr. Reuel, do you have that in writing?"

"Yes."

"OK. I will tell Trevor to proceed. This is all new to me so I am not sure exactly what to expect."

"That's fine, Dr. Garrett, this is all new to all of us. How did you get to Denver so fast?"

"Trevor pays me a retainer and keeps a company plane ready for emergencies. I think Trevor is ready to begin."

Gamiel marveled at the resources already expended to save a woman they had never met. He said, "Please go-ahead. We are out of time." Gamiel returned to the ICU.

Back in Gamiel's backyard laboratory, Trevor Nibley, one of the world's leading physicists, business tycoon, decorated Naval Officer, Retired; and now Unified Field research specialist in partnership with Dr. Gamiel Ben Reuel, began issuing commands into the software that controlled the T-L-E Door. Ben's suspended orb from his science project rotated as before through the opening vortex and the

T-L-E Door opened exposing a view inside the ICU of family members gathered around a bed with a patient. Trevor took the phone from Dr. Garret and began talking.

"Gamiel, we can see you across the room as we view the patient's bedside. I am moving the coordinates to the patient. As I do, I will let Dr. Garrett direct my focus. I am putting the lab phone on speaker so we can both talk and hear your report and you can hear Dr. Garrett's comments."

Gamiel marveled as he looked around the room and saw no evidence of any disturbance, yet Trevor was here in the room with them as they spoke. He leaned over to Mark and whispered, "Trevor is beginning the scan."

Mark said, "That's incredible. I can't tell anything is going on."

Dr. Garrett spoke to Trevor. "This is amazing. Please move around the patient's head. Yes. Massive contusions, massive... Trevor, can you move so I can see underneath her head where it lays against the sheet?"

Trevor did so...

Dr. Garrett gasped in amazement. "Yes. That's perfect. There is evidence of some damaged cranial connective tissue, but I cannot be sure without X-Rays."

Gamiel moved away from the group again and spoke quietly into the phone, muting his voice with his hand, and asked, "Trevor, are you satisfied with your experiments? Do you believe you can move this open door inside human tissue mass without disturbing anything?

Trevor answered, "Yes."

Gamiel said, "Dr. Garrett, you are about to view actual living organ tissue inside a patient's body which I believe will offer more pertinent information about this patient than any X-ray ever will. With your permission, Trevor will move your view to any position and magnification you specify inside the patient's body."

Speaking to Gamiel, Trevor said, "I need you to go up beside the patient and make sure none of my activities are disturbing the observable space-time matter."

Gamiel stepped back near Mark and whispered, "Can you ask them to let me stand by her head?"

Mark spoke to the family members who parted for Gamiel to stand next to her head beside the bed, cell phone in his pocket using a hands-free device in his ear.

Gamiel said, "I can see no disturbance."

Trevor said, "OK. Dr. Garrett has asked me to look inside the injured area of the cranium. I am re-calibrating focus and moving inside her cranium space."

Dr. Garrett said, "Amazing. Are you sure the patient is experiencing no additional induced trauma?"

Gamiel replied, "None. I can see no evidence of intrusion."

Gamiel looked around the room at the family members watching him. He wondered what they were thinking. He looked over at Mark and motioned for him to come near.

He whispered in his Mark's ear. "Mark, does anyone here think I am some kind of miracle healer; do they believe I am going to save this person?"

Mark whispered back, "They are all hoping for a miracle Gamiel. The only one who knows anything is Jarmo. Please do not worry. They understand we do what we can."

Gamiel listened to Trevor who was already talking into his ear, "Gamiel we are moving about inside the injured flesh – and I have gone up and down the magnification scale without once loosing focus. Dr. Garrett is speechless. He is taking notes."

Dr. Garrett spoke up. "Gamiel, can you get the attending physician into the room to talk with me? I think we have a chance of saving this woman."

Gamiel said, "Mark, quick, get the doctor in here."

Mark left the room and came back with a petite Finnish lady who spoke good English with a thick accent.

Mark said, "Gamiel, this is Doctor Rinnekari." <pronounced Re'-Neigh -Car -E>

Gamiel said, "Thank you Doctor. Would you mind speaking with Dr. Garrett?" He switched off the hands-free mode and handed the phone to Dr. Rinnekari.

Mark said, "Dr. Rinnekari, I realize this is most unusual, but I ask you to trust me."

She took the phone, and said, "This is Dr. Rinnekari."

Dr. Garrett introduced himself and said, "I know this will sound fantastic to you, but I have a way of looking into your patient's injury from where I now stand. I have been told she has been given no hope of recovery. However, I have discovered something X-Rays and Cat-Scans might miss. If you will try what I suggest, you may save this person's life. I can't do it myself, nor do I expect you do anything you do not feel is right; but, I ask you to consider whether it is worth the chance this patient may survive."

Dr. Rinnekari was amazed but skeptical. However, the name Mark Leppänen – Member of the Finnish Council of State, Minister of Education, was widely recognized. He was also trusted in his own community – his family name locally respected. The fact that he was in the room personally asking for her cooperation persuaded her to listen as Dr. Garrett explained his proposed procedure.

Dr. Rinnekari said, "Dr. Garrett, I will assemble my staff and perform your procedure. Mark, I need to move the patient into the operating room immediately. Please ask all family and friends to return to the waiting room."

Dr. Rinnekari kept Mark's phone and took the hands-free device Gamiel handed her as she ushered everyone out the door while the interns and nurses quickly prepared the patient, rolled the bed out the door and down the hall.

Outside in the waiting room, Rachel sat next to Gamiel and quietly asked, "Gamiel, what's going on? Did Trevor use the 'T-L-E door' to look at Grandma Laaksonen's injuries?"

Gamiel replied with muted voice, "Trevor could not describe it. Dr. Garrett took notes and explained things to Dr. Rinnekari. Beyond that, I don't know. I only hope it works. I tried to find evidence of intrusion and there was none. Do you realize what that means?"

"Are you saying you can look inside someone's body through the T-L-E door and that person can't feel a thing?"

If this works, that is exactly what I am saying."

Mark beckoned Gamiel who stood and walked over where he stood by Jarmo.

Kaila came over and sat by Rachel. The two women had formed an instant bond of friendship that transcended culture and language.

Kaila asked, "Rachel, do you know what is going on?"

Rachel looked at her, wondering how to explain, or even if it was safe to say anything. She answered, "I don't understand the science and technical terms, and I can't say how it works, but a medical doctor of one of our friends back home is recommending a miraculous procedure he believes will save your sister's mother."

Kaila looked down and said, "I believe in miracles. My sister is coming to believe, but she is not of our faith. What faith are you?"

Rachel said, "Gamiel comes from Jewish heritage. I was raised in a Christian home – we had no affiliation with any denomination. Gamiel and I share a belief in God and a faith in his goodness and mercy."

Kaila smiled and said, "Then we have much in common. I am a convert to Christ's church. So is Mark. We both joined shortly after Alexi was born. We believe in healing and other manifestations of God's love, and in the ministering of angels. I felt a divine presence in the room tonight. It seemed to be centered around your husband."

Rachel asked, "What do you mean by a "presence?"

Kaila answered, "I don't know who you are, or what Gamiel does, but your husband is a great man. The spirit whispered to me that you and your husband have a very special mission."

Rachel pondered upon Kaila's words, reflecting upon both the historical and future implications to her and Gamiel for having opened the Trans-Light-Element door. As she did so, future prospects both grand and frightening opened to her mind.

Time passed slowly; minutes seemed like hours. Just 30 minutes later, Dr. Rinnekari came out and spoke with Jarmo in Finnish. Jarmo and Laila went into the recovery room followed by other family members.

Dr. Rinnekari beckoned Gamiel and Mark into her office. Looking squarely at Gamiel, she said, "I don't know who you are, but Dr. Garrett has just coached me in pioneering a new procedure he guarantees me is not in any medical journal. The only reason I have consented to do it is because of the personal esteem I have for the Leppänen and Laaksonen families. Dr. Garrett says he is not at liberty to tell me how he was able to view Mrs. Laaksonen's injuries through an imaging device located in the United States. Are you?"

Gamiel shook his head, saying, "I am sorry, but neither am I."

Mark asked, "Will she live?"

"Yes, I am sorry, I forgot to tell you. The procedure was a success; the patient has revived. It will be at least a week before we can think about releasing her."

Dr. Rinnekari continued, "I can't fault you for saving that woman's life; but, I do not have sufficient data to record the procedure I used tonight in my official records. Unless a medical procedure has been approved by competent authority, even if it accidentally works, it could be considered malpractice. Do you understand the position I am in?"

Mark said, "Yes, but don't you allow for miracles – acts of God – I mean not everything can be explained by medical science – and not all your patients survive despite everything you can do. Isn't there something you can reference from your approved procedures that might justify your actions?"

Gamiel searched Dr. Rinnekari's face for some clue to understanding and trust. He asked, "Dr.

Rinnekari, what happens if you simply ascribe this success to an act of God."

A look of surprise crossed her face, and she asked, "Are you suggesting God had a hand in this?"

Gamiel said, "I believe he did. There are many ways to tell this story. May I suggest that you give Him credit for everything you cannot explain and rejoice in the preservation of the life of your patient?"

Dr. Rinnekari said, "You are a wise man. Mark has assured me he trusts you completely; but, I still have to find a way to explain to my peers why I deviated from normal procedure. My own medical practice could be called into question. The mere fact that it worked, and the patient recovered could be labeled an accident by the medical board."

Gamiel replied, "You have Jarmo's signed permission to use your professional judgment. You also consulted a leading physician from the United States about this procedure both before and during the operation. I suggest you simply explain the procedure you used and why you believe it worked, and leave the rest in God's hands. Your pioneering effort helped save a life – and can now be verified and repeated by your peers."

Dr. Rinnekari replied, "I will consider your advice Dr. Reuel; but, someday I really would like to understand how Dr. Garrett could see from his laboratory on the other side of the world without any instruments – what none of us here could find with the best instruments money can buy. How do I explain that?"

Mark said, "Dr. Reuel is conducting very sensitive research under Presidential protection. I wish we could tell you more. I must ask you to take an oath of silence about his research. Will you do that?"

Dr. Rinnekari looked pensive, and said, "I will need a letter from the Eduskunta granting immunity from any malpractice considerations."

Mark said, "I can arrange that."

Dr. Rinnekari said, "Thank you. I must go now."

Later, after family and friends concluded their visit, Gamiel and Mark were walking out of the hospital behind Rachel and Kaila. Laila stayed with Jarmo. It was agreed Seppo would remain at the Leppänen home and play with Joseph until tomorrow afternoon.

As Mark and Gamiel walked outside returning to the car ahead of their wives, Gamiel asked, "Do you think the good doctor will be silent about our part in this?"

Mark answered, "She really has no alternative. If she attempts to disclose our role in this miracle, it will make her medical report seem implausible. She is a good person and a very good doctor. She will find a way to explain her success."

Gamiel replied, "How long will it take to get the letter from the Eduskunta?"

Mark said, "I will write it as soon as I get home. A signed copy will be on her desk tomorrow morning."

Gamiel smiled and said, "You Finns don't waste any time, do you?"

Mark smiled back, and said, "Time never stops, Gamiel, you know that."

The drive home was pleasant. Gamiel kept dozing off. Mark noticed and let him sleep in between comments. Rachel and Kaila talked most of the way about their children and plans for the summer.

Nearly half way back to the Leppänen estate, Mark's phone rang. The shrill sound awoke Gamiel from his slumber. Kaila took the call, talking in Finnish. She handed the phone to Mark.

Mark's rich voice spoke in his native tongue, "Terve, Mitä kuuluu?" <mee tä coo-luu>

He listened in silence then, in Finnish, said, "Thanks, Pekka. We will be home as fast as we can." The family car became a government cruiser, immune to speed limits.

Gamiel asked, "What's wrong?"

Mark replied, "Security detected an intruder on the grounds."

Chapter 9
Intruder Alert

B en and Joseph were happy to finally retire to their room for the evening. Ben looked forward to a new dawn after good night's rest. Monday would be Joseph's first visit with his new Doctor. That was the main reason the Reuel Family had come to Finland.

Joseph was already fast asleep. The Sauna had completely relaxed his tired body. Ben smiled at how the Finnish foods excited Joseph enough to eat more than usual. Ben felt his own stomach wishing he had eaten a little less.

Welcome sleep was tugging at his conscious thought when he heard loud Finnish voices outside his window. At first he was afraid they might wake up Joseph. Then Alexi came into his room and said, "Ben, come quickly."

Ben slipped on his house shoes and quietly closed the door as he entered the grand hallway. He asked, "What is all the commotion?"

Alexi said, "Security just told me they spotted an intruder. You need to shut your windows. Tell Vanessa. Is Joseph asleep yet?"

"Yes."

"OK. You tell Vanessa. I will shut your windows."

Ben knocked on Vanessa's door. She opened, and asked, "What is all the noise about?"

Ben said, "There is an intruder! Shut and lock your windows!"

Vanessa turned and hurried to her window. Just as she was closing it, she thought she saw a dark human form running down the driveway. Locking the window tight, she turned and followed Ben into the hallway. Looking around, she asked, "Where are Joseph, and Seppo?"

Ben said, "Joe is asleep in bed."

Alexi said, "Seppo is getting ready for bed. He is with Koira."

One of the security staff approached Alexi speaking Finnish rapidly, looking very agitated.

Vanessa asked, "What is he saying?"

The servant left. Alexi answered, "He said they chased someone who was trying to get in the library from the back patio. They don't know how he got to the house without setting off the alarms."

Ben said, "And I was hoping to get a good night's rest."

Vanessa answered, "How can you rest at time like this?"

Ben said, "Easy! All I have to do is close my eyes and I will be gone in seconds."

Vanessa shook her head and asked Alexi, "Have you tried reaching your parents?"

"Security tried but the phone was busy."

"So what do we do now?"

"I suggest you stay in your rooms with the windows closed and locked. A security guard is coming to stand by your doors. Father has given those instructions to keep you safe where ever you go. You did not know it, but they were right behind us the whole time we were in Lahti this afternoon."

Vanessa looked at Ben with sobering concern.

Ben said, "I am going to bed. This day has been too long already. Thanks Alexi. I am looking forward to a good night's rest."

Vanessa said, "Good night little brother."

Ben was too tired to protest the word 'little'. He went back in his room and closed the door.

Alexi said, "Good night, Vanessa. It has been wonderful meeting and getting to know you and your family."

"Likewise... Will you be staying at home tomorrow? Or, do you have things to do?"

"Well, it is summer vacation. School is out. I don't start class in the University until mid-August. I guess we do whatever we can as long as my parents approve."

"OK then. I can't wait to see what Finns have for breakfast on Monday mornings."

Alexi laughed, and said, "Around here, since you are a guest, you may probably have anything you ask for."

Vanessa thought about that, and said, "Sometimes it is better to just accept what is given without asking too much."

Alexi smiled and bowed, saying, "Nobly spoken. Until breakfast?"

"Until then. Goodnight Alexi. Thanks for the great Sauna and for taking us to meet your friends."

"You are welcome. Good night."

Vanessa smiled and closed her door.

About 15 minutes later, Mark turned his car onto the grounds from the main road. There were several guards standing at strategic locations on both sides of the gate, inside and outside the grounds. Mark did not stop to question them. Another five minutes and he pulled up under the overhang at the front door in the circle drive and gave the keys to one of the attendants.

The parents went quickly inside as the attendant parked the car in the garage. Once inside the house, Mark questioned Pekka. After getting the full story, he joined the Reuels to check on their children.

Kaila checked on her own children. Opening Alexi's door first, she spoke quietly in Finnish.

"Alexi? Are you awake?"

Alexi replied in Finnish, "Yes. I couldn't sleep."

"How did things go tonight?"

"It was great, Mother. The Reuels really liked the Sauna. The house staff was superb. Supper was delicious. The Reuels are the best. I think Ben wants to learn to speak Suomi."

"How did Joseph and Seppo get along?"

"…like they had known each other for years."

"What happened when the intruder came?"

"Nothing dramatic. Vanessa said she saw someone running down the driveway to the highway."

"Were the younger children frightened?"

"No. Joseph was already asleep. I did not alarm Seppo. Security took care of everything very well. There was never a time we felt unsafe."

"That is good."

"Did Vanessa enjoy the Sauna? Her mother told me she did not want to try it."

There was a pause… then Alexi asked, "Mother, is it possible to know your future wife – I mean – before anyone really knows or talks about it?"

Kaila caught her breath. This was her 18 year old son talking about marriage. She composed her thoughts and said, with a slight smile curling her lips, "Yes, but how did Vanessa enjoy the Sauna?"

"Oh, she loved it. She said she was going to ask her father to build a Sauna when they got back home – only she wasn't sure if they could because that might mean having to install a swimming pool, too."

Kaila laughed, and asked, "Do you like Vanessa?"

"Very much. I don't know why, but it seems like I've known her all my life."

Mother and son had a quiet moment before Kaila continued, "Are you asking me if I think Vanessa will be your future wife?"

Another short moment of reflection before Alexi said, "Not really; and, I don't want you to worry about my plans for going to school and serving a mission. I plan on doing both."

Kaila breathed a silent sigh of relief in her heart and listened as her son talked.

"Mother, I can't really explain everything I felt today. One thing was made clear to me; Vanessa is supposed to become my wife – and I plan to ask her three years from now."

Kaila was amazed and fearful, yet grateful her son was coming to her with these thoughts. She asked, "Does Vanessa know how you feel?"

"No; or at least I have not told her a word about this. As for what she is experiencing herself, I cannot say. She has not said anything to me. I think it is really too soon to share anything like that with each other."

There was a short pause, then Alexi asked, "Will it be alright if Vanessa and Ben come to Helsinki with Koira and me – and Timo and Niina?

Kaila thought before she answered, " I don't know. That is something Dr. Reuel will need to answer. His family is here under the protection of the Finnish government and I don't know what security practices they may need to follow."

"Oh. I guess I will talk with Father."

"That would be best. Your father has extended the hospitality of our nation under his own cognizance. If something should go wrong, your father could face disciplinary action. So, for now, please keep all your feelings in perspective. I hope you can sleep now. Good night, Alexi."

"Goodnight"

Kaila turned to go when Alexi asked, "Oh, I am sorry I forgot ask earlier. How is Great Aunt Pauliina?"

"Kaila turned and said, "By a miracle she revived and will be discharged in about a week. Perhaps we can discuss everything tomorrow. It was good of you to ask."

"I am so glad to hear it. When may we go visit her?"

"In a couple of days."

"That is very good. Good night, Mother."

Kaila closed the door and peeked in on Koira and Seppo before returning to the grand hall where she found her husband and Gamiel. She asked, "Where is Rachel?"

Gamiel said, "Vanessa could not sleep, so Rachel is visiting with her."

Mark said, "Pekka showed me the video records. It looks as if our intruder swam ashore from the lake. He climbed onto the docks from the pier by the boat house. Unfortunately, he was able to get off the grounds before anyone got a good look at him. He was wearing a black skin-diving suit with complete head ensemble and breathing mask, so none of the videos got anything more than a form and body size. I have contacted the police. This is the first time anyone has broached the government warning sign buoys. There will have to be a complete internal investigation. May I suggest we all go to bed tonight? Gamiel, I know you wanted to have Sauna – what about tomorrow evening?"

Gamiel replied, "Sounds good to me. I think I will turn in. Good night." He walked across the rotunda and went inside his room.

Kaila looked at her husband and said, "There are more things brewing than you know my husband. I think we should all retire for the evening and pray tomorrow is only half as busy as this day has been."

Mark and Kaila walked towards their room, talking about the intruder and how well their children got along with their guests.

Thus ended one of the longest Sunday's the Reuel family could remember. Gamiel laid his head on his pillow expecting to fall fast asleep when Rachel spoke in the darkness next to him, "Our daughter is in-love."

Gamiel answered, "I know."

Rachel asked, "If you knew, when were you planning to tell me?"

Gamiel said, "Well, I didn't really know – I just observed. How did you know?"

"She told me."

Now was Gamiel's turn to feel left out. "What did she say?"

"Alexi is the most perfect person she has ever met. She knows he likes her by the way he treats her and talks to her. She said the spirit whispered to her today to honor her future husband."

Gamiel sat up in bed, and said, "Rachel this is serious. You did not see her this morning when she first met Alexi. If she is thinking God is giving her fore knowledge of her husband, we may have problems."

"Gamiel calm down. I visited with Vanessa a half hour this evening while you and Mark were chasing that intruder. She knows the time is not right. For some reason, she seems to think it will probably be about three years. She isn't sure yet, but she wants to go to Helsinki with Alexi and his friends next week and begin application to the University. Alexi tells her that people come to Finland from all over the world to go to school because tuition is free – if they can pass the entrance exam. She wants to see how hard it really will be for an American who does not speak Finnish to attend Helsinki University."

Gamiel lay back down. His little girl was growing up – and becoming a responsible adult, too. He said, "I will talk with Mark tomorrow. He probably knows how to enroll Vanessa if that is what she wants. With the income we now enjoy from Trans-Light-Element, I don't have any concerns about paying for it. Frankly, I can't think of a finer learning institution on the planet."

Rachel giggled, "You're biased, aren't you?"

Gamiel said, "No, just better informed."

Rachel smiled to herself and said, "Right. Dr. Gamiel Ben Reuel, – inventor of Trans-Light-Element and the T-L-E Door, able to see into burning buildings and human brains, best informed expert on international universities."

"OK wife. Don't get carried away. I am very tired. How about we just go to sleep?"

"I second that motion, husband." Rachel was asleep before Gamiel

Gamiel was slumbering deeply within minutes. His dreams carried the burdens of fatherhood and a daughter who was already talking marriage. It was too soon, as it always comes far too quickly – especially to your only daughter.

Chapter 10
Drop Shipment

B en stood up from tying his shoes and said, "Joseph, let's get breakfast! Alexi said he would make 'pannukakku' today!"

"Oh boy! Some more delicious weird Finnish food." Joseph hurried getting dressed as best he could in his weakening condition.

"Why do you keep calling Finnish food 'weird'?"

"That is what Vanessa said it was."

"Well, don't say that anymore. It might offend our hosts. Besides, it is some of the best food I have ever eaten. Don't you agree?"

"Sure. What does 'weird' mean?"

"It means strange – and sometimes not very nice. That isn't what you think of Finnish food, is it?"

"No way! It is not weird. Do you think we need to tell Vanessa?"

"Nah. I think Vanessa learned a lot yesterday. She seems different. I can't explain it yet. Are you ready to go eat now?"

"Yep."

"OK then."

The two brothers left their room, closing the door, and walked into the grand hall. Ben enjoyed the feeling of the grand old mansion. He sensed a happiness that permeated from the very walls – even more; somehow, everyone who lived and worked here was happy. He had never seen so many happy people all under one roof.

The sun was already high in the sky sending warm rays through the dome skylight. The boys wasted no time getting to the kitchen.

"Hei, hei, Ben. Mitä Kuuluu?" <mee tä coo-luu>

Ben smiled at Alexi, grateful he remembered Ben wanted to start talking Finnish. Ben remembered immediately what that phrase meant – literally, "What is heard?" Translated for meaning and intent, in english, one might say, "What is going on?" or "How are you doing, today?"

Ben remembered the standard response, and replied, "Hyvää kuuluu," meaning, "Good is heard."

Alexi smiled and said, "Very good. You will be talking Suomi in no time."

Joseph asked, "Is that a cock coo pan?"

Alexi laughed, and asked, "Do you mean Pannukakku? <Paw' knew cock cuu>"

"Yes. What is it?"

"Pancake."

"Oh. It looks different from the pancakes Mom makes."

"That's because this is a Finnish pancake. Most Americans refer to them as Swedish Pancakes, but we don't mind. They still taste good."

Alexi demonstrated excellent cooking skills. Soon a batch of Finnish pancakes (similar to Crêpes) were ready for toppings of choice. Kaila came into the kitchen and smelled breakfast already on the table.

"Thank you, Alexi. That looks wonderful. How are you this morning, Ben? Did you enjoy the Sauna last night?"

"Oh it was great! Wasn't it Joseph?"

"Yes. Sauna is fun. Can we do it again today?"

About that moment, Rachel came into the kitchen and said, "If Doctor Mäkkinen says it is OK, you can do the Sauna whenever it is offered. How are you Kaila?"

Kaila responded cheerfully, "Well, thank you. What time is your appointment with Dr. Mäkkinen?"

"3 pm; however, Gamiel and I wanted to arrive about an hour early and tour the care facility first before our appointment."

"Understandable! You will be in our prayers. You have wonderful children."

Rachel looked at her boys with gratitude for their hosts praise.

Koira came into the kitchen, and asked, "Mother, do you know where Seppo is?"

"Why... No! Alexi, did you get Seppo up this morning?"

Alexi said, "No, I let him sleep. Isn't he in my room?"

Kaila answered, "Not when I looked in. Where do you think he is?"

Joseph said, "I think he is in the library."

Koira and Kaila went to the library. Rachel followed. Ben left Joseph in his chair at the table eating pannukakku and followed everyone into the library. Alexi continued getting the table set for breakfast.

Kaila called, "Seppo, misä olet?" <where are you?>

Koira called, "Seppo!"

Ben walked over to the large raised area where desks hid the bottom of the ladders that ran around the perimeter of the library shelves that extended from the floor to the 7 meter <approximately 21 feet> ceiling.

There at the bottom of the ladder sat Seppo, reading a book.

Ben called, "Here he is. He is reading a book."

Kaila came around and spoke in Finnish, "Seppo, didn't you hear us?"

Seppo looked up, and smiled, replying in Finnish, "I was reading this book. It has pictures of Joseph's home. Look!" (Katso! Kas!)

Ben understood that Finnish interjection and looked at pictures of Denver and the Rocky Mountains. He was amazed at Seppo's ability to find a book about a place he had just talked about yesterday. Ben asked Koira, "Does he know how to read?"

"Remarkably well for his age; we talked yesterday about Joseph's home and I showed him that book. He must have really liked it."

Kaila said, "OK. Let's go eat breakfast. Seppo. Halluatko syödä?" <Do you want to eat?>

"Kyllä. Menkämme nyt. <Yes. Let's go now.>

The small crowd returned to the kitchen to be seated around the large breakfast table. Mark had already entered and was just sitting down by Joseph who was already eating his second pancake.

Gamiel walked into the room just after everyone else and said, "Good Morning!"

All echoed a return greeting, not quite in chorus but close.

Ben was fascinated with the table. It seemed very rustic. He asked, "How old is this table?"

Rachel was embarrassed by the question, and spontaneously replied, "Ben?!"

Mark said, "It is alright Rachel. Ben is very observant. This table belonged to my Great Grandmother. I have refused to let it leave the family. Every year I have to repair something or other on it so we can keep using it. Great Grandmother Leppänen had 13 children. For many years, all of them, including my Grandfather Leppänen, sat around this table at the old family farm near Seinäjoki."

"Where?"

"Seinäjoki is a city northwest from here not far from the Gulf of Sweden, near Vaasa. My father had to pay his Uncle Tuovi dearly for this table; but he finally named a price our greedy great uncle could not refuse."

"Cool!" Ben was appropriately impressed.

At that moment, Vanessa joined the two families in the kitchen, apologizing, "I am so sorry; I slept in and nobody awakened me." She glanced over at Alexi as if seeking approval.

Alexi smiled, and said, "You are just in time. The pancakes are hot."

Everyone was seated and Mark offered a blessing on the meal in Finnish. Ben felt a familiar warmth during the prayer – a feeling he remembered from his own prayers. The food was passed all around. There was more than enough. Each had grand comments about the chef.

Alexi smiled and said, "Really, it was nothing. Mother was the one who showed me how to do it."

Rachel noted how Kaila glowed.

Ben asked, "Dad, have you heard from Trevor today?"

Despite the sudden turn of topic, Gamiel looked at his son with understanding eyes and said, "No. This morning Mark and I plan to survey the grounds and make some decisions. You are welcome to come along."

"Thanks." Ben was elated. They were finally going to do something about Trans-Light-Element. He could hardly wait.

Kaila spoke up, "Mark, all the women want to go with me this morning to visit the open air market in Asikkala. I was telling Rachel about the quaint little restaurant by the canal bridge. Do you mind if we stop there for lunch today?"

"That will be grand. Are you taking the younger boys, too?"

"Of course. We will be back right after lunch. Then Gamiel and Rachel need to leave early to look things over before their appointment with Doctor Mäkkinen."

"Yes, of course. Gamiel, you and Rachel can use my car. I will have matters of State to attend to today. I may even be required to go into Helsinki this morning. I can take the late morning commuter train. It is actually faster, and I don't have to look for a place to park."

Gamiel said, "Thank you Mark. Will you have time to discuss the laboratory before you leave?"

"Yes, right after breakfast."

Vanessa and Koira helped Alexi clean up the breakfast dishes. Joseph and Seppo went into the den to play with Seppo's toys and look at books. Rachel and Kaila visited in the garden room where she showed off her kitchen garden. Rachel was impressed with the variety of vegetables growing in this northern soil in the warmth of a solar room.

Ben tagged along with Gamiel and Mark. The conversation drifted from politics to science and finally to the matter at hand, Trans-Light-Element.

"Gamiel, I don't see why you can't use my basement. It is very spacious and mostly empty. I can get someone to remove everything. It is a natural location for your lab.

Gamiel replied, "Thank you, Mark, but I don't want to expose your home to unpredictable events related to Trans-Light-Element research. We are venturing into new untested waters every day. Anything could happen. Ben can tell you T-L-E is full of surprises."

Ben nodded.

Gamiel continued, pointing, "I like that old barn out there."

Mark blurted, "...that old thing? It might fall on top of you."

"It won't after we get the generators up and fabricate new internal walls out of T-L-E.

"Will it change how the barn looks?"

"You won't even notice any changes on the outside; and I promise to preserve the rustic ambiance on the inside. Then, after we start fabricating T-L-E, I believe we will be able to make new buildings in short order, out of the elements that surround us. We can even go underground, if you wish."

Mark shook his head. "That is incredible. How soon before Trevor starts sending your first lab components through the new T-L-E door?"

"I hope tomorrow. We don't have much time. As soon as we can get up and operational, we can really beef up your security here. With a functioning T-L-E generator site, I believe T-L-E can be configured to selectively deny access based on your inputs."

Mark looked around, looked at his old barn and said, "My father used that old barn to keep livestock and hay. The previous owners had it built in the early part of the last century out of imported oak planks. It is solid as a rock, just old and weathered, with a lot of leaks. I got out of the livestock business - just did not like it. Now, it just sits there."

"That old barn will be a perfect cover for my lab. No one will suspect the inside of that building is the Finnish connection to the T-L-E Spaceport."

Mark shook his head and said, "Well, I guess I will keep my basement then."

Gamiel looked at his wrist to check his watch, and then remembered it was missing. He shook his head and said, "I wish I knew what happened to my watch.

That is the most puzzling thing. What time do you have now Mark?"

"10 am."

"Well, it is 1 am in Denver right now. I don't expect Trevor will be up, yet, but I would like to get on the internet and fire off some emails so he can start working them first thing after he wakes up."

"Sure, use my office. I need to hurry and catch the train."

Ben was fascinated by the old barn. He asked, "Dad may I go over and look inside that barn?"

Gamiel looked at Mark.

"Sure," Mark said. "There is nothing in there but a bunch of old farm implements."

Gamiel nodded his approval.

Ben took off at a trot, eager to explore, ready for action.

The two fathers returned to the house discussing their plans for the remainder of the day.

Once inside the old barn, Ben noticed sunlight peeking through knotholes and warped siding. His quick breaths from the short run drew in the musty odor from old dry hay mingled with an old lingering hint of cows and sheep. Rusting plows and pitch forks hung from the wall since a bygone era in which men labored for their daily sustenance to store up enough to last through the long dark Finnish winters.

A large mother cat with kittens defended a cozy warm corner; where they absorbed the rays of the morning sun while the kittens nursed. A bridle dangled from an old nail in the large equestrian stall where the hoof mark impressions in the dried mud and scarred sides of the wooden stall wall gave Ben the feeling a horse would be coming back any moment. He imagined what it would have been like to harness a horse to the old wagon now falling apart in the open space across from the stall with one remaining wheel intact. The old structure was huge with a center open space large enough to park six large wagons top heavy with hay.

Ben noticed hay straw and grains of salt where farm workers must have tossed them from the wagons to the hay lofts. He recalled reading how in old times farmers salted the loose layers of hay in the lofts to prevent spontaneous combustion. They would spread about 2 or 3 feet thick in the loft, then salt, then another 2 feet or so with another sprinkling of salt until the wagons were empty or the loft was filled.

The old barn roof seemed very sturdy construction, designed to withstand the weight of heavy snows. The barn was well built, just as Mark had mentioned. Ben moved to the very center to get a better feel for the weathered timber – huge oak beams imported for this once impressive building. As he was looking for any leaks in the roof, he heard a distinct 'thud' behind him.

Turning about he saw a very large crate sitting in the exact center of the barn where none had been before. Ben moved close to inspect the inscriptions on the side, written in English.

"**From: Nibley Enterprises, Ogden, Utah**"
"**TO: Reuel Research Laboratories**
Asikkala, Finland"
"**Mode of Transport: T-L-E Drop Shipment**"

There was a series of thuds. Ben turned around to see three more crates. As he was looking, he saw another drop out of thin air from about 2 feet above ground. The soft dirt in the barn absorbed the impact of the crates. Billowing dust clouds rose for the first time in decades of non-disturbance.

Ben ran as fast as his legs could carry him to tell his father.

Michael Irvin Bosley

Alternating Log Pole Shingling of a Finnish Barn Roof

Image was photographed by and belongs to the Author

Chapter 11
New Discoveries

S unlight beamed through one of the holes in the eaves of the old barn onto the letter in Gamiel's hand like a spotlight. Ben stood by impatiently as his father read without a word.

Nibley Corporation
Nibley Enterprises, Nibley Security
1 am, Monday
Doctor Gamiel Ben Reuel, President
Reuel Research Laboratories, Incorporated
T-L-E Space Port, Incorporated
Asikkala Finland Field Office

Dear Gamiel,
I have been monitoring your conversation with Mark for the past half hour; acted immediately on your decision to drop-off equipment in the barn. This letter announces the first shipment through a working T-L-E port. I know; it is too early for me to be up – but the reality is I got a good nap yesterday after church and couldn't go back to sleep.

I also got a call shortly after midnight from Tom Clarington, my Chief Engineer back in Ogden. He made an unexpected breakthrough late Saturday evening after my first letter to you. I will spare you all the research data in this letter. You can log on the encrypted Corporate Website at your leisure and take all the time you need to review his report.

Let me say the constraints we faced on Saturday have been overcome. It was all a matter of calibration and compensation for time-space variations. This is where we stand now:

1. T-L-E Door calibration is controlled through a series of algorithms that depend upon precise

location coordinates – and the earth's magnetic field fluctuation parameters of the coordinate in question. A quick review of our current data about the earth's magnetic field parameters enabled my research team to tighten up the T-L-E Door. This will become critical as we plan deliveries to other planetary bodies – a lot of astronomical variables for which we have no data right now.

2. Your medical experiment earlier this morning was extremely valuable to our research effort. I passed on the results of our activity to my research team in Ogden and they came up with a complete calibration control matrix. This also gave us more concrete test data about how to orient the Door, as you will see from the way we were able to drop-ship our crates straight from my warehouse in Ogden.

3. This brings me to another news flash. Our Unified Field Lab in Ogden opened a second Vortex in accordance with your synchronized field containment ratios you gave me permission use. This time, we focused the phased array directly into the floor of the warehouse. While this T-L-E Door was open, we were able to hang the crates directly over this T-L-E 'man-hole' and lower them right into Mark's barn. Because of the progress I mentioned in paragraph 1, above, all we had to do was release the crates and Tom's new calibration formula's handled the rest. I think we let them fall about two feet. Next time, I plan to just set them down gently before releasing.

4. Your first priority will be to set up a T-L-E Security parameter around the Leppänen grounds. This brings me to our final – possibly most amazing new discovery about T-L-E itself: We can make it invisible! No, I am not going to explain all the scientific reasons how this happens. Read it yourself in Tom's research white paper report, on our secure shared on-line webpage.

5. Let me know if anything got damaged in shipment. We will send a replacement.

Ok, I guess that is all – except for this final post script. One of Tom's brightest lab techs is working on a process for controlling multiple ports within a single doorway. Simply speaking, this means we may be able to use one T-L-E Door to send and receive packages from multiple addresses simultaneously. We are working on a range of Door sizes. I envision a time when we can drive a freight train through a T-L-E Door and never leave the track. Think about driving a space-proofed pressurized train from tracks on the earth seamlessly onto tracks on the Moon, or Mars!"

T-L-E space suits could be fabricated and equipped with micro-gravity control matrices that would allow an Astronaut to walk through a T-L-E door right into space and maneuver where ever he wants.

Consider T-L-E thermal underwear that is so sensitive it can conform to the size and shape of any human body – AND not only adjust automatically to any climate for cooling as well as heating, but – get this, act as the perfect ultimate personal body armor. <OK – You are probably thinking I am getting carried away with too many projects; but hear me out>.

This T-L-E material seems like it can be programmed to take any shape and any size. If that is true, and we can learn how to shape and program it, we can make personal armor suits that will protect the wearer from collisions, speeding bullets, falling boulders, airplane crashes, knives, lasers, you name it – so far T-L-E seems impervious to damage.

Gamiel, I am sorry, but my mind is being carried away into ecstasy over the limitless potential of personal T-L-E body armor. It makes the perfect environmental containment suit – because it would be virtually indestructible. The wearer could dive to the deepest depths, walk on the hottest surface of any alien planet, or no surface at all suspended in deep space. We might even be able to visit the Sun!

I think we could find a way to ship breathing atmosphere through mini-T-L-E doors in this all-purpose diving / space suit. That brings me to another line of thought. What do you think about the potential of microscopic T-L-E doors? What if we could dispense medical subscriptions into a patient at exact molecular and perhaps – get this – maybe even sub-atomic coordinates. Dr. Garrett is following up with research into this application. My lawyers are researching our legal liabilities.

Gamiel, cancer treatment would be revolutionized by pin point targeting of mutated cells. One T-L-E Door could be programmed to target every molecular location of a single human body with billions of dedicated micro-ports tailored to fit the body of the individual patient! Think what this might mean to young Joseph! More about this later!

This much is certain; we can send both large and small packages to precision delivery points – your desk top <or perhaps even your vest pocket – that is still a bit tricky unless you are standing still>, the seat of a moving aircraft – or spacecraft.

We are on the verge of being able to just walk through a T-L-E Door to any measurable and predictable location – be that a moving car, airplane, spacecraft, or planet …just as long as we can predict a continuous future space-time real coordinate and account for all the magnetic, nuclear, and gravitational field parameters at that location. Yes, my head is spinning. Is yours?

OK! You need to hurry up and get your torsion-generators on line so we can start beefing up Mark's security. I have received reports that Ungman may have somehow learned you are in Finland. Now you know why I couldn't sleep.

Sincerely,
Trevor Nibley

P.S. I almost forgot; open the box marked, **"Bug Detectors."** One of my bright lab techs made some 'buttons' out of T-L-E with program instructions to search for electronic surveillance devices. If there is anything monitoring your space, these buttons will start vibrating. Put one in your pocket and give one to all your family and friends. When you want to turn them off, simply press the center of the button with your thumb and forefinger.

Gamiel read the letter for third time then handed it to Ben who read it with eagerness. Ben's jaw dropped as he reviewed all the possible applications for T-L-E. He handed the letter back to his father and asked, "Do you really think T-L-E can help cure Joseph?"

Gamiel answered, "That is for the medical doctors to decide. It won't do to get anyone's hopes up over an untried theory. So, please, don't mention that to your mother, or anyone. What is more, don't talk about anything in Trevor's letter with anyone. Do you understand me, Ben?"

Ben swallowed the lump in his throat and said, "Yes sir."

Gamiel folded the letter and put it in his safe – which Trevor had packed in one of the crates. Then he and Ben examined all the equipment carefully.

Satisfied there was no damage, Gamiel said, "It looks like we can start building our Finnish Laboratory."

Ben asked, "When do we start work?"

Gamiel replied, "This evening after Sauna. You will be in charge of this equipment until Mother and I get back. Until we fabricate T-L-E walls, the only thing keeping us safe is Mark's security staff. If what Trevor says is true, Ungman himself could have been our intruder last night. It is a good thing Mark's security was on the ball."

Ben said, "They do really good."

Gamiel replied, "Yes, I agree. However, for now, only you, Mark, and I are cleared to know what this equipment does. Understand?"

Ben nodded. He checked his watch. It was now Noon. "Dad, does this mean I can't go with you to check Joseph into the hospital?"

Gamiel put his hand on his son's shoulder, and explained, "Joseph will only be over-night for testing. Tomorrow, we will bring him back home after his first treatment. Then he will go through a series of scheduled treatments. There will be times when Joseph may be very weak and exhausted, perhaps even suffer pain. You will have opportunities to visit him while he is undergoing his treatments. Today, I need you to watch the lab."

Ben reflected on how any other time he would be elated at the responsibility his father was handing him. He paused to consider what might be the purpose of conflicting desires and opportunities. After a moment, he decided they were all part of a much larger test – a test of the soul. A new part of his mental and emotional development suddenly awakened to a deep abiding hope that he would prove equal to this larger test.

Father and son walked out of the barn. Gamiel closed the old doors, dropped the huge cross beam, and pulled a towing chain around the beam and bracket to keep it from being lifted, and secured the chain with a very large padlock.

"This padlock will only slow down anyone trying to get in. If anyone tries, just call security."

Ben nodded.

They walked together along an old path that lead back to the well-manicured grounds around the mansion house. The pasture was full of tall grasses, shrubs, berry bushes, and an occasional tree. Birds sang early summer songs Ben loved to hear. Then he heard sounds that told him the ladies and children had returned from their morning outing.

Rachel stepped onto the back patio from the Garden Room and said, "Gamiel, Dr. Mäkkinen is on the phone for you."

Gamiel took the phone. Ben went inside to bid Joseph off.

Joseph and Seppo were playing with a hand copter they got from the open market earlier that morning. Ben asked, "What is that?"

Joseph answered, "A propeller. We twist it in our hands like this and it flies."

The little toy lifted quickly into the air bringing a spontaneous burst of laughter from Joseph and Seppo.

Ben said, "Let me try."

Ben rubbed his hands in opposite directions against the vertical rod connected to the propeller. It climbed nearly to the glass skylight of the grand hallway dome.

Joseph said, "Wow! That was high."

Seppo flew the toy next. It went nearly half as high.

Koira came in from the front door, and asked, "Ben, are you going to the hospital, too?"

"No. I am staying to..." Ben caught himself, and changed what he was going to say in midsentence, "to help Alexi load the wood and stoke the Sauna."

"Oh. Vanessa, are you going?"

"Yes. I am." Vanessa gave Ben a curious look.

Ben smiled and put his hands in a classic time-out crossed T position. That was an agreed Reuel Family symbol for Trans-Light-Element.

Vanessa understood and said, "That is kind of you Ben. Perhaps you and Alexi can find Dad's missing watch, too? What are you doing today, Koira?"

"Nothing. Do you think your Mom and Dad would mind if I come with you?"

Vanessa said, "I am sure they wouldn't."

Despite Koira's Finnish accent and sometimes irregular rhythm, Ben was impressed with her vocabulary and command of the English language.

Ben asked, "When are we planning the boat ride on the lake?"

Koira said, "I am not sure. We need to check with Alexi and Timo."

Ben said, "OK. I will ask Alexi."

Gamiel came into the hall and said, "Vanessa, Mother and I have to leave now. Dr. Mäkkinen has to perform an unscheduled surgery this afternoon. He wants to see us with Joseph at 1 instead of 2. We have just enough time to make it."

Vanessa asked, "Can Koira come with us?"

Gamiel replied, "If her mother says it's OK."

Koira ran to get her mother's permission.

Vanessa grabbed her purse from her room.

Rachel came out of her room with Joseph's suitcase; she asked, "Joseph, are you ready?"

Joseph answered, "Yes ma'am. Is it time now?"

"It's time."

"Good. I am glad we are finally going to see my new doctor. I want to get well."

There was a quiet pause on everyone's part. Ben noted the moment and prayed for his big hearted brother. He said, "Yes, Joseph, we are all very glad you will be getting well soon."

Koira came back with her purse, and said, "OK. Äiti said I can go."

Ben watched his family leave with regret. He wished he was going with them.

Alexi came and stood next to Ben as they waved Koira and Ben's family good bye. Touching Ben's elbow, Alexi said, "Seppo is with my mother. Would you like to come help me stoke the Sauna?

"Sure, where is the wood?" asked Ben.

"We keep the wood in a large shed next to the boathouse – where it is close and easy to toss from the wood box into the firebox."

"Then let's do it, right after lunch. I am famished."

The two young men worked together preparing lunch, then sat down and visited about many things while they were eating.

Ben looked his watch and said, "Wow! I did not realize we took a whole hour for lunch."

By the time they cleaned up the dishes and started loading wood, another thirty minutes had passed.

Ben tossed the wood, Alexi caught it and dropped it in the firebox. Things were going pretty quick. After about 15 minutes of tossing and dropping, Ben paused to ask, "How long since your last firewood delivery?

"This morning. Why?"

"So we used all the wood yesterday and this is all new wood delivered today?"

"Yes."

"So, what is this?"

Alexi peeked in the woodshed. He saw a new green backpack on top of one of the newly stacked woodpiles. He started to reach in and pull it out, when Ben grabbed his hand.

Ben said, "This must have been placed here by the wood delivery man. There is no other explanation. I would not touch it. It could be an explosive device."

Alexi pulled his cell from his side pocket and dialed a two digit code. Speaking in Finnish, Alexi said, "Pekka, hei. Jo – tulle saunalle nopeasti!" (Come to the sauna ASAP!)

Ben looked at Alexi who explained, "Pekka is coming."

It was less than 20 seconds when Pekka rounded the corner of the Sauna at a run.

He stopped and listened as Alexi explained in Finnish, "We think this backpack could have a bomb inside!"

Pekka pushed both boys away from the shed quickly ushering them back to the house. He did not use his cell or any other electrical device. Once they were inside the house, he pulled a fire alarm next to the back door as he was shouting in Finnish "Bomb! Bomb! Everyone go out the front door! Go outside!

Within minutes, Kaila, Seppo, and the rest of the house staff were standing with Alexi and Ben in the front yard while Pekka formed a bomb squad detail from house security and ran back around to the wood shed.

Ben realized with a start the barn he was supposed to be watching was now out of sight. He prayed no one was using this distraction to snoop around the barn. He also prayed Pekka and his team would not detonate the bomb, if that was what it was, and that no one would be injured. He peered anxiously into the dense forest around them wondering who really placed the back pack in the woodshed and why?

A typical Rustic Old Out Building in Finland
(*...much like the old woodshed*)

Image was photographed by and belongs to the Author

Chapter 12
Bond of Trust

D octor Juri Mäkkinen leaned back in his chair to observe the unique American couple who sat before him. He said, "Mr. and Mrs. Reuel, I want to first assure you my staff will do all that is humanly possible for Joseph; however, we cannot make any promises. The will of God and the reality of Joseph's condition must be acknowledged from the start. We both agree that if we do nothing, Joseph might expire from his condition fairly soon; or, he could get better on his own. With that in mind – we cannot assume that any action on our part will only improve his condition. In some cases, the treatment itself presents greater harm. My first rule, always, – do no harm."

Gamiel and Rachel sat alone with Dr. Mäkkinen in his modest office on the outskirts of Lahti. His accent was decidedly Finnish; his English impeccable. They could both see there were no fiscal pretensions in this man's life. He was a dedicated physician from the old school – devoted to his patients and not much concerned about getting rich. While it was obvious he was well paid, his office was not ostentatious. Behind the doctor, they watched through glass bay-doors as Vanessa and Koira played with Joseph in the park overlooking a stand of beautiful pine trees north-west of the hospital complex. Gamiel guessed close to fifty other children were enjoying the warm sunshine, too; adding a festive feeling to the day.

Gamiel looked at Dr. Mäkkinen and said, "We understand. Our intent is to take actions we know will help Joseph; and, of course avoid anything that might make things worse. We plan to be here for Joseph until he has recovered. We only ask that we be allowed to participate in this treatment plan wherever possible."

Dr. Mäkkinen smiled at his new found friend. He did not make friends quickly, but something about Gamiel created an instant bond between two professional men that went beyond the constraints of professional science. "Mr. Reuel, you and your wife have complete access to my clinic – and may assist in anything not barred by law or the rules of the medical profession. Naturally, you must respect insurance rules – and government laws and policies which are a part of the Finnish Social Medicine institution."

"Without reservation," replied Gamiel.

"Good – let's bring young Joseph in and find out how he feels about all this. After all, the patient always comes first."

Gamiel and Rachel stood as Dr. Mäkkinen stood and opened the glass doors behind him to call one of the staff on the grounds. According to prearranged directions, she went over to Vanessa and Joseph and escorted them into the office.

Joseph came in quietly and leaned against his mother while Vanessa stood by her father.

Dr. Mäkkinen stepped around his desk, leaning over and extending his hand towards Joseph in a manner that made him think of Santa Claus, and introduced himself, "My name is Dr. Mäkkinen, how are you today, Joseph?"

Joseph took the cordial handshake and said, "I am fine, Sir. Mother says you are going to help me get well."

With a twinkle in his eye, Dr. Mäkkinen replied, "Well spoken, young man. Your mother is a wise person. I am going to ask you a big favor. If I do all I can to help you get well, will you do all you can to help me, too?"

"Yes, of course."

Dr. Mäkkinen continued, "Sometimes, I may have to ask you to take some medicine that tastes terrible, or makes you feel terrible. Sometimes you may have to stay overnight in my clinic in a strange bed – maybe even without your mother around. Could you do all that?"

Joseph looked at his mother with big round eyes, and said, "If Mother says."

Rachel hugged her baby boy, and said, "I will be here, Joseph, even when you have to stay all night in a strange room."

Dr. Mäkkinen smiled and looked at Gamiel with admiring eyes. All mothers would say that, most all would do it, but it always impressed him when a couple such as Gamiel and Rachel presented themselves in complete unity and devotion as he saw today. He could tell this experience, come what may – would be filled with the right love – crowned by endless vigil.

He opened the glass door and summoned the orderly who had brought Joseph and Vanessa in, and said in Finnish, "Please ready Joseph's room and prepare accommodations for parents and visitors."

The loyal nursing staff orderly left quickly to carry out Dr. Mäkkinen's instructions.

Dr. Mäkkinen looked at Vanessa, and asked, "Are you the big sister?"

Vanessa nodded.

Dr. Mäkkinen continued, "I spoke with Mark Leppänen earlier this morning. He tells me you are looking for a good college to attend. Have you considered University of Helsinki? The Faculty of Medicine there is, in my humble opinion, the best in the world. You strike me as someone who will make a very good doctor."

Vanessa blushed and replied, "I am really not sure what I want to major in."

Dr. Mäkkinen replied, "Then you must do your homework and find out what really interests you. If you are looking for a professional career, make sure you choose something you love." He then turned to Gamiel, and asked, "Did you mention you have some suggestions – about Joseph's treatment?"

Gamiel looked at Rachel and back to Dr. Mäkkinen and said, "Yes. I would like to discuss them alone, if that is alright. Rachel and I have already discussed them."

"Certainly."

Rachel stood and said, "Vanessa, Joseph, let's go visit with Koira. I believe she is waiting for us in the sitting area."

When the office doors closed, leaving Gamiel alone with Dr. Mäkkinen, Gamiel asked, "Doctor, are you open to recent scientific breakthroughs which might aid your research – not only in behalf of young Joseph – but all your patients?"

Dr. Mäkkinen looked at Gamiel with cautious eyes; yet trusting. He studied the back of his hands for a moment while his own thoughts took in all the ramifications of the question. Then he replied, "I am restricted by laws that govern the practice of medicine in Finland. While I am naturally disposed to any new way of saving lives and promoting health – I must draw the line at conducting research on living patients. There are those licensed to do that – with patients who sign permission – I am not one of those. What do you have in mind?"

Now it was Gamiel's turn to consider how far he could trust this man. He decided to bait the hook and study the nibble. "Dr. Mäkkinen, I have discovered a scientific breakthrough that could be used to save my son's life. If it works, it will save thousands – perhaps millions. Will you consider allowing me to introduce this into Joseph's treatment plan?"

Dr. Mäkkinen replied, "Gamiel, please tell me what you think I can do for Joseph."

Gamiel breathed in relief, and added, "I will be asking you to sign a non-disclosure agreement with me backed by the government of Finland before I divulge the nature of my research. As Joseph's father – I will also sign whatever papers you require to make it legal for you to use my research in your treatment program for Joseph. One condition I must insist upon – and that is complete control over the operation and application of the process. Naturally, you will retain complete discretion as to when or whether you choose to use it in your personal practice. Once you understand what I am talking about, I believe you will want to make this a permanent aspect of your practice."

In the course of human relations, there often forms that bond of perfect trust between two persons that goes beyond words or even comprehension. This was one of those moments. Dr. Mäkkinen said, "Where do I sign?"

Gamiel presented a Finnish Government non-disclosure agreement Mark had provided and asked the doctor to sign. It was composed in short, concise, well-structured Finnish. Dr. Mäkkinen read it once; picked up his pen from his desk, and signed it.

Pulling one of the T-L-E bug detector buttons from his vest pocket, Gamiel pressed the center and let it run a few moments to insure no cell phones or other listening devices were within range inside or outside the office. After he was satisfied the area was truly private, Gamiel returned the device to his pocket and leaned back in his chair as Dr. Mäkkinen settled into his. For the next half hour, omitting the drama involving Trevor, Ungman, and Gillespie, Gamiel related an abbreviated version of the story of Trans-Light-Element interrupted only occasionally by strategic questions from Dr. Mäkkinen.

"Do you have a diagram of the equipment you will bring into the treatment room?"

Gamiel smiled and replied, "Actually, Dr. Mäkkinen, this process is so non-intrusive – neither I nor my equipment will need to be present in the same room.

Juri Mäkkinen raised his eyebrows, and said, "I would like to visit your lab when it is ready, and witness a demonstration of your claims."

Gamiel smiled and said, "As soon as possible, sir, I shall ask Mark to arrange such a visit."

Conversation continued at length. Suddenly, Dr. Mäkkinen looked at his watch and said, "I am sorry, but I am scheduled for surgery in thirty minutes. I have to go meet the patient and get scrubbed."

As they both stood up and shook hands, Juri Mäkkinen said, "I think I see your lovely wife and children over by the garden. Why don't you exit directly from here?"

Gamiel said, "Thank you."

Slipping quietly out the glass bay doors, Gamiel hurried over to Rachel's side as she was ending a phone call on her cell. He asked, "What's up. Who was that?"

Rachel answered, "That was Kaila. She says they found a bomb in the Sauna wood shed!"

Gamiel looked shocked. "What!?"

Rachel put her hand on Gamiel's arm, "Everyone is OK Gamiel. She said Pekka is leading a bomb squad to dismantle and remove it. The police have been called. Mark has been notified. He is on the train back to Lahti. Kaila asked if we could go get him. We need to take Joseph inside now."

The couple went over to where Joseph was playing. Gamiel took Joseph's hand, and asked, "Are we ready to get started, Joseph?"

Joseph looked up with trusting eyes, and replied, "I was wondering when we would."

Vanessa dropped to her knees and hugged Joseph, saying, "I will be staying with you this first night. Everything will be OK."

Parents held Joseph's hands as he walked between them. Koira and Vanessa followed them inside to find a place to sit and visit while Gamiel and Rachel attended to Joseph's arrangements for the night.

Koira asked, "How long will Joseph have to be here."

Vanessa looked at her and said, "I think I heard Mother say something like six weeks. I guess it all depends on how Joseph responds to treatments. We will stay as long as it takes."

The two young women sat down and visited until Gamiel and Rachel came back. Vanessa hugged them goodbye as they left with Koira to go get Mark at the Train Station.

Typical Train Station - "Waiting on the next train to Helsinki"

Image Photographed by and belong to the Author

Chapter 13
Helsinki

Vanessa, Koira, and Niina sat on a three person bench on the train looking across at Ben, Alexi, and Timo. Conversation had continued nonstop from the moment they boarded the train at the Lahti Rautatiaasema (Railway Station).

Ben was thrilled by the scenes flashing by the window next to him. He admired the small villages, farms and brightly colored Summer Cottages on lake front properties in the distance. The steady rhythm of the car wheels greeting each new rail segment was soothing. He was looking forward to their first outing in the city of Helsinki.

Ben commented, "This moves along pretty fast. I see a lot of people riding the train."

Koira replied, "Yes, most people use the trains and busses in Finland. It costs less than driving a car."

Alexi added, "You can purchase annual passes and hop on any train or bus going anywhere in the country. It is very convenient."

Vanessa asked, "Do you make this trip often?"

Koira answered, "More so now since we are older and our Father is in the government. We sometimes ride to meet him for lunch or supper when he cannot come back home. There have been times when he had to stay in Helsinki all week."

Timo said, "There is much to see in Helsinki. Alexi, how long do you think it will take us at the University?"

Alexi replied, "Well that depends on how many questions Vanessa needs to ask the registrar."

Vanessa smiled and said, "I will try to keep it brief. Dad asked me to come back with an application he can review and sign. Of course, your father's endorsement won't hurt."

Timo asked, "Alexi, did Pekka find out who put the backpack in the woodshed? Was it really a bomb?"

Ben looked on with amusement as Alexi explained. "It was not a bomb. We don't know how it got there. When we called the wood delivery service, they said they would talk with the driver. When they called us back, they gave us the driver's name. Pekka called and talked to him. He said he delivered the wood but knows nothing about a back pack. So, how it got where it was, we don't know yet. Pekka and his security staff are investigating."

Ben prodded, "Tell them what they found in the backpack."

Alexi answered, "Toilet Paper."

Timo asked, "What?"

The girls all shook their heads.

Vanessa asked, "Where was the back pack made? What store did they buy it in? Was the toilet paper still in the store package or unpacked?"

Timo interjected, "Good questions. Was it a brand new back pack? Did they unroll the toilet paper to see if it had anything in between the rolls?"

Alexi raised his hands, and said, "All good questions. Maybe we should ask Pekka to let the Lahti Detective Club handle the investigation?"

Everyone laughed.

Koira said, "Well maybe we should anyway. This sounds too strange."

The other girls nodded their heads.

Ben smiled and thought to himself, "As soon as Dad can get the T-L-E laboratory in full operation –

everything would be different. They would soon know the answer to a number of perplexing questions."

Peering out the window, Vanessa was surprised to see the train was pulling into the Helsinki terminal. She said, "Wow! We are here already!"

As the group alighted, Ben felt a charge of excitement and fascination with the sights and sounds of the bustling train travelers. They passed through the doors off the boarding platform at ground level and took the escalator up the main floor and walked through exit doors into the front grand hallway of the old Helsinki Train Station.

Alexi led the group out the front door onto the street and crossed over to the city tram rail where several different routes were featured by number. He said, "This is the tram that takes us to the University."

It wasn't long before the next Tram arrived and they got on. Many people were getting on and off the tram at every stop. All of them looked preoccupied with their own agendas talking in Finnish, a few in Swedish, and some in Russian. Some passengers glanced politely at the group speaking English with a little more than mild curiosity.

At some point, Ben noticed one man dressed in the same kind of street clothes as everyone else who seemed to be watching them. He could not remember how long he had been there. Leaning over to Timo, Ben whispered, "Don't look now, but I think that guy is watching us."

Timo smiled and whispered back, "Of course he is watching us. We are riding with a couple of Americans. You stand out like sore thumbs."

Ben couldn't help himself. He broke out laughing.

Soon, their stop came up and they got off near the University and walked up to the main entry way.

Alexi guided them into the registrar's main office and approached the clerk on duty.

Speaking in Finnish, he said, "Hello, my name is Alexi, my father is Mark Leppänen."

The clerk looked up at the mention of the Mark's name. He was well known in academic circles besides the fact he currently served as the Minister of Education on the Council of State.

Alexi explained in Finnish, "This is Vanessa Reuel. She is 18, just graduated from high school and is now visiting from America and wishes to attend Helsinki University in the Fall."

Ben's gaze was drawn to the badge on the Clerk's lapel – labeled "Opiskelijarekisteri" with her name above the label – Ansa Siponen. He looked at Koira who whispered in his ear "Student Registrar."

Ansa was a pleasant young adult with radiant complexion and well groomed light golden brown hair that fell lightly just below her ears. Her manor was amiable yet precise.

Ansa replied in English, "Vanessa, I am so pleased to meet you. Alexi tells me you wish to attend Helsinki University?"

Vanessa smiled and said, "Yes. My father wants me to bring an application form back to him so he can complete his part and sign it."

"Your father may do that if he wishes, but it really isn't necessary. You are of age, and Alexi's father's endorsement will be more than enough to approve your admittance. However, we will still need you to pass an admission examination. When would you like to take it?"

Vanessa pondered for a moment, then said, "I don't know. My schedule is still somewhat unplanned."

Before Vanessa continued, Alexi said, "We can probably be back this same time next week. What times do you have open?"

Ansa answered, "We have two available slots on Tuesday next week, three on Wednesday."

Vanessa answered, "Let's set a date for next Tuesday and if I need to reschedule, can I call you?"

Ansa said, "We will need at least 48 hours' notice if you plan to reschedule or cancel. The demand for testing slots is high. The exam takes two hours. It starts at 9 am and 1pm. Which will you prefer?"

Vanessa said, "Well, let's schedule it for in the morning. I always test better in the mornings."

Ansa finished the registration on the computer and set the appointment. She then looked at Alexi, and said, "Please tell your father I just sent his office a workflow notice – so we can have his endorsement. That will practically guarantee Vanessa's acceptance letter. I presume we can mail it to your home address?

Alexi said, "Yes, our home in Asikkala. Do you have the address?"

Ansa replied, "Yes. Vanessa, here is a copy of your completed registration application for your father. He can initial it. You can bring it and just show it when you take your test."

Vanessa said, "Thank you" and took the document folding it neatly before putting it in her purse.

Ansa added, "It was so good to meet you, Vanessa. I hope you end up in one of my classes. When you finish the test next week, you can select your curriculum schedule – online.

Ansa handed Vanessa a University business card with important points of contact and her appointment on the back. Pointing, she said, "Your authorization access key is on this card, right here. Create your account as instructed – then make up your own password when you are done. Classes start the first week in September."

Vanessa took the card, saying, "Thank you."

Alexi turned, giving Ansa a wave, everyone else waving too, and said, "Hei Hei! Näkemiin!"

Koira, Timo and Niina also said, "Näkemiin!"

Ben and Vanessa waved not feeling comfortable enough with their command of Finnish to utter the sounds in public.

Ansa smiled, and waved back, saying, "Näkemiin!"

The young people left the building and returned to the sidewalk outside. The weather was perfect for an outing.

Timo asked, "Where do we want to go now?"

Ben looked around and checked the copy of the city touring map he had picked up from the train station, then asked, "How far is it to the open air market from here?"

Koira answered, "Ah! The Kauppatori! Not too far. It is just a few blocks. Shall we walk?

Niina said, "Walking is good. Vanessa, you will like the ice cream kioski."

Timo said, "Yes. Jäätelö! I can't wait."

Vanessa looked at Alexi, and asked, "Will we have time to visit the Sibelius monument?"

Alexi smiled, and said, "Sure! We can take one of the tour buses that goes around town and see all the famous places in Helsinki."

Within 15 minutes, the group had easily walked to the main market square next to the public harbor front dock. New sights and sounds of stall venders vocally engaging the teaming throng of curious tourists greeted them. It was midday and the market was filled with visitors from many countries, all anxious to find a token gift for some friend or family member back home.

Alexi commented, "On most days there are more tourists here than Finns; and several of these Venders are from places all over Europe. They come to market handcrafts, photographs, paintings, you name it. Some are here to sell their home grown fruits and vegetables. For instance, this is a Spanish Peach, and I am almost certain the man behind the counter is a farmer from Spain."

Alexi spoke to the Vender in Finnish, and asked, "Good morning Sir! Are these peaches fresh from Spain this week?"

The Vender replied in Finnish with a heavy accent, "Yes. Fresh from the farm. Would you like a bushel?"

Alexi smiled and said, "We are on foot and cannot carry so many, but, if these have been washed, may we have just six peaches, please?"

The Vender smiled, and said, "Of course." Then he packed six of the largest juicy peaches from his carefully stacked display into a brown paper bag and handed them to Alexi. "For you, today, that will be only six Euros (€6)."

Alexi smiled and pulled a €10 coin from his pocket and gave it to the Vender who promptly returned €4 in coins to Alexi.

The group continued walking around the market, eating their peaches, intrigued by the large variety of offerings.

Timo commented, "That peach was good, but not enough. How about getting lunch here? There are several prepared food stands; fish, hamburgers, potatoes, vegetables, - just looking at all this makes me hungry."

Everyone laughed. Koira suggested, "Let's do some shopping here first, then grab lunch before we leave the Kauppatori."

Everyone agreed.

Niina said, "Ben, here is the Harbor Tour. It runs several times a day and takes you out by Suomenlinna, the "Fortress of Finland" on an island just off shore. It is a world heritage center with a history that predates your American revolution – starting about 1748."

Ben squinted against the sun reflecting on the waves to see the many islands off the Helsinki shoreline. He asked, "How long is the tour?"

Timo answered, "About two hours."

Vanessa commented, "Ben, maybe we can plan to take that tour when we come back for my exam next week. I really want to see the Sibelius monument today."

Koira agreed and so did Ben. The group explored the rest of the market, milling slowly around the vender bins and tents with tireless enthusiasm. Vanessa took out her camera and began capturing images.

Eventually, the group broke apart as the girls pursued common interests. Handmade shawls, purses, hats, complimented higher priced coats and furs being presented to interested buyers.

Vanessa was keenly interested in the arts and crafts. She found several artists. Some were painting landscapes, and others, portraits. She stopped in front of a gifted artist who was rapidly producing caricature portraits of enthralled customers with incredible detail.

Alexi just happened to be rounding the adjacent corner next to the girls, so Vanessa asked, "Alexi, would you like to get a portrait with me?"

Alexi responded, "Sure. How much are they?"

Ben followed Timo to look at hats, knives, and boots. Ben's interest was captured by the reindeer skins on display. There was also a curious science project vender vocally engaging shoppers as they walked by. Ben could not resist engaging him in a lengthy conversation.

After a brief moment, Ben said, "Timo, look at this, a solar powered weather station! This would be fun to put together."

Timo smiled at his friend, recognizing the scientist coming out in Ben, and asked, "Yes, but from what Koira tells me, you are already a gifted scientist. This is for kids. Besides, would you have time to do this and help your father, too?"

Ben grinned sheepishly, and said, "It's hard for me to resist things like this."

Soon, Vanessa and Alexi appeared with a portrait of the two of them. She showed Ben, and asked, "What do you think?"

Ben looked at it carefully, and commented, "This guy is good. We should get Mother and Dad down here and get a portrait of them, too."

Vanessa agreed. After an hour of shopping and buying small items they could carry back home, the group came back together and walked over to one of the burger vender mobile trailers. Inspecting the menu, each began placing their orders.

Soon their food was ready. They found an empty table with chairs under one of the tents, and sat down to enjoy their selections. Conversation was casual over the delicious entrees. About halfway through their meal, Timo noticed a man sitting under another tent directly across from them.

Timo leaned forward towards Alexi and quietly said in Finnish, "I think that guy to my left has been watching us. I noticed him several times this morning while we were shopping."

Alexi glanced all around in such a way to allow his roving eye to observe the man ever so briefly as he continued looking all around, then casually turned around to concentrate on his meal. He had seen enough.

The suspect was clean shaven with tanned complexion, short hair under an Australian looking hat, sun glasses; wearing a bright blue pressed shirt, casual light brown khaki trousers with a black belt, and sturdy brown leather hiking boots. His hands were relaxed on the table in front of what looked like an empty plate. He seemed free of any shopping bags or camera. His pockets were not bulging either. Alexi decided he was not a shopper – quite possibly could be following them.

Between bites, Alexi quietly asked, "Ben, do you recognize that guy in the blue shirt?"

Ben was sitting next to Alexi but in such a way with his legs crossed and relaxed that the stranger was already naturally in view as he answered, "Not really, but he does not strike me as a Finn."

Vanessa quietly commented, "I have seen him ever since we arrived at the market. His bright blue shirt makes him stand out in the crowd. That Australian hat and dark glasses make it easy to spot him. I am sure he is a tourist. Wouldn't you normally expect someone who is trying to follow us to want to blend in?"

Timo agreed, "Perhaps he is just a curious tourist. I mean, we are obviously Finns, but I am sure Ben and Vanessa are clearly American by their accent and dress. That might draw his attention more than normal."

Niina smiled at that, "Yes, but give them time and a few shopping trips and they will become Finns."

Koira laughed, and said, "They practically speak Finnish now… and will soon know more about Finland than any American I know."

Ben smiled, and said, "I would like to be a Finn."

Vanessa smirked at her brother, and said, "You are more a Finn than you realize. And the guy across the way is not. I think we should at least keep an eye on him."

Alexi got up and went over to the Vendor and paid for a few after meal treats. As he carried them back to the table he took a long look at the curious man in the blue shirt.

Sitting back down, he looked at Ben and asked in a low voice, "Does that guy seem to be talking – maybe on a hands-free device?"

Ben glanced at him and said, "Yes. It is hard to say who or what he is looking at with those shades, but I would say we need to get up and head over to Senate Square and catch the bus before it is too late to see the Sibelius monument."

"Agreed."

Everyone got up together and dumped their refuse in the waste container, quickly walking away from the tent towards the street. The traffic was steady so they had to wait for it to clear before crossing.

At the last minute Timo decided to get in line at the Ice Cream Kioski as it was next to where they were crossing the street. He remembered how much he wanted a strawberry cone and decided to purchase cones for the group. He waived everyone ahead. The line was short, and he was soon paying for his order.

As he was paying the vendor, Timo noticed the stranger in the blue shirt walk by and stop at the street. Traffic cleared and the stranger crossed. The vender finished dipping the cones and gave them to Timo in a carry rack. Timo took the rack and bolted across the street behind the suspect.

The girls had walked well ahead of Ben and Alexi and were engaged in a casual conversation as they crossed the street and turned up the street towards Senate Square just a block away.

Upon reaching the other side of the street, Ben felt a loose shoe string and bent down to tie it as the girls kept walking. Alexi waited on Ben.

Out of the corner of his eye, from his inclined position, Ben spotted the man in the blue shirt crossing the street. As he stood up, he said, "Don't look, but Blue Shirt is following us."

Timo was concerned the ice cream would melt before he could catch up; but, now did not want to catch up too quickly.

Alexi and Ben moved on quickly to catch up to the girls. Timo was keeping a slight distance behind the stranger who seemed to be in no hurry but was clearly going the same direction. If he knew he had passed Timo, he did not seem to be concerned.

As Alexi and Ben caught up with the rest of their group, Alexi quietly spoke to Koira in Finnish, "Don't look back. We need to walk quickly over to the tour bus and get our tickets. Blue shirt is following us.

Koira nodded and walked between Vanessa and Niina, touching their elbows, and said in English, "It looks like the bus may be getting ready to leave. Let's hurry over and get our tickets.

Timo saw the group hurry ahead and stepped up his pace. He was afraid he might pass 'Blue Shirt' until he saw him also quicken his pace. Timo nearly ran to catch up.

Vanessa said, "These are double decker busses. How neat!"

Alexi quickly purchased six tickets and handed everyone a ticket as they got on the bus. The driver spoke in Finnish to Alexi, and said "It is past time for me to leave."

Alexi responded, "Timo is coming."

The driver looked at the young man with the ice cream and said, "I am sorry, but he cannot bring the ice cream on the bus."

Alexi and Ben both looked perplexed as they waived at Timo to hurry. The man in the blue shirt paused a second somewhat baffled by the waiving. He and Timo arrived at the bus at the same time.

Alexi spoke in Finnish, "Timo, the driver says we cannot take the ice cream."

At first, Timo was dismayed. He had so wanted to taste the ice cream and now he had a hand full of cones he could not eat. Then a mischievous grin crossed his face as he turned to face the stranger in the blue shirt, and spoke in his best English, "Excuse me sir, can you take these? The driver says we cannot eat them on the bus."

The man in the Australian hat, dark glasses, blue shirt, khaki pants and sturdy brown hiking boots was completely caught off guard as Timo handed him the rack of slightly melted ice cream cones.

Timo said, as he hopped on the bus, "Thank you so much. We really have to go now. I am sure those kids over there will love the ice cream."

The bus quickly departed slightly behind schedule while everyone in the group looked out the windows at the surprised stranger holding the ice cream.

Michael Irvin Bosley

Scene from the Tour Bus Downtown Helsinki

Ice Cream Kioski on Kauppatori Market Square, Helsinki

Images photographed by and belong to the Author

~ 128 ~

Chapter 14
Musical Heart of Finland

Alexi and Ben were amazed at Timo's quick thinking. Niina looked at her brother with admiration. Spontaneous bursts of laughter escaped everyone's mouths as the bus pulled away from Senate Square.

Koira said, "That was close. How strange he wanted to get on the same bus as we!"

Vanessa agreed.

Ben sat in silence wondering who the stranger was. Dad had been right about this trip. The risks they were taking began to loom larger in his mind. The fun he felt earlier in the day began to be replaced by feelings of insecurity and anxiety.

Alexi sensed Ben's change of mood, and said, "Hey! Cheer up, Ben. With Timo and me around nothing bad can happen."

Ben smiled and asked, "So, you don't think we should head back?

Alexi answered, "I think we should finish our tour but keep our eyes open. Vanessa really wants to visit the Sibelius monument."

Ben nodded as he scrutinized the other passengers on the top deck of the bus with them. Everyone had on their earphones completely absorbed in the recorded tour. He realized he was missing it and quickly put on his earphones and joined the tour.

The recording described Embassy housing, the Finnish Yacht Club, public Sauna, and many other points of interest. At length, the recording announced they were approaching the Sibelius monument.

As the group got off the tour bus, and began to make their way to the monument, Vanessa sensed a level of excitement she had not felt in many years.

She giggled as they walked under the sculpture and admired each intricate detail of the representation of organ pipes standing up from the ground. Everyone admired the sculpted likeness of Jean Sibelius.

Vanessa worked her camera taking pictures from every angle; capturing poses from each member of their small group. Then everyone walked over to the small visitor appreciation center down near the water. Inside they found the walls covered with a mural presentation of the dedication ceremony presided over by then President of Finland standing next to the artist.

Koira said, "Vanessa, see, this is the artist presenting the final work to the President of Finland. This monument embodies the Musical Heart of Finland."

The young people took in the images, dates and historical facts presented in the visitor center. Then they went back outside.

Timo looked at his watch, and said, "We probably need to catch the Tram back to the Train Station. It is getting late."

Alexi agreed. Everyone walked back to the street and waited for the next tram. It wasn't long before it arrived and they boarded the bus single file.

Ben was surprised he was beginning to feel a little tired. He sat down next to Timo and asked "How often do you come to Helsinki?"

Timo answered, "Maybe once every two or three months with my mother. She knows one of the vendors and comes to help them when they take their produce to market."

Ben asked, "Is it always this busy with so many different nationalities?"

Timo nodded, and said, "Summer is usually this busy. However, there is something in Finland for visitors every season. We are becoming the America of Europe. Everyone wants to visit Finland. Many come here from other countries because we have a good economy with plenty of work. There is also free tuition and many other benefits of living in Finland."

Ben glanced at Alexi sitting next to Vanessa. They were reviewing the paper Ansa had given her.

Koira and Niina were sitting across from Timo and Ben. Koira looked at Ben, and said, "There are lots of sports events here in Finland, too. Are you still coming to our soccer practice tomorrow? Our team is practicing for the Juhannus Day tournament."

Ben smiled, and said, "Yes, I wouldn't miss it. Joseph wants to play, too, as soon as he can."

Ben felt more relieved when the Tram stopped in front of the train station. They jumped off and walked through the front doors of the grand old building. Timo and Ben went to the public pay restroom facilities while Alexi accompanied the girls into the ticketing office.

Niina and Koira sat down on one of the couches to wait for Alexi to help Vanessa purchase her advance return ticket for next Tuesday. They and their brothers already possessed passes that let them ride all year round. The ticket office was a very large room with high classic ceilings and large windows at the front of the train station.

Looking around, Niina and Koira conversed in Finnish, commenting on some of the customers waiting. Koira glanced outside through one of the large front windows. She was startled to see the man in the blue shirt walking from the Tram to the front door of the Train Station.

In Finnish, she said, "Niina, look. It is him, again."

Niina was astounded, and asked, "Should we get up and go tell Alexi?"

Koira looked at Alexi very busy talking with the ticket sales clerk, and said, "Not yet. Let's go to the main foyer and watch where he goes."

The two girls exited the ticket office casually trying to spot the man in the blue shirt. It wasn't hard. He was heading directly towards them. They quickly turned aside at a service kioski and asked the customer service attendant about the brochures.

Koira watched Blue Shirt out of the corner of her eye. He walked past them into the ticketing office. The girls cut short their conversation and quickly returned to their seats in the waiting area.

Back inside, they found another couch to sit and watch. If he had recognized them, he never let on. The man pulled a numbered service ticket and sat down to wait right behind Alexi and Vanessa.

Alexi and Vanessa finished their business at the counter and paid for their tickets, and left the counter never looking behind them.

Koira watched with concern as the man was obviously watching Alexi and Vanessa. But he made no move. Soon his number was called and he went to the counter, occasionally looking back at the retreating couple. It was then he also noticed Koira and Niina, looking right at him.

The lady at the ticket counter asked in English, "Sir, can I help you?"

He turned to conduct his business.

Koira and Niina quickly got up and latched arms with Alexi and Vanessa to walk them faster back into the main foyer.

Niina said, in Finnish, "Alexi, don't look now but the man in the blue shirt just came in and sat down right behind you. He was watching you. He also just spotted us. I think we should hurry to get on our train and go home."

The conversation continued in Finnish for a few moments, as they walked faster towards the waiting area outside the restroom facilities.

Alexi explained in English to Vanessa, "Blue Shirt is in the ticket office. He seems to be following us."

Vanessa was concerned as she looked back at the ticket office. "I hope Ben and Timo hurry."

As if on cue, the two young men appeared.

Alexi explained the situation to Timo in Finnish, then said to Ben, "We need to hurry. Blue Shirt is right behind us."

The group hurried downstairs back out onto the rail departure docks and scurried over to their train.

Ben waited to be the last to board, looking back as he did so. He did not see the man in the blue shirt. He quickly got on the train.

It was not time for the train to leave, so everyone was on pins and needles anxiously glancing out the window, wondering if Blue Shirt would actually board their train to continue following them.

After a few moments, Timo spotted him walking directly to their train. They headed down the main aisle to put as many sections between them and their stalker as possible. Timo held back to watch which car Blue Shirt would board. Fortunately, he boarded the closest car on the end. Timo walked quickly to catch up with the rest.

Alexi asked, "Did he get on the train?"

Timo answered, "Yes. First Car."

Ben suggested, why don't we all sit in separate seats but close enough we can see each other? He will be looking for us to be together and may not spot us if he comes down the aisle."

Timo said, "That is a good idea, Ben."

Each one found a place to sit by themselves but within easy view of the others. They sat by strangers who were curious but were typically Finnish and too polite to probe into other people's business.

It wasn't long before Blue Shirt came down the aisle. Ben spotted him first and signaled the others. Each sat quietly reading or looking out the window.

Timo sat in more secluded seat and stuffed his hat and jacket under the bench. He casually thumbed through a magazine he had brought onboard hoping he would not be spotted sitting next to a stranger. It seemed to work. Blue Shirt walked right by with no sign of recognition.

Timo thought he seemed anxious – perhaps even desperate. Then Blue Shirt spotted Vanessa and sat down in a seat two rows away. Timo caught Alexi's gaze and looked at where Blue Shirt sat. Alexi nodded. The train ride continued, seemingly much longer now as each sat alone in silence.

Ben thought he would burst. He wanted to just get up and introduce himself but decided it best to wait. He saw Alexi texting on his cell and guessed he was probably contacting Pekka or his Dad.

Finally the long train ride ended. Each got off separately. Timo watched Blue Shirt and got off after he did, once again following him.

Vanessa joined Ben. Koira and Niina caught up to Alexi. Everyone paused together just outside the Lahti train station doorway.

Niina asked, "Where is Timo?"

Alexi said, "He got off last. He is following Blue Shirt."

Ben looked around, this time a lot less casually, giving Blue Shirt a stern look, but smiling to see Timo following close behind.

Suddenly from a group of passengers previously unnoticed, a non-descript man dressed in faded pants and a wrinkled shirt who appeared to be a local Finnish resident approached the group and asked in Finnish, "Excuse me, but can you help me? I am trying to find a friend of mine who should have got off the train. Did you see a man carrying a red umbrella?"

Ben sized the stranger up, not comprehending his words, yet he felt something was not right. He moved closer to the girls in a protective posture.

Alexi answered the man in Finnish, "No. We did not see anyone with a red umbrella. Who are you?

Pointing to the train, he continued in Finnish, "My name is Juri Tarkonen. I was supposed to meet my brother here on this train. But he has not appeared and it looks like everyone has got off and the train is leaving."

Even as he spoke the train left the station. All in the group naturally looked in the direction he was pointing. They could see Blue Shirt coming toward them with a quickened pace and Timo nearly running to keep up.

Suddenly, the stranger grabbed Vanessa and yanked her away from the group. A menacing expression crossed his face as he spoke harshly in clear English, "Don't anyone move."

Everyone was caught off guard.

Ben was stunned at how quickly this stranger had reacted. He started to run into him as hard as he could.

The stranger said, "Don't even try it, Ben. Your sister is going with me."

Alexi was very angry, and moved as if to arrest their assailant, but the stranger brandished a small pistol freezing him in his tracks.

All the while, Timo was running to catch up to Blue Shirt who by now was sprinting towards the group. Because the stranger was watching Ben and his group from a side angle to the direction of the train, neither he nor the others could see Timo and Blue Shirt.

In a flash, the man in the blue shirt sprinted without a sound into a flying tackle that knocked the breath out their assailant breaking Vanessa free as they hit the ground. She ran towards Alexi who immediately jumped into the fray assisting Blue Shirt to subdue Vanessa's would be kidnapper.

Timo caught up in time to help as handcuffs were secured. Ben picked up the pistol that had been knocked out of the assailant's hand when Blue Shirt hit him.

Blue Shirt looked at Ben, and asked, "Do you know how to use that, Ben?"

Ben said, "I have been trained in the use of firearms." He brandished it carefully making it clear he was now in control of the situation.

The assailant glared at Blue Shirt and asked, "Who are you?"

Blue Shirt answered, "My name is John Burkwell. I work for Trevor Nibley. I have been following you all day. I was afraid you would make your move while these kids were on their tour bus ride. But I caught up to you getting on the train."

"Now, we are going to the police station. I need all you kids to come with me to make a statement so we can get this fellow locked up. Ben, if you don't mind, I will take that weapon. You are under age and not licensed to carry it in Finland."

Ben was still cautious. Holding tightly to the weapon, he asked, "How do we know you are working for Trevor?"

John handed Ben a business card, and said, "Call him yourself."

Ben looked at the card and gave up the weapon. Above phone numbers Ben recognized, it read:

John Burkwell
International Private Detective, Bounty Hunter,
Process Server, Protective Services Consultant,
Nibley Security, Inc.

Author Cameo Appearance at Senate Square, Helsinki

Sibelius Monument, Helsinki Finland

Image photographed by and belongs to the Author

Chapter 15
Turning Point

Gamiel rode with Mark to the train station. Pekka followed them in a separate security task force vehicle with two Finnish government agents. Mark had received numerous urgent texts from Alexi saying they were being followed.

When house security had interrupted his work in the laboratory with the news, Gamiel had stopped what he was doing and locked up the lab to join Mark and Pekka immediately. His thoughts were caught up in the anxiety of the moment as he chastised himself for letting Ben and Vanessa go to Helsinki. He was feeling responsible for bringing his troubles to Finland to endanger his dearest friends.

Mark, guessing what was on Gamiel's mind, said, "Gamiel, don't be so hard on yourself. These young people have handled this situation very well. Consider the life experiences they have gained. We will meet them at the train station and Pekka will see to this stranger in the blue shirt."

Gamiel had to smile at that. He found it almost comical this fellow would be so obvious – yet, wondered if there wasn't something ominous in that alone.

The traffic moved along quickly. Soon they were approaching Lahti train station, when a text came in from Alexi.

Gamiel asked, "What does it say?"

Mark handed him the phone. In Finnish, it read, "Take us to police station. Waiting at train station. Will explain."

Gamiel looked at Mark, questioningly.

Mark touched a button on the control screen of his car, and spoke in Finnish, "Pekka, change of plans. We are picking up the children and taking them to the Police station. Alexi will explain, but I think you should be ready for the unexpected. Go ahead of us and get into position."

Pekka drove quickly around Mark and Gamiel and sped ahead to the train station.

Gamiel asked, "It sounds strange! What do you think happened?"

Mark shrugged, and said, "Alexi said he will explain when we get there.

Gamiel nodded, his lips pursed, and said, "You know, when I opened the Trans-Light-Element vortex, I never dreamed it would cause so much trouble. I am wishing now I had never done it."

Mark said, "Gamiel, there is something I did not tell you when you first arrived. You were very tired and I decided to wait."

Gamiel looked at his friend, waiting.

Mark said, "You remember I mentioned the assassination attempt on President Salmo?"

"Yes."

"Well, the trial is set for next month, and our agents have noticed an increase of nefarious activities presumably intent on intimidating witnesses. One thing I did not tell you is I was also on the list of assassination targets."

Gamiel replied, "Why would anyone want to hurt you?"

Mark answered, "In the past, I have been involved with matters of State that included national security. You were aware of that when you were here before. Now, it seems some of those past events made enemies I never knew. Trevor has been helping me, as well– with President Salmo's permission. Trevor recently learned these assassination conspirators have connections with Carl Ungman."

Gamiel stared at his friend, listening with heightened levels of intrigue as Mark continued.

"In fact, Trevor told me the London Imperial Planet Corporation is a cover for a plot to seize control of all world governments. Trevor believes your Unified Field containment ratio is key to their plans. Several top Nibley Security agents have been operating in Finland with the President's permission for over a month now."

Gamiel sat in silence, suddenly aware of a much larger concern than his backyard laboratory project.

Another 5 minutes passed too slowly as the car finally arrived and pulled up to the curb where Alexi and Vanessa were standing with Ben and Koira.

Mark got out and asked, "Where are Timo and Niina?"

Alexi answered, "Their parents just came and got them. They were already running late to a family event."

Mark looked around and spotted Pekka, then asked, "Where is the man in the blue shirt?"

Alexi said, "He called a taxi and took his prisoner to the police station."

Mark gave Alexi a questioning look, then said, "You can explain it on the way over. Get in the car."

The young people were very grateful to climb in and buckle up, once again in the safe care of their parents.

Mark got behind the wheel again and signaled Pekka on the government comm-link to follow him to the police station.

Gamiel greeted their new passengers, and said, "You have had quite an adventure today. Who wants to tell us what happened?"

Ben was the first to speak up. "We had a great time in Helsinki. I guess we may have over reacted to the guy we first thought was following us. Turns out he was following the real guy who was following us. Alexi can explain better."

Alexi did explain. He briefly recounted their first encounter with the man in the blue shirt at the market square. Everyone laughed when he described how Timo handed off the ice cream cones. They raised eyebrows over the episode at the Helsinki train station, but were astounded by events at the Lahti train station.

Mark and Gamiel were stunned when Vanessa described how the new stranger had grabbed her, how he knew their names and was going to kidnap her.

Ben picked up the story, "Then the guy in the blue shirt tackled this guy in a flying leap setting Vanessa free and causing the bad guy to drop his pistol. I got the gun and held it while Timo and Alexi helped him put the guy in handcuffs."

Gamiel was bursting at the seams and had to ask, "So, who is this guy? Where is he now? What did you do with the gun?"

Ben answered, "I gave the gun to Blue Shirt. He said his name is John Burkwell. He said he works for Trevor. Here is his business card."

Gamiel took the card. Shaking his head in amazement, he said, "I should have guessed Trevor was already on top things. I am sure glad he was."

By this time the car was approaching the police station. Mark asked, "Gamiel, this is bound to get publicity I think you wish to avoid. Do you want to come into the police station with me and give a statement, or just wait?

Gamiel answered, "Oh I am coming in; but, I am going to let you do the talking, if you don't mind."

It was a curious sight as Mark, a well-known public figure entered the police station with his children followed by a strange unknown American and his children.

Alexi spotted John Burkwell standing at the counter giving the clerk a report. The bad guy was nowhere to be seen.

Alexi led his father over to Mr. Burkwell, and said, "Sir, this is my father, Mark Leppänen."

The two men shook hands, as Mark asked, "Where is the assailant?"

John answered, "The police have him in custody. He calls himself Juri Tarkonen. All I need is a statement from yours and Dr. Reuel's children. I want to file a charge of stalking with malicious intent, assault and battery, brandishing a deadly weapon against minors, and attempted kidnapping. In order to make those charges stick, I need statements from each of these young people."

Mark motioned for Gamiel to come over. Ben and Vanessa followed.

Mark said, "Gamiel, do you want your children's names on the public record?"

Gamiel answered, "Not if the public can see it. Isn't there a way to seal the record?"

John spoke up, "Yes. It just needs a Presidential order."

Mark leaned over and spoke to the clerk in Finnish. After a brief conversation he turned back to Gamiel and said, "I can get President Salmo to sign an order to hold this man indefinitely for trial. The President can also order this Police record sealed in the interest of National Security. Let Ben and Vanessa register a formal complaint. Their names will not be published."

Gamiel said, "Alright."

All the youngsters sat down to write out their statements and sign them. As they were thus engaged, Gamiel turned to John and began questioning him.

"How long have you been working for Trevor?"

"About 10 years, now. Trevor is a fair and generous employer."

Mark asked, "How long have you been watching our children?"

John answered, "Since they got off the train this morning. I was on detail following the man who calls himself Juri Tarkonen. Trevor told me to not let him leave my sight.

Mark asked, "Did Trevor explain why?"

John answered, "Trevor told me Juri is an operative for the Imperial Planet Corporation. He received a tip Juri was acting point man for Carl Ungman."

Gamiel was stunned. How could they have discovered where he was so quickly? He began to suspect a leak. He said, "I am grateful to you and Trevor. I honestly don't know how he keeps up with everything given the heavy research workload he has right now."

John smiled and said, "Trevor has a lot of helpers who report to him daily – in some cases, hourly. It was a good thing because I found Juri at the train station today waiting for your kids. As soon as they got on the Tram headed to the University, he started following them."

Ben was listening while he was writing, and looked up suddenly realizing Juri was the same stranger he thought was looking at them on the tram. He added that to his written statement.

John continued, "I was Juri's shadow all day. I thought I had everything under control until your kids gave me the slip in Senate square. That was pretty cute. Too bad Timo couldn't come to the station. I owe him for six ice cream cones." John grinned and looked over at the young people busy writing.

Alexi, Ben, Vanessa, and Koira looked up at John together and chuckled merrily.

John continued, "Luckily, Juri also missed that bus and chose to go to the train station and wait for them to return. He watched for them and got on the train after they did. I followed him. He had to wait until they got off the train at Lahti to make his move. I think he has connections here – probably the same ones who told him which train to watch for in Helsinki."

Gamiel looked around the police station trying to spot any suspicious onlookers, then asked, "Does Trevor know who this contact might be? Could he be here now and we not know it?"

John smiled, and said, "You are a very suspicious man, Dr. Reuel. I can tell you there is no one in this room who is connected to Juri's club. I have been in country long enough to distinguish bad guys from happy citizens. Right now the only bad man here is Juri."

The youngsters turned in their written statements. Mark leaned over the counter and directed the clerk in Finnish to seal the statements and put them in the safe. He gave him a card and told him a member of the Presidential detail would be by later today with the order from President Salmo.

The group left the station. Ben spotted Pekka immediately. He was obviously talking on a hands-free device. Ben looked around and noticed two other possible security agents. He touched Alexi's arm and nodded towards Pekka.

Alexi smiled and nodded back.

Gamiel turned as they were leaving, and shook John's hand, saying, "John, thank you again for doing your job so well. People like you restore my hope in our future."

John smiled, "You are too kind, Dr. Reuel. I have worked with Trevor in the field. He knows his stuff. Believe me. You have the best possible combination of friends and security here in Finland. My people are all over this. You have my card. Don't hesitate to call me."

Chapter 16
Mysterious Diver

Ben lounged in one of the deck chairs on the Leppänen lake barge as it cruised slowly toward an inviting lake shore. He contemplated the events of their train ride to Helsinki last week. Since then, he and Joseph had signed up to play on the 'football' league in their respective age groups. His first day at practice had been challenging. Learning the calls and the plays in Finnish took him three practice games to finally get it. Joseph only needed two practice games to get his.

Ben watched Alexi teaching Vanessa how to drive the boat. Niina and Koira were talking with Timo in Finnish as they stood along the railing admiring the shoreline.

Timo called to Ben, and asked, "Ben, do you like to fish?"

Ben smiled and answered, "Sometimes."

Timo said, "My father takes me fishing in these waters every year. This is our lucky spot. Do you want to try?"

Ben said, "Sure."

The two opened the storage bin to locate rods and tackle. Alexi left Vanessa's side to help retrieve the fishing tackle. The young men soon presented enough gear for everyone.

Vanessa said, "Koira, this is fun. How often do you take this boat out?"

"I don't know, many times in the summer. Not when it is too cold. When the lake is frozen we go ice skating. Father likes to go out on the lake and watch the Juhannus bonfires from this barge on Friday evening before Juhannus Päivä."

"So, is 'Juhannus Päivä' always on a Saturday?" Vanessa asked.

Koira answered, "Yes, but the celebration starts on Friday. In most of the old orthodox churches in Europe and Scandinavia, the birth of Saint John the Baptist is commemorated 6 months before Christmas. Like Christmas Eve, we also count the evening before Saint John's birth on June 24th.

Vanessa asked, "But the 25th is not always on a Saturday. How do they know which Saturday?"

Koira said, "The Summer Solstice comes on the 21st of June. Many of the old pagan customs surrounding that day have merged with the celebration of Saint John's birth so now we see a mix of all these ancient traditions in our 'Juhannus Päivä' celebration."

Vanessa nodded as Koira continued, "The closest Saturday to June 25th is scheduled on everyone's calendar years in advance. Friday evening before is filled with festivities – and traditions that have originated from Sweden, old Karelia, and Estonia, and other countries. Most of the shops start to close on Thursday when many go to their summer cottages to prepare."

Koira motioned towards the shore line as she said, "See, people are adding final touches to their bonfires on the lake shore. Tonight all along the shore as far you can see will be midsummer bonfires."

Vanessa nodded as she gazed at the distant shorelines with busy workers. They looked like ants.

Koira continued, "See the shore by our dock? Our bonfire will be ready in time for our celebration after we eat tonight."

Alexi said, "Vanessa, take us in a little closer to this shore."

The barge glided to within 50 yards of the dense wooded shoreline.

Alexi said, "Cut the engine and drop anchor."

Vanessa turned off the boat motor. Silence prevailed as the engines stopped.

Vanessa asked, "How do I drop anchor?"

Alexi said, "Push the button with the picture of an 'Anchor'.

Vanessa blushed and pushed the button. There was a splash and not long after a sudden strong tug on the anchor rope held the barge in place.

It was unusually warm for mid-June. The young people all stood in the welcome shade of the canopy that covered most of the deck on the barge and baited their hooks. Once the fishing lines were in the water and the rods were secured to stanchions in the deck along the rails, they all settled down into comfortable chairs watching their lines as conversation drifted around the events of their lives.

Ben mused upon how time had passed so quickly. Joseph was into his third week of treatments; the new T-L-E doorway was nearly completed. Dr. Mäkkinen had informed the Reuel Family that Joseph's treatments were moving ahead of schedule because of the unique capabilities Gamiel's research had made possible. Ben really wished he was back in the laboratory but his mother had insisted he take time to be with his friends and lead a 'normal' life. Ben was glad he did. He really did enjoy fishing. It had been a long time since he could remember going with his dad. He hoped they would do it again – perhaps once more right here in this spot if the fish took the bait.

Koira asked, "Ben, how are your laboratory experiments progressing?"

Ben answered, "Well, I can say that every day, we learn something new – and Dad is ecstatic over the new products and services they are pioneering. Maybe next week, I can talk more about them. Right now, Dad wants me to keep everything under wraps."

Vanessa gave Ben a curious look. She was aware of most of the new developments but often wondered why everything had to be so secret. She herself had taken every opportunity to visit with Alexi between his running errands for his own dad and making final preparations college. Their trip back to Helsinki had been successful. She was smiling inwardly at how easily she had passed the entrance exam.

Alexi asked, "Timo, what is happening with your detective club? Are you still holding meetings?"

"Oh yes. In fact, I wanted to talk about that today. Niina and I want to ask all of you to join our club. We don't chase dangerous criminals like the Hardy boys did. We investigate harmless mysteries. For instance, once we helped a school mate find her missing cat; another time we recovered a stolen bike. Last week, we helped our next door neighbor find his football shoes. He left them in the public Sauna."

Everyone laughed.

Timo continued, "We also help investigate petty crimes at school. Our focus is on perfecting scientific investigation techniques not sending people to jail. We would love it if you would join us."

Alexi answered, "It sounds like fun, but time is a real problem."

Vanessa replied, "It sounds like fun to me, too. I suppose Ben and I have a little time – at least we could talk about it today."

Ben asked, "Do you have Detective Classes?"

Timo answered, "Sherlock Holmes 101."

Everyone laughed, again.

Ben asked, "When can we get started?"

Niina answered, "How about right now?"

Just at that moment, Ben's line jumped, so he jumped to man his rod. In minutes, a fine lake trout was dangling from the line inside the hand net. Alexi helped Ben remove the hook and place the fish in the keep. Ben re-baited his hook and dropped it back in the water. This was more like it; good fishing and exciting conversation.

Conversation refocused and soon Timo was conducting class. The afternoon sun slowly drifted west on this long Finnish Summer day. Occasionally, someone's line would jerk and another fish was brought on board.

Prompted by the topic of their discussion, Vanessa asked, "Ben, has Dad found his watch yet?"

"No."

"Does he have any idea where it went?"

"Nope, and none of the house staff can find it either."

Timo listened carefully and asked, "Alexi, do you think your father would mind if our Detective Club tried to find Dr. Reuel's watch?"

Vanessa stood up to check her line. Alexi stood to help her as he answered, "I don't know. Father doesn't like a lot funny business on the grounds. It can interfere with security; but, I will ask him."

Ben looked across the water at another barge that had quietly dropped anchor about a hundred yards from their position. He could not see anyone topside.

"Alexi, do you have a pair of binoculars on board?"

"Alexi looked over at the barge and said, "Yes, I will go and get them."

Timo went over to the rail next to Ben and peered at the barge, then said, "It looks like one of the rentals from the Lahti Marina at the southern end of Vesijärvi Lake. If it is, he had to bring it through the Vääksy Canal."

Alexi came up with his binoculars and peered over at the barge. Then he handed the glasses to Ben. The girls became curious and came over to listen to the conversation.

Ben asked, "Alexi, do you remember when it first arrived? How long has it been here?"

Alexi answered, "It was not there a half hour ago. I remember checking my watch and noting we were all alone this side of the point."

Ben looked through the powerful lenses at the barge. He could see the deck clearly. There was no gear topside – no evidence anyone was planning to do anything on the deck. He could not see through windows of the cabin – and detected no motion. He scanned the sides to see the anchor rope. He noticed a rope ladder hanging in the water. Handing the glasses back to Alexi, he asked, "Is that rope ladder supposed to always hang over the side like that?"

Alexi looked and said, "No. It is normally stowed in the cabin. I know because I rented one of those last year for our Football Club party in Lahti. Ah hah, I see something – yes there is a diver. He is putting his hand on the rope and starting to climb up."

Ben took the glasses back and looked. Everyone else could see the diver by now as he climbed up on the deck. Ben watched as he removed his air tanks and dropped them to the deck. Then he removed his head gear.

Ben handed the glasses back to Alexi and asked, "Do you know that person?"

Alexi looked and said, "No. I never saw him before."

Alexi gave the glasses to Koira, who looked and said, "Me neither."

Timo and Niina both looked. They did not recognize the diver, either.

Ben watched through the glasses as the man weighed anchor and began steering his barge towards Vääksy Canal very quickly.

Timo commented, "Alexi, does that look like a normal rental barge?"

Alexi answered, "No, it appears to have an extra fuel tank and much larger outboard."

Timo said, "On second thought, I don't believe that is a rental barge. It must belong to one of the wealthy Marina Club members."

Ben said, "I think we need to head back."

Vanessa looked at Ben curiously.

Alexi concurred and said, "Let's weigh anchor."

The young people reeled in their fishing lines and stowed the fishing tackle away back in the storage bin. Koira covered the fish keep and put it on ice as Alexi steered the barge on a course for home.

Vanessa stood by Alexi at the wheel and talked as the others sat under the canopy discussing past and future exploits of the Lahti Detective Club.

Ben frequently glanced across the lake at the rapidly retreating barge until it was out of site. He wondered if it was the same diver who had intruded upon the grounds.

Ben said, "Dad needs to know about this."

Michael Irvin Bosley

Quiet shore along Asikkalanselkä near the Leppänen home

Image photographed by and belongs to the Author

Chapter 17
Increased Safety Measures

The concern that showed on Gamiel's face was genuine. He listened as Ben explained everything. Then he asked, "Did he look like Carl Ungman?"

Ben answered, "No. It wasn't him. The diver had dark hair and a different face. I can't really describe it, but I would recognize him if I saw his face again."

Gamiel shook his head and said, "I will have to talk with Trevor."

Ben looked around the new lab inside the old barn where they were sitting and asked, "How soon before we open a new vortex here?"

Gamiel smiled, and casually replied, "Monday afternoon. I will need your help."

"Wow! That soon? I can't wait!"

Gamiel replied, "We will have to wait for Trevor to open the Door in Denver first. Our hope is to be able to monitor and control this opening from the other side. Once it is open both ways – it should be a cinch to walk back and forth."

Ben asked, "Do you mean we can just walk back and forth like it was just down the street?"

Gamiel smiled and said, "Yep, that's the idea."

Ben said, "Then lets open doors all over the place so we can go places without having to take long car rides – although I think I still like riding in planes. Just think! Our adversaries would never be able to keep up with us! Poof we are in Finland; Poof we are in Denver. Wow!"

Gamiel smiled at his son's enthusiasm, then put his hand under his chin and thought a moment before commenting, "Speaking of security, I think I can program T-L-E to follow you around everywhere you go. The next time something like this mystery diver happens, I can be right there watching. If any funny business starts, I can stop it with the touch of the keyboard."

Ben smiled and asked, "Really?"

"We will know more on Monday after we open the Finnish Connection."

Ben could hardly wait. He was itching to finally start researching T-L-E again. He asked, "How does the T-L-E security system work?"

Gamiel smiled and said, "We programmed T-L-E to setup buffer zones via the normal entry points – front driveway, boat docks, helipad, etc. – through which every person coming onto the grounds is profiled. I have linked every phone book on the planet to other public records inside the T-L-E profile discriminator. Trevor has provided me a direct link into his security profile database, as well, which has access to FBI and Interpol computer records.

If the person has a known profile that presents no threat, then T-L-E admits that individual on the property under a temporary honor system. T-L-E also monitors everyone on the grounds for specific behaviors. If suspicious behavior is flagged, I am notified. I check and if I have a problem with what is going on, I notify security. They take it from there."

"What about when you are not here? Who checks then?"

"Trevor's Security Staff."

"Oh. All the way from Ogden, Utah! Wow! T-L-E isn't affected by distance. What about someone sneaking onto the property from the fence or the lake?"

Gamiel sighed, and said, "Well that is a different matter. There is no buffer zone for them. Anyone who is not already on my 'fully trusted' list attempting to enter the grounds from unusual directions creates a suspicious behavior flag. That person will run into a T-L-E force field. I get notified and so does Mark's security staff – automatically. Not only do these sneaky intruders get detected, they are encased in a T-L-E containment area so they can't get out. Then along comes security personnel who are not affected by the force field (and have no idea it exists) and they apprehend the poor unsuspecting intruder."

Ben asked an obvious question, "What happens if someone tries to land from the air?"

"T-L-E will allow helicopters to land on the helipad – but nowhere else. Aircraft attempting to land without permission will be forced into a containment security zone and enveloped by T-L-E and sealed shut until Security arrives. Anyone attempting to parachute will be physically guided by T-L-E into a single isolation envelope until security has time to deal with them.

Ben shook his head in wonderment as Gamiel continued, "T-L-E absorbs, stores, and redirects all incoming energy. Excessive kinetic energy from a bullet or a cannon, heat from the sun or a match, a laser beam or a nuclear bomb, high winds – hail, hurricanes, tornadoes, and lightning – all is captured and absorbed and used to strengthen the T-L-E force field."

Ben pondered his father's words and said, "Wow! It would seem we have a perfect blend of force field and intelligence protecting the grounds."

Gamiel nodded his head, and continued, "There are other strategies programmed into the T-L-E security system – sophisticated subroutines that block entrance into this laboratory by anyone from anywhere – even unauthorized access through another T-L-E portal."

Ben sat amazed. He thought he had been following the work his dad and Mr. Nibley were doing – but this was fantastic. He was ecstatic and wished Monday was already here. Ben asked, "Has there been any news about Carl Ungman?"

Gamiel shook his head. "Mr. Ungman is an elusive shadow. However; we have learned a great deal about his organization. Mark told me just this morning that several key members of Imperial Planet's Berlin Office have recently entered the country. Finnish Intelligence officers have been monitoring their activities. The General Manager of their Helsinki Field Office has been entertaining Corporate Executives and setting up 'job interviews' with new Finnish employees. All of them attended a private corporate party at the Lahti Marina only yesterday."

Ben sucked in his breath, and asked, "Do you think they had anything to do with the mysterious diver this afternoon?"

"Yes."

Ben's concern reached new levels of anxiety. He asked, "How soon will T-L-E be able to monitor us when we leave the grounds? Is Joseph safe?"

Gamiel smiled, and said, "It will still be a couple of days before I can turn on the new T-L-E Security System, but Joseph is safe. He has two body guards at the hospital in Lahti. After we program the T-L-E roving security monitor, we will not need them."

"Wow!" Ben was truly wowed by everything his father told him. He could not wait to see the security demonstration.

Father and son worked through the late afternoon connecting torsion generator filters, cleaning up, and putting tools away.

Gamiel said, "By the way, Trevor and I worked out a way to send small packages and letters through a T-L-E slot from here. It is not the same as opening a full vortex door, but I was able to send a couple of letters out today."

Ben paused, and said, "That's Great! I should write Leslie." He was reminded of something else, and asked, "What about the Trans-Light-Element Orb we used in our lab back home to stabilize the vortex? Do we need one to open the door on this side?"

Gamiel replied, "Trevor and I want to see if the one back home will somehow show-up when we open both the Finnish and Denver Vortices in-sync. If not, then Trevor can send another from the hoard of balls we hid from Dr. Gillespie."

Ben remembered the day just three weeks ago when they opened the first T-L-E portal. He asked, "What made those spheres hang suspended in my room that morning? I would sure like to find out why they did that."

Gamiel replied, "Yes, that was a mystery. I expect we will find out soon enough, but not today."

Ben said, "When?"

Gamiel replied, "In the Lord's good time. Tomorrow is 'Juhannus Päivä' and Jarmo's mother, Mrs. Laaksonen, is coming home from the hospital this afternoon. The Leppänen family is planning a very special dinner with all their relatives this evening to welcome her home."

Ben said, "That's wonderful."

Gamiel said, "I think we have done enough in the lab today. Why don't you go see if Mother needs any help."

Ben stood up and walked over to the door, turning back he asked, "Will you be long?"

"No, I just need to double check this final test sequence and put a few things away."

Ben said, "OK," and walked to the house.

Gamiel watched his son leave the lab, his heart filled with love for a son who honored his parents.

Putting his rag and tool down on the table in front of him, Gamiel raised his head and looked into heaven and prayed aloud in the privacy of his seclusion, "Lord God of Israel, God of Abraham, Isaac, and Jacob; I have been remiss in my honor to thee. You have given me knowledge and favored me with discovery and understanding even though I have not attended synagogue – or even taken my wife and children to a church of her liking. I have many questions. Mark's family seems well grounded in their devotion to thee and blessed in so many ways. Why is my family being put through these great trials?"

Gamiel bowed his head and laughed to himself, as he verbally echoed the thoughts that came to him even as he asked the question, "What trials? Where in hast thy family been sorely tried? Was it in the true friends I sent thee? Was it in the protection I gave thee through the instrumentality of my sons, Trevor Nibley and Mark Leppänen? Was it in bringing you to a most beautiful land and people to help you find a cure for your son, Joseph? Tell me, let us reason together – in which of these great trials has your family been sorely afflicted and chastened?"

Gamiel was quiet for a moment, then continued in the privacy of his heart, "Nay, Lord, I was wrong. I am blessed above all. Thou hast taught me patience in my inconvenience. Please forgive me for complaining. Teach me to walk in thy ways. Help me harken unto thy voice as did Abraham. Help me be patient. Grant me wisdom. Show me how to use and protect this terrible power thou hast led me to discover. I fear lest it be turned to evil."

There was silence as Gamiel looked around the laboratory, still in partial disarray – so much work yet to finish. He suddenly felt very tired and said, "This weight is more than I can bear alone."

Almost immediately, to his heart came a warm reassurance he did not expect – and the clear impression upon his thoughts, "You are not alone, Gamiel."

In the sobering solitude that followed, Gamiel remembered a verse from his childhood;

"18 Behold, the eye of the Lord is upon them that fear him, upon them that hope in his mercy;

19 To deliver their soul from death, and to keep them alive in famine.

20 Our soul waiteth for the Lord: he is our help and our shield.

21 For our heart shall rejoice in him, because we have trusted in his holy name.

22 Let thy mercy, O Lord, be upon us, according as we hope in thee." (Psalm 33, KJV)

Light dispelled the darkness. Excitement for the discovery of Trans-Light-Element lifted him up as hope once again returned to quiet the noise and settle his troubled heart.

Gamiel Ben Reuel walked out of the old barn and closed the door. As he was locking up, in the solitude of the moment he prayed out loud, "Thank you for sending me such great friends as Mark and Trevor. Please keep them and their families safe. Amen."

Traditional Juhannus Midsummer Maypole
Image photographed by and belongs to the Author

Chapter 18
Juhannus Päivä

Unaware of his father's prayer, Ben entered the Leppänen kitchen garden doorway to find a busy kitchen full of visitors – many whom Ben had never met. He waived as he recognized Mrs. Laila Laaksonen and young Seppo.

Koira spotted Ben and came over greeting him with an inviting smile. "Terve, Ben."

Ben said in his best Finnish he had been practicing all week, "Terve! Mitä kuuluu?" (Health! What is heard?) (How are you?)

Koira answered with a grin, "Hyvää kuuluu. Entä Sinullakin? (Good is heard. (I am fine.) (And what of You as well?)

Ben answered back, "Oikein hieno!" (Just Fine!)

Both youngsters laughed, and Koira said, "Your Finnish is sounding more and more like a Finn every day."

Ben gazed at Koira with new awakening adoration. She was becoming something more than a family friend. He was puzzled and confused by his feelings for Koira. His loyalty to Leslie Richards kept him from exploring those feelings. It was clear Koira liked him, too. He wanted to preserve that friendship.

Mrs. Reuel and Mrs. Leppänen walked past them, and Ben asked, "Mother, is there anything I can do to help?"

Mrs. Reuel answered, "No we are doing fine, Ben. Go enjoy your time with our hosts."

Ben and Koira went into the great hall to greet the other guests. He guessed there must have been at least a hundred people mingling together. Yet, there was room for more.

It was an uplifting feeling to experience the sounds of happy voices and quiet laughter of family and friends rejoicing over Grandmother Laaksonen. The hall was filled with quite background music Ben recognized from his Dad's home collection. The composer was Jean Sibelius. His famous "Finlandia" overture was just beginning.

Alexi came over and asked, "What did your father say about our mysterious diver?"

Ben said, "We think he is connected with our intruder."

Timo came over and asked, "Ben, did your father find his watch yet?"

Ben remembered seeing his Dad's bare wrist and said, "Not yet."

Timo looked at Alexi, and asked, "When will your father be home?"

Alexi answered, "Soon, but I won't get a chance to ask him about looking for the watch until after our guests have gone home. That may be tomorrow sometime."

"OK."

Time passed quickly as the young people mingled together and milled around the reception hall greeting relatives, introducing Ben and Vanessa. Ben was beginning to feel a little uneasy over how long it was taking to get started with dinner when Mark Leppänen entered the front door to the grand hall.

Pekka greeted him; and after conferring briefly in lowered voices, Mark called out something in Finnish. Ben noticed how quickly everyone stopped talking and listened. He felt Koira's close presence as she touched his arm and said, "Father just asked for everyone's attention."

Walking over to Mrs. Laaksonen and taking her hand, Mark continued his remarks in Finnish. Koira quietly interpreted at Ben's side. Ben noticed Alexi was doing the same for Vanessa. Gamiel had just entered the reception hall from the kitchen with Mrs. Reuel and Mrs. Leppänen. He was speaking in Mrs. Reuel's ear. Ben guessed he was interpreting for her.

Translated, Mark said, "Honored family and friends. Good Saint John's Day (Hyvä Juhannus Päivä) to all of you."

The crowd returned his greeting in one voice, "Hyvä Juhannus Päivä."

Mark continued, "Thank you for coming. President Salmo asks me to convey his regrets at not being able to attend our celebration as he had planned. He is visiting his son who lives in Michigan – who decided he wanted to be married today."

Laughter rippled through the small crowd.

Mark continued, "We are gathered here today to give thanks for the miraculous recovery of our dear Aunt Pauliina Laaksonen."

Facing Mrs. Laaksonen, Mark said, "Aunt Pauliina, we are very glad you are with us today. It is a happy coincidence that today also happens to be your name day (Nimi Päivä)."

Pulling a small package from his pocket, Mark presented it to his guest of honor. At that same moment, Pekka appeared at his side with a large bouquet of flowers.

Mark continued his remarks as he gently laid the bouquet in Mrs. Laaksonen's arms, "These traditional gifts are an expression of our love for you. Kaila, will now escort you to the banquet table. All of you please follow and take your assigned places at the table."

Ben noticed, for the first time since he had been at the Leppänen's home, the servants opening grand doors into a spacious room with a very long table. The doors to the room, when closed, blended so perfectly with the walls it was not possible to recognize the doors or even suspect the large room hidden behind them. On the table were more than a hundred ornate place settings and beautiful pottery vases along the center filled with fresh flowers about every 10 feet from end to end. Inside the room, intricately engraved walls were neatly adorned with old family portraits some of which must have been at least a hundred years old.

As the guests assembled, curtains were drawn along the lakeside of the grand room exposing a large bay window affording a spectacular view of the sloping tree studded landscape down to the lake. The double glass window panes stretched from the top of the 16 foot ceiling to the floor. Ben observed the large woodpile under final phases of construction at the water's edge. Soon all would be ready for the traditional 'Juhannus Päivä' bonfire celebration.

If he had not seen it with his own eyes, Ben would not have imagined so many people seated around the same table. Amazingly, no one was excluded from this grand family gathering. In less than five minutes, all the guests found their seats and the gentle conversations ceased.

Ben noted that he was seated to Koira's right, his father and mother were seated immediately to Mark's right, and Pauliina Laaksonen was seated next to Mrs. Leppänen's left, who was directly left of Mark Leppänen. Alexi sat left of her; and Vanessa sat left of him. He also noted similar seating arrangements for most of the other guests.

Mark, standing at the head of the table, raised his glass of clear water, and said in Finnish, "In the tradition of our fathers before us, I invite you to raise your glasses of water distilled from the lake Päijännejärvi – in memory not only to our Leppänen ancestors – but to each of our extended family lines and their fathers and mothers. I especially wish to recognize the presence of a very beloved friend and his family – Dr. and Mrs. Gamiel Ben Reuel and their children – Vanessa, Ben, and their little Joseph who is not with us this evening because he is undergoing treatments for a life threatening condition. As we rejoice over Aunt Laaksonen, I would ask you to remember young Joseph Reuel in your prayers, as well."

All seated raised their glasses high and spoke in Finnish, Koira translated, "To Aunt Laaksonen, Little Joseph, and our esteemed Fore Fathers."

Ben followed suit with a lump in his throat for Joseph as everyone sipped from their glasses and returned them to the table. Mark then turned to his son, and asked, "Alexi, would you please offer our prayer for a blessing on this feast and upon all concerned?" Mark sat down as Alexi stood up.

Ben looked up once in the prayer just to see if everyone else was praying. He was surprised that even the children bowed their heads and closed their eyes. Only the very young toddlers were looking around. Ben closed his eyes again and bowed his head until Alexi concluded his offering. The prayer was in Finnish, but he heard Joseph's name twice and felt a strong reassuring presence that warmed his heart.

A chorus of voices echoed "Amen" and the house staff immediately began bringing the food from the kitchen, placing serving dishes in the center of the table so the guests could help themselves. Feasting began in earnest, attended by warm conversation. Ben found himself entranced by the ambiance of the occasion. He was grateful for Koira's kind attention with translation and social commentary. Several times he could not help laughing at her observations.

The meal passed in satisfaction. At length Mark stood and spoke in Finnish to his guests. Koira at Ben's side said, "Everyone continue feasting as long as you wish. I am going to inspect the bonfire. Please join me when you are ready. We will light the fire at 10 pm tonight."

The house security staff opened the large French doors to the outside veranda and steps leading down to the lake shore. Mrs. Leppänen joined her husband as he exited the dining room. Ben noticed his mother and father were among the first of several others who stood and followed. Ben and Koira got up and followed them. Alexi and Vanessa were close on their heels. The remaining guests sensed the time was passing quickly and the line began to form at the door behind them.

At length, the inspection complete, it was time, and Mark handed the torch to Gamiel who accepted the honor of touching the kindling which quickly grew into a bright roaring inferno.

Ben asked, "Do Finns light bonfires like this every year?"

Koira answered, "Yes. It is an ancient tradition."

The evening progressed with traditional music and dancing. Ben decided he really liked this mid-summer festivity. It reminded him of harvest balls back home. It wasn't long before all members of Lahti Detective Club spontaneously gravitated around each other for the final song and dance of the evening. Ben felt their happiness seemed complete and he wished it would not end. He felt a bond with these youth he had never felt with any other in his life. While the rest of the family visitors spoke Finnish – the 'club' members conversed in English out of courtesy to Ben and Vanessa.

Timo asked, "When shall we meet next? We need to resume our search for Dr. Reuel's missing watch."

Alexi looked at Vanessa, and said, "Tomorrow is Juhannus Päivä. Most families have planned time together. Isn't Joseph coming home for the weekend?"

Vanessa said, "Yes," then looked at Ben, and asked, "Are you and Dad working together tomorrow?

Ben said, "I don't think so. I was looking forward to playing in the Juhannus Päivä tournament. I think Joseph wants to come to the game, too. Also, I heard Mom talking about wanting us to attend church with Mark's family on Sunday. Why don't we plan on meeting Monday night. Meanwhile, I can find out what else Dad remembers about his watch. Where are we meeting?"

Alexi said, "I think we can meet at Timo's house. Is that alright with your parents, Timo?"

Timo answered, "Yes, of course. We will see you at the football game tomorrow."

The young people separated to go home with their families as the crowd began to disperse. The house staff wanted to get things cleaned up early and go home to get ready for their family celebrations on Saturday.

Vanessa walked with Alexi to help him put things away before everyone retired for the evening. Ben helped Koira as they assisted the kitchen staff to bring in the last dishes off the dining table and toss used napkins and table clothes into the laundry chute.

Ben and Kaila met Mrs. Reuel in the grand hallway where she was helping Kaila thank all the

Guests for coming – getting their coats and hats, and generally making all wish they did not have to leave.

Ben asked, "What time is Joseph coming home tomorrow?"

Mrs. Reuel answered, "We are going to get him at 9 am and take him to see the soccer game. Are you still planning to play on the team?"

Ben answered, "Yes – and here they call it football."

Rachel Reuel smiled at her son, and said, "Whatever."

Ben laughed as he and Koira walked out to say final goodbyes to the guests who were leaving.

Gamiel helped Mark and Pekka with security arrangements and made sure the bonfire was burned down and under control.

Alexi walked Vanessa to her room, and said, "It has been a wonderful day.

Vanessa said, "One the best I can ever remember. Are you still playing in the tournament tomorrow?"

"Of course! Ben and I have been practicing and worked out a little surprise move we believe will win the game for sure."

"I can't wait to see it."

There was an awkward pause… Alexi had moved a little closer to look into Vanessa's eyes. Vanessa felt his closeness and said, "I am glad we came to Finland Alexi. I better get to bed so I don't sleep in and miss the game tomorrow."

Alexi released her hand, blushing as he realized for the first time how tightly he had been holding it. He said, "I am very happy you came to Finland. I can't find the right English word to tell you how much I have come to love you and your family."

Vanessa smiled and said, "Goodnight Alexi."

She closed the door gently leaving Alexi outside with his heart pounding. He turned and walked slowly to his room feeling a little embarrassed yet elated.

Alexi paused to listen to the house staff preparing to leave for the remainder of the weekend holiday – and to his own mother and father as they walked around the house greeting each of the staff thanking them for working overtime to make their family celebration a success – and wishing each person individually a happy mid-summer break.

Alexi caught a glimpse of Dr. and Mrs. Reuel going into their room and noticed Koira saying goodnight to Ben before she went to her room. He watched Ben walk to his room and quietly close the door – and wondered what Ben might think if he knew about Alexi's feelings for his sister. Then it occurred to him it was probably no secret by now.

After getting a quick shower and dressed in his pajamas, Ben knelt beside his bed and offered a long tired prayer of gratitude. He closed with, "Please grant Joseph will have a good day tomorrow. Let him be healed - and I will do a better job next year to make sure he does not miss any more Juhannus Päivä celebrations. Amen."

Ben realized what he just said – and decided that Finland had become an inseparable part of his life. Yes, they would surely want to come back next year – and many more – or perhaps celebrate the day in a Finnish American community.

As he slid between clean sheets and laid his head on the soft fluffy pillow, Ben wondered what it would be like in a Finnish American home – as he fell fast asleep dreaming of playing soccer with his brother, Joseph.

Michael Irvin Bosley

Ceremonial Bonfire marks the Juhannus Festival.........

Image photographed by and belongs to the Author

Chapter 19
Finnish Football

Joseph's delightful laugh could be heard up and down the stadium seating as it greeted the players ready to begin the game in the field. Mrs. Reuel smiled and hugged her son. Gamiel sat on the other side of his son enjoying the warmth of the sunlight in the cool Finnish Summer morning breeze as he put his arm around both.

Out on the line, ready for the Referee to start the game, Ben heard Joseph and smiled. This was going to be his best game of the year; marked by a promise of healing and happiness.

Mark turned around and looked up from the row in front of Gamiel and explained, "This is an informal junior league holiday special game for families, visitors and guests. It is not so much about winning as it is learning how to play better. This local stadium is a convenient place where local teams help prepare young players to join the national junior league football club. Football does not enjoy as much popularity as ice hockey in Finland – but our family likes it. These two local team names are Asikkalan Explorers and Lahden Leaders."

The referee called the players to attention in his rapid staccato tone. He reminded both teams of the rules of sportsmanship in Finnish Ben could not follow. Ben could understand a few words and the names of the teams. Soon, the game was afoot.

Ben remembered the Finnish calls Alexi had taught him, moving skillfully into rehearsed positions – kicking the ball into the control of fellow team members.

Alexi sent the ball far and high straight down the field to their goal then moved swiftly to his next choreographed position. Another team member kicked and would have scored but for the swift action of the opposing Goalie (Ben remembered, in Finnish he is called, "maalivahti.")

The play continued, as Ben recovered the ball launched by the goalie and dribbled it up field – but a fast opponent gracefully kicked it out from under him and ran it to their goal scoring deftly before the Goalie could recover

Ben felt crestfallen. The opposing team had scored on him. He redoubled his efforts and recaptured the ball again this time running it all the way to the goal. But the opposing 'maalivahti' was very agile – stopping his drive with a long fast dive. He retrieved the ball and kicked it high and clear nearly all the way to the distant goal as the players ran to catch up to the ball. One of the opposing team kicked it hard and high just inside the goal – but this time, Timo, their home team goalie, caught it just before it entered the goal zone and tossed it to Alexi waiting on the side.

Alexi and Ben teamed up to deliver the ball between desperate opposing players whose swift feet and skillful ploys were no match for the rehearsed strategy of this unstoppable duo. Even before the goalie realized it, the ball was in the net and the scoreboard ringing a small sweet victory in Ben's ears.

The crowd roared as Joseph jumped up to say, "That's the way to do it Ben!"

Vanessa was sitting on the row below next to Koira and her family – thrilled by the game. She turned to Joseph and said, "You tell him, Joe!"

The game continued, with a few more scores by the opponent; but, every time Ben and Alexi teamed up they just could not figure out how to beat their secret code. Excitement mounted as the last minutes of the game came and the opposing team was close to breaking a tie. Ben deftly stole the ball running single handedly down the full length of the field as other players raced to catch up.

Ben was wondering how to beat the goalie when he saw Alexi rush into their pre-arranged position for set up to the unstoppable scoring run. The crowd was on their feet roaring in anticipation. The energy lifted their tired bodies into perfect synchronization. The ball sailed past the desperate goalie center of the net just before the buzzer sounded the end of the game.

All team members lined up to shake hands and trade compliments. Every opposing team member told Ben in their best English how much they admired his good sportsmanship and determination as they shook his hand. Some asked if they could practice with him and Alexi to learn their secret.

Ben smiled at that, and said, "Thank you. Ask Alexi. He is the mastermind."

Families greeted their champions on the field with excited remarks about the suspense they felt during the game – heaping admiration and praise on all the players for their personal success.

Later, after the players had showered and changed, the two families met outside the playing field and decided to go get lunch at a local diner near the Vääksy Canal Bridge – not too far from their home.

It was a half hour drive from the ball park. Getting out of their car, they walked towards the front door of the restaurant. Joseph noticed the draw bridge was up, and said, "Dad, look! The road is sticking up in the air!"

Gamiel answered, "Yes that is a draw bridge. It rises up to let boats pass through the canal between the lakes. See, there is one passing even now."

Everyone stopped to watch as the lock gates opened to let a small private yacht pass from Lake Vesijärvi to Lake Päijännejärvi."

Ben noticed one of the passengers looked a lot like the mysterious diver. He immediately stepped over to Gamiel and said, "Dad, that man in the red shirt looks just like the diver I saw through the binoculars yesterday."

Gamiel looked up and watched the man in the red shirt. He had not taken notice of them. The boat continued and Gamiel counted the number of people on board. They all seemed like normal Finns out on a holiday pleasure cruise on the lake. But he remembered the man in the red shirt.

Everyone went inside. Mark worked out the seating arrangements with the waiter. The place was not large but offered ample cozy table space for everyone. The waiter took their orders amidst light conversation about the game – some in mixed Finnish and English.

Gamiel never felt so at home with another family before. He was overwhelmed with gratitude towards Mark and his family. They had taken them in at a moment's notice and made them instant family members. Where else in the world could he find so kind and noble friends?

Vanessa sat next to Alexi and talked about highlights of the game and the happy crowd of sports fans that had filled the stadium. Koira sat next to Joseph engaging him in conversation about the secret code Ben and Alexi used to win the game. Ben sat on the other side of his little brother listening intently and chiming in occasionally.

Kaila and Rachel were locked in a discussion about how to manage a busy schedule and still keep up with sports, school, and affairs of State with Mark. Mark came to join them after making sure the waiter understood all their needs and wants, sitting next to Gamiel.

Mark looked at Gamiel and said, "You may recall, in 1982, our nation finished construction on a ten year tunneling project called the Päijänne Aqueduct. It was quite an undertaking to carve a solid granite 120 kilometers long tunnel. From a point not far from here, that tunnel drains pure clean lake water all the way to the Helsinki metropolitan area. The mouth of the Päijänne water tunnel is 25 meters below the surface of the lake about 300 meters out from this Vääksy Canal right here in Asikkala."

Gamiel nodded, and said, "Now that you mention it, I do recall some discussion about repairing this tunnel some time ago."

Mark continued his remarks, "The tunnel gradually drops elevation from 70 meters to 26 meters. This provides a natural gravity flow all the way to the man-made Silvola reservoir and from there to Helsinki's water treatment plants in Pitkäkoski and Vanhakaupunki."

Gamiel commented with awe, "Wow! Were they able to harness the tunnel for power production?"

Mark answered, "The energy from this gravity flow yields seven million kilowatt-hours of electricity each year through the Kalliomäki hydro-electric power generation plant.

Gamiel whistled. "Impressive."

Changing topics, Gamiel remarked, "I understand the Finnish Detective Club is looking for my watch." A gleam of amusement danced in his eyes as he glanced at Ben and the other youth. Everyone was so busy talking with each other, no one heard Gamiel but Mark.

Mark said, with a smirk, "Yes, every member of my staff was cross-examined yesterday – as was I."

Gamiel smiled and said, "One of them came up to me taking notes asking very astute questions. Who knows, my watch might turn up, yet."

Mark grinned broadly and said, "Our children and their friends are happy people with a purpose Gamiel. They will be running the country in few years. In a way, I look forward to retiring and watching them run."

The waiter brought their food and everyone turned their thoughts to feeding hungry bodies. Gradually, conversation resumed as hunger pains subsided.

Vanessa looked at Koira and asked, "Isn't there a small art gallery nearby?"

Koira answered, "Yes! Do you want to see it?"

Vanessa nodded her head and looked at her mother.

Rachel looked at Kaila and asked, "Is there an entry fee?"

Kaila answered, "Yes, but it isn't much. Do you think Joseph would like to see it, too?"

Rachel looked at her son, and asked, "Joseph, do you want to go with us to look at some artwork?"

Joseph thought about it, then looked at Ben.

Ben smiled back at Joseph and said, "That sounds like fun, Joe. Who else wants to go?"

Alexi looked at Vanessa who was nodding her head and gave in, "Oh, I guess we guys can go with the ladies to the Art Gallery."

Joseph looked at his mother and said, "Yes!"

Everyone worked on the last bites of their meal. Some were done before others and excused themselves.

Alexi took Joseph to the men's room while the ladies made a quick stop by the curio shop before going to the ladies room.

Gamiel finished his food last and leaned over to Mark and quietly said, "Ben told me a man in a red shirt on the boat that just passed through the canal looks a lot like their mysterious diver from yesterday."

Ben heard his dad's remark and stopped to listen, watching attentively as Mark asked, "Did you happen to see the name of the Yacht?"

Gamiel pulled out his pen and wrote what he remembered seeing on a napkin. Ben leaned over to see what was written.

"Keisarillinen Maa"

Mark and Gamiel both stared at the name in recognition. Even Ben was surprised he could translate it.

"Imperial Earth"

Asikkala Vääksy Canal Bridge Span raised

Michael Irvin Bosley

Asikkalanselkä shore - Päijännejärvi (Päijänne Lake) - east of Vääksy Canal near the Päijänne Aqueduct.
(*Not far from the Leppänen family estate...*)
Images were photographed by and belong to the Author

Chapter 20
Safety Concerns

On the far side of the planet, in another time zone later that day, another conversation was taking place across the dining table over a casual Saturday evening home cooked supper.

The food was nourishing but not exciting. Leslie Richards was watching her Aunt Norma quietly stitch a small hole in her favorite blouse. Her mother was talking about the latest pranks and nonsense going on in the halls of government on Capitol Hill.

Denise Richards looked at her daughter and realized she was not listening to a word she said. As she stopped talking and the silence spoke loadly, Leslie looked up with a mild expression of embarrassed interest.

"Mom, I am sorry. I don't know what's wrong. I can't seem to focus lately."

Mrs. Richards recognized the symptoms and smiled at her daughter. It had been three weeks since the Reuel family left in a big hurry with no forwarding address and no letter from Ben.

"How would you like to go with me tomorrow? I am visiting a local hospital to see what help they need in their new Cancer research center."

"I don't know. My summer plans are still in a mess. I kind of wanted to just walk around the park and think. I have a lot to do before college prep in August."

Mrs. Richards consulted her feelings before venturing out on this ledge with her daughter. Finally, she just put it out on the table for discussion. "Leslie, you know Ben is barely 16 years old. In many ways, he is still a child."

Leslie looked at her mother, surprised that she would even mention it. She was about to reply when the doorbell rang. Mrs. Richards got up and walked to the door. A quick look through the peek hole revealed a woman standing there with a plate of cookies.

Opening the door, Denise greeted the stranger with "May I help you?"

"Hi Mrs. Richards. My name is Laura Nibley. I am staying with my husband for a week to help him keep the Reuel home tidy while they are away. Trevor asked me to come by with this note from Rachel."

Leslie appeared behind her mother at the mention of the Reuels and asked, "How is Ben?"

"He is doing great; getting used to a new language and culture is keeping him busy. He spends a lot of time helping his Dad in the lab. Little Joseph seems to be responding well to treatments. They asked me to let you know they are safe."

Leslie said, "That's good news." The tone of her voice gave away her disappointment over no letter from Ben.

Denise took the note and said, "Thank you. We were wondering how they are getting along. Won't you come in?"

Laura handed the cookies to Leslie and said, "Thank you, but I need to finish laundry and get supper on. There are several hungry young men working with Trevor at the house. I know it looks quiet, and that is how Trevor wants it, but things are pretty busy. There is a lot going on and Trevor is in contact with Gamiel every day."

Leslie answered, "Please tell Ben I will be going to college in August. When do you think they will be coming back home?"

Laura replied, "We don't know the answer to that question, yet. The past three weeks have been filled with concerns for their safety. I am sure they told you?"

Denise answered, "Not in so many words, we had understood the reason they left so suddenly was for young Joseph's treatments."

Leslie could tell Laura felt a little awkward at maybe saying too much. She said, "It's OK Mrs. Nibley. I understand. I just miss Ben, a lot. Tell him I hope he is happy and well.

Laura Nibley smiled and said, "I better get back. Maybe we can visit more next week?"

Denise answered, "Any time. No need to call, just knock. I am returning to the District in July. Recess starts in August, but I took time off in June to be home with my daughter. There is a lot of work yet and rumors of cancelling our recess if we don't get something done."

Laura said, "Thanks, I will bring word when I get it. Take care." She turned and walked back down the sidewalk towards the Reuel home. Mrs. Richards closed the door.

Leslie carried the cookies into the kitchen table, and asked, "What does the note say?"

Denise opened the note. It was hand written in a neat cursive that was clearly Rachel Reuel's hand writing. She commented, "No Post Mark? It must have been included in another package. Oh, that's funny, the note is dated today?"

Mother and daughter looked on at the note together as Denise read out loud.

"Dear Richards,
By now you must think we have completely forgotten you. Nothing could be further from the

~ 183 ~

truth. Gamiel and Ben are very busy in their new laboratory. Our hosts have been too gracious. We are safe and well – learning a new culture and working to keep up with a busy schedule. We have regular meetings with Joseph's physician.

I wish I could tell you where we are, but Gamiel says we need to wait a little longer. Our Joseph has been responding well to the cancer treatments. Vanessa is possibly looking at staying here and attending University in the fall.

Our hosts have become fast friends. You would really love them. I have been trying some new recipes and hope to share them with you when we get back. We miss all of you and pray you are safe.

Gamiel says be cautious and keep your eyes and ears open. He fears your friendship with us could be a source of trouble for you. So I want to ask you to please be careful. If you have any questions, Trevor Nibley can answer them.

All our love,
Rachel Reuel.

Mother and Daughter looked at each other, both thinking the same thing. Leslie spoke first, "We need to go over and talk with Mr. Nibley, Mother. Something isn't right."

Denise agreed, saying, "Let's clean up supper and walk over."

Later that evening Laura answered her doorbell. There stood Leslie with her mother. Denise asked, "May we come in, Laura?"

Laura said, "Of course." Her visitors stepped inside as Laura closed the door.

"Trevor, we have guests. Could you come in the living room for a moment?"

It was only a few seconds later when Trevor appeared in a white lab coat and lab shoes with his patent smile that never ceased to win friends and create trust. With extended hand, he said, "Senator Richards! So wonderful to have you over. I guess you read Rachel's note?"

"Yes. We have some concern over Rachel's last comment – about taking care?"

Leslie added, "She said you could answer our questions?"

Trevor gestured towards the sofa, "Won't you sit down?"

With everyone seated, he began, "Apparently, I understand Ben has shared quite a bit of his father's work with Leslie. Has Leslie discussed this with you?"

Denise looked at her daughter and said, "No. I had no idea."

Leslie blushed, and said, "I'm sorry Mother, but the Reuels told me it was extremely confidential. I had to wait for their permission to even discuss it."

Trevor, recognized his blunder and intervened, "And Leslie is right. The matter is not only confidential – but highly charged with personal risk to anyone who knows anything about it. However, as Gamiel's trusted friend, and as the one he has placed in charge of security for his work – I am sure he will not mind my sharing a few details with you, Senator."

Denise looked at Trevor in a new light, and asked, "Does this concern matters of national secrecy?"

"No. The government knows nothing about this, yet. We plan to brief them – as soon as we are ready.

However, it does involve national security. In fact, it involves the safety and security of the entire planet not to mention the stability of our Solar System."

Mother and Daughter looked at Trevor, transfixed, as he began to relate the highlights of what happened in the first week of discovering Trans-Light-Element. He related how his research laboratory had combined with Dr. Reuel to form a new consortium for peaceful application of all the capabilities of T-L-E.

Looking at Leslie with an amused smile, Denise said, "Thank you, Trevor, for enlightening me. I see why Leslie was so tight lipped about this. It is good to know she can keep a secret."

Looking at Leslie, Trevor added, "Yes, very good to know. I am always looking for bright intelligent help in my company – especially people who know how to keep a secret."

Leslie gave Trevor a questioning look.

Trevor declined to disclose where the Reuel family had gone explaining that not knowing made it safer for both families. He concluded his brief summary of events by saying, "This brings me to the most important concern Gamiel and I have; and that is the fact that his enemies could target you if they find out you are close friends. They might try to use you to get Gamiel to cooperate with them. I am glad you came over this evening. I was just about to call you myself and get your permission to add you to my protective services – above and beyond any Federal protections a Senator enjoys these days."

Denise paused, then asked, "What will that mean? Please explain what you are offering."

Trevor answered, "The short answer is you will hardly even know we are around. We work behind the scenes out of sight. We stay away and clear of anything you specify. We make sure you are safe and keep you informed. I understand you already have some level of Federal and State security. Look at my services as a sort of supplemental health plan. I would be happy to come by with an Account Representative from my company on Monday. Will that work for you?"

Denise answered, "Yes, please do. Meanwhile, you have my permission to go ahead and start watching over things."

Trevor said, "I will get in touch with my service department tonight. I have to contact another detail to begin monitoring your home. They should have everything setup sometime Monday afternoon."

Denise smiled and said, "That will be fine."

Looking at Laura, she said, "Please tell Rachel and Gamiel thank you from us for their kind note. Thank you, Laura, for your cookies. I sampled one before walking over. I don't think they will last long."

Laura gave her an amused look, and replied, "There is more where those came from."

Denise stood up. Leslie followed. Laura Nibley stood up with Trevor. The group walked slowly back to the front door trading not so small talk and courtesies.

Laura opened the door, and said, "Please come by anytime. We have been feeling isolated here with all the secrecy Trevor is enforcing."

Denise said, "Thank you for all you are doing to help the Reuels in their work and for helping keep both our families safe."

As they stepped outside, Leslie said, "Tell Ben to be careful. I am looking forward to seeing him again, soon."

Laura smiled, and said, "We will, Leslie."

As Leslie and her mother turned to walk back down the sidewalk, the Reuel front door closed quietly.

Mrs. Richards, acting on a sudden unexplainable prompting, stepped up her pace and said, "Leslie, I think you should come with me back to Washington, tomorrow. We need to pack tonight and leave in the morning, first thing!"

Leslie asked, "What about Mr. Nibley's offer to keep us safe?"

"We can't be too careful. From everything Trevor told us, we are in as much danger as the Reuel family – possibly more. I will let Trevor know our change of plans tomorrow."

As soon as they came back in their own front door, Mrs. Richards opened her lap top and began looking for the earliest flight back to Washington. As she was pondering when to leave, it occurred to her that her sister, Norma, could possibly be in as much danger as they were.

Denise Richards went into the living room to sit by her sister and talk.

Leslie went up to her room to pack. She came back down a half hour later, and asked, "How long do you think we will be gone?"

Denise looked up from her conversation with Norma, and said, "I don't know. Norma has agreed to go stay with your Uncle Max in Saint George, Utah. We can't take off and leaver her here alone, under the circumstances. So, until we can all get packed, and I can get Norma on a plane tomorrow, you and I will probably not be able to leave until tomorrow evening."

Leslie said, "OK. I will plan on taking enough clothes to last a couple of weeks." She returned upstairs to finish packing.

Denise went back to her laptop to finish arranging flights for everyone as Norma went upstairs to pack.

Senator Richards closed her laptop and sat thinking. Picking up her cell phone, she called a number she only called twice a year, or so. Perhaps it was time to patch up her relationship with her brother.

The voice answered on the distant end, "Hello?"

"Max, this is Denise. I am sorry to call so late, but some matters have come up and I need your help."

"Certainly, Denise. What is wrong?"

"I am taking Leslie back to Washington with me. I have just learned we are possibly in danger and need to ask if you can take Norma in and watch her until the situation is under control."

"Anything. What kind of danger?"

"I can't say right now. I have booked Norma on the first flight available. It should arrive around 9pm tomorrow evening. Is that too late?"

"No. Not at all. What else can I do to help?"

"Pray. This is bigger than both of us. I will keep you informed."

"OK Denise. You are in my prayers. I will pick Norma up at the airport tomorrow evening. You call me if anything else changes. I can be there to help at a moment's notice."

"Thank you, Max. I am sorry I have not called and talked more often."

"Don't worry about that. Take care of that lovely niece and tell her, Uncle Max loves her."

"I will. Good bye."

"Good bye."

Denise hung up; surprised at how easy that was. She got up and went upstairs to start packing.

*** *** *** *** *** *** *** *** *** *** ***

Gamiel and Rachel sat in church together for the first time in many years. The Reuel and Leppänen Families came early and sat together in the center section of pews filling up nearly all the sitting space available in the fifth row back. The Reuel Family decision to attend church with their Hosts had been a natural progression as friendship and common danger bonded these two families together.

Ben sat next to Joseph on one end. Vanessa was sitting between Alexi and Koira on the other. Their parents sat next to each other in the middle.

Timo, Niina and Aki came in with their parents, Mr. and Mrs. Seppälä, and sat in the next row back on the end next to Alexi and Vanessa. Vanessa turned around to greet Niina and Timo with a happy smile.

The prelude music was soft and uplifting. Aside from occasional enthusiastic greetings and visiting between arriving members, there was a reverent feeling in the room.

Mark and Kaila stood up suddenly when Jarmo and Laila Laaksonen made a surprise appearance with Seppo. Kaila worked her way past Alexi on the end and went over to give her sister an emotional hug. Seppo went and sat by Joseph. Jarmo and Laila sat by the Seppälä family. It was a joyful tearful moment for Kaila and Laila. Mark shook Jarmo's hand and gave him a hug.

Gamiel and Rachel stood and shook all their hands. Then all were seated as the meeting was coming to order and the prelude music concluded.

The meeting proceeded in Finnish. Ushers brought headsets to their guests instructing them what channel to select for the English translation.

Gamiel was able to pick up some of the Finnish directly but found the flow of new vocabulary and conjugations overwhelming – so he was grateful for the headsets. He listened to the speakers with interest, and found some of the comments profoundly moving and thought provoking. He was especially touched by the ordinance of the sacrament.

Gamiel and Rachel looked at each other more than once with common amazement at many of the new concepts that came to light during the meeting.

Ben listened with absorbed attention – hanging on to every word the translator spoke. Occasionally he looked over at Vanessa. She was equally attentive. He did not notice until after the meeting how quiet Joseph and Seppo had been the whole time.

Chapter 21
Missing Pieces

D etective Grand was just finishing dinner. It was one of those rare occasions he was able to prepare his own meal on a Sunday afternoon. Home cooked vegetables out of his own backyard garden, salmon on the grill, honey on dinner rolls, and grape juice. He was enjoying the last sip of juice when the call came over his cell. Time of call reported 6:39 pm.

Putting his glass down, he answered, "This is David."

"Sir, we just received an alert you requested."

"OK. What is it?

"Ungman is back in country."

"Alright! Start the plan we discussed and let's get this guy this time. Tell dispatch I will be out the door as soon as I can get my go bag and close up the house."

So much for the quiet time he had planned at home. He gathered up his dishes and dumped them in the sink with the intent washing them later. He walked around the lonely house making sure his doors were all locked and gathered up his car keys and other personal items with his suit jacket. Grabbing his emergency 'go-bag' that had a little bit of everything and anything one might need on a sudden unplanned trip, David turned out all unnecessary lights.

It was 7:07 pm when he paused at the front door. The picture of his departed wife gazed down upon him. He smiled and said, "Alice, I still hear your voice telling me to be careful and come back home. I think I am going to take a vacation and go see our son in Texas. I am growing a little tired of the fight. I will be back later. Don't wait up for me, OK?"

The hot summer sun was less than two hours above the setting horizon as he eased into his unmarked police cruiser and punched the computer log that activated the recording devices and cameras. He sighed. Things had changed a lot since he first started working on the force. Now his team had to cross every **T** and dot every **i.** He hoped Mr. Ungman was not being very careful tonight.

Additional monitoring reports came across his phone including the continuous updates on Ungman that said he was on a plane scheduled to land in Colorado Springs at 7:30 pm.

As David put his car in gear he touched the keypad function key that placed a call on the police band to dispatch. The answer came back immediately, "Yes Sir?"

"Who do we have at the Colorado Springs airport?"

"Detective Hernandez."

"Please alert him to activate task force Charlie Union."

"Yes sir. I just transmitted the alert code. He should be calling you in a few moments."

Detective Grand said, "Thank you," then dropped the call. Less than thirty seconds elapsed before the expected call came through. It was 7:17 pm.

"Sir, this is Carlos. What flight am I looking for?"

"Flight 1083 out of Reagan International, arriving at 7:30pm."

"We're on it."

"Carlos, please watch yourself. Don't make your move too soon. He is a fugitive from justice – a foreign national traveling under an assumed name and a forged passport. You don't have to read him his rights. He escaped from my custody once before. I want him back. You will need all seven members of your swat team on this. Cuff him and bring him to me."

"Don't worry. We are not letting this guy slip through our fingers this time."

Detective Grand said, "Out here."

The phone call dropped. Silence prevailed against the background of his supercharged police engine and the road noise. An occasional car passed as he made his way over to the Reuel family residence.

Part of the plan included additional monitoring of the Reuel home. He called up the map on his smart phone. Again, the special police app reported real time location cell phones that were powered up. This time, there were only two. One was a private unnamed corporation. David knew whose that was. The second reported the owner, Laura Nibley.

That caught the Detective off guard. He wondered how long she had been there.

Another app, recently installed, monitored other intense signaling in and around the home. Significant signals activity was coming out of the backyard. Some of the frequencies were off the chart. This was new.

****** ***** ***** ***** ***** ***** *****

Carlos Hernandez stood at the exit ramp from flight 1083 as it pulled up to gate A2 Colorado Springs Airport at 7:30pm Sunday evening. He was holding up a sign with the assumed name Ungman was using on his passport. The operative they intercepted had been carrying it when they picked him up.

Carlos was amazed how Detective Grand had known. He aspired to emulate the success of a legend. Someday, he, too, would know what Tracker Grand knew. Today, he was content to be part of his success. If all went well, Ungman would be in his custody shortly. Six plain cloths undercover officers were strategically stationed ready to close in.

Passengers began to disembark. Carlos had alerted the Airline and Airport Security of this operation. Everything was in place. People began to file across the threshold; women, children, old men, businessmen, grandparents, teenagers, all walks of life, every different sort of clothing, suits, dresses, blue jeans, dungarees, shorts, sandals, boots, dress shoes. Some wore hats, some wore wigs. Some had too many bags, some had no bags.

When the last passenger crossed and no one responded to the sign, Carlos waited patiently having been briefed on Ungman's crafty methods. He could walk right by you looking like somebody else. Question was, did the operative have a secret code for identifying himself? If so, the sign was not going to be enough.

Carlos signaled his backup to make sure Ungman was not standing nearby watching him. Once that was clear, Carlos walked down the ramp and spoke to the Flight Attendant.

He asked, "Sir, can you confirm this plane is empty? I was supposed to meet someone and he did not get off."

The Attendant said, "I checked every seat and every baggage compartment. No one else but me and the pilot."

Carlos showed his badge and said, "Then you won't mind if I take a look?"

The Attendant said, "Be my guest."

Carlos walked the entire length of the passenger compartment and checked all the lavatories. As he was turning to walk back up the aisle, one of emergency exits caught his attention.

"Excuse me."

The Attendant looked up from his work.

"Can you come look at this, please?"

Walking back to the end of the plane, the Flight Attendant asked, "What you got?"

"Why is the emergency exit showing it has been opened?"

The Flight Attendant took one look and picked up the phone. "Hello, this is MacMichaels, Chief Steward. Before you write your flight report, I need to you come look at this."

The pilot got up and came through the secure hatch, closing it behind him. Then he walked back to the end of the plane.

Carlos showed his badge and introduced himself. "I am Detective Hernandez assigned to Colorado Springs Police special task force. We are in pursuit of a fugitive last seen boarding your flight. He did not get off your plane at the gate. This emergency exit looks like it has been opened. Can you explain this?"

The pilot answered, "That's not possible. I get an alarm in the cockpit when these doors are opened!"

Carlos tapped his police radio transmitter and said, "Jenny, this is Carlos. I need a detail inside the plane. It looks like our bird flew the coop. Could you get Detective Grand on the line?"

Airport Security descended on the plane and cordoned off the entire gate area outside and inside. The entire air crew was summoned for a lengthy interrogation. A full report would be out by morning.

Detective Grand called, "Carlos, what happened?"

"Don't know. I never saw Ungman leave the plane and we seem to have an emergency exit that was tampered with presumably after the plane landed. If it was Ungman, he could have left the plane as much as a half hour to forty five minutes ago. My guess is he had an accomplice pick him up on the tarmac and left the airfield as a part of the crew. He could be half way to Denver by now."

"OK. So our fox has slipped through our hands once again. Pack up your team and report back to Denver. I have another detail that requires your immediate attention."

*** *** *** *** *** *** *** *** *** *** ***

The Reuel residence doorbell rang at 7:57pm. Laura went to answer. When she opened the door, Denise Richards stumbled into the room sobbing deep tears carrying a single sheet of paper with a short type written note.

Laura called loudly, "Trevor!"

Trevor Nibley was there in a flash. They got Denise to sit down on the couch and finally calm down enough to tell her story.

"When we left here last night, I decided to take Leslie back with me to Washington today. I took my sister to the Airport and got her on the plane to St George so she would be safe with my brother."

Trevor listened without interrupting.

Denise continued, "We tried to get a flight out this morning, but the 9:30 and 12:30 flights were booked; some sort of convention. So we booked the next available. I had to run a couple of quick errands after I loaded my sister on the plane before I came back home to get Leslie. Oh, I wish I had just come back immediately. Now what will I do?"

Denise broke down into tears again.

Laura brought Denise a cool damp cloth to dry her eyes.

Denise calmed down, and said, "Leslie stayed to finish closing up the house. I just got back home and found the door wide open, the house trashed, and this note."

Trevor took the note and read it.

At that moment, the doorbell rang again. It was 8:11 pm.

This time, one of the Nibley Security Agents answered the door.

Trevor heard a familiar voice, "Hello young man, I believe we have met once before. I am Detective Grand. Do you mind if I come in?"

Michael Irvin Bosley

Chapter 22
Kidnapped

"Good Morning, Trevor. Isn't it just a little late for you?" Gamiel was feeling for his watch, and mentally reminded himself it was still missing. He then looked at the T-L-E world time clock on the console that indicated every time zone around the globe.

Ben smirked. It was bright and early Monday morning a few minutes past 8 am. Back in Denver, that meant it was barely past 11 pm on Sunday. He and his father had opened the barn laboratory and fired up the generators early to get ready for the big event. Today was the day. If all went well, the first Trans-Light-Element doorway between two places would be successfully opened.

They had just started reviewing the initial test sequence when a phone call came in over the new micro-vector T-L-E-Telecom Port. Ben was admiring the design of the telephone handset against Gamiel's ear.

Gamiel's countenance clouded instantly. His voice became distressed. "What's that?! Please repeat slowly!"

"Trevor, that's preposterous! You mean someone just walked right into Senator Richard's home and kidnapped Leslie?!!!"

Ben bolted upright. His whole frame tense and ready to jump into action. "If Ungman harms Leslie… …When did it happen?"

Gamiel turned on the T-L-E Console speaker, and said, "I have Ben here with me. When did this happen?

Trevor's crisp voice coming over the T-L-E phone line sounded as if he were standing in the room with them. "About 7pm our time here. We have been working with Detective Grand and the FBI."

Gamiel asked, "Do we need to postpone our experiment this morning?"

Trevor answered, "No. We need this experiment to work so we can find Leslie!"

Ben nodded his head vigorously. He was ready to open the door and go home right now.

Gamiel said, "Let's do it."

Trevor said, "It is settled, then. Gamiel tune up those torsion fields and let's open this gate."

Ben helped his dad run through the checklists. Soon, the new Unified Field Torsion Generators were on line and in-sync. It wasn't long before a new vortex appeared on the far wall of the old barn just as it had in their laboratory in Denver. Gamiel made some final adjustments and asked, "Trevor, what is happening on your side?"

"We are just starting your original T-L-E Door program sequence. The orb is circling as I speak. If our coordinates are matched you should see the orb enter your space any second now."

Ben watched the swirling vortex through the monitor screens of the control center. Suddenly the vortex cleared. Before them appeared a new clear T-L-E Door about 10 feet in diameter – perfectly circular, with the bottom of circular arc unseen slightly below the floor along the inside wall of the barn that now formed a natural threshold between the two laboratories.

Just the other side of threshold stood Trevor Nibley smiling like a kid at Christmas time. He pointed to the orb as it passed into the Finnish laboratory for a brief moment then disappeared.

Trevor rolled a bowling ball across the threshold. Gamiel picked it up and rolled it back. Then, one of Trevor's lab technicians released a canary through the port. It flew around the Finnish Lab and roosted in one of the old barn rafters.

A childish grin crossed Gamiel's face. He said, "Trevor, I am going to walk across the threshold and back again."

Trevor answered, "I guess somebody has to do it. It may as well be you. This is your contraption. However, I think you should send the canary back first just so we can rule out any compound back and forth affects, if you know what I mean?"

"I do know what you mean, my friend, but I doubt I can catch that bird."

Ben looked at his father with sudden fear. What if something did go wrong? He stepped up and asked, "Dad, can I go through, first?"

Gamiel answered without hesitation, "No! The risk is too great. I should go through first."

Ben grabbed his dad's hand and said with urgent conviction, "But you've already been in the vortex. If there are any unknown affects, it may act doubly on you."

Trevor said, "The boy has a point, Gamiel."

Gamiel said, "Dash it all, Trevor, why didn't we get this cleared up before now. Ben, help me coax that bird back down here."

Ben found an old ladder and leaned it against the barn wall. While Gamiel held the ladder still, Ben climbed up slowly to retrieve the canary. It moved over to his outstretched hand with no complaint. He climbed back down the ladder and gently coaxed it through the T-L-E door into Trevor's waiting hands.

Trevor passed the canary to one of his staff who examined it carefully.

"Everything checks out. This bird appears to have suffered no ill effects."

Trevor looked at Gamiel and said, "It is your turn, now, Gamiel."

Ben looked anxiously into his father's eyes, pleadingly.

Gamiel smiled at his son and said, "OK Ben. You deserve to be the first human being to cross the T-L-E threshold."

Ben spun on his heels and walked briskly into their back-yard laboratory. Turning to stand by Trevor, he said, "Dad, it was just like walking into another room. I didn't feel a thing."

Ben wanted to run outside into the dark night and go try to find Leslie.

Gamiel knew his thoughts and said, "Ben, I need you to walk back across now. There is nothing you can do there now. You have to be here when I walk across in case something happens so we both don't get stranded on the wrong side."

Ben looked longingly out the door of his father's familiar laboratory. Outside that door was his yard and home. Down the street was Leslie's home. Somewhere someone was holding his dear friend in peril. It took all the strength he could muster to walk the few feet back to Finland.

Gamiel said, "I know how hard that was for you. I promise you. After we get T-L-E working, we will find Leslie."

Gamiel turned and walked across to stand in his old lab pausing to shake hands with Trevor across the threshold as he walked to stand in the old barn in Finland.

Trevor said, "Fantastic. We finally did it Gamiel. This is history in the making and we did not even think to bring a movie camera."

Gamiel smiled, and said, "Yes we did. Every instant is recorded on both sides by laboratory cameras. If fact, I believe T-L-E itself is making a subatomic record of all our words and deeds."

Trevor smiled and said, "You make it sound like T-L-E has intelligence."

Gamiel looked at his friend in surprise and asked, "But, Trevor, I thought you of all people already understood; intelligence is found in the elements at all levels. Trans-Light-Element is no different."

Trevor nodded and asked, "But, Gamiel, surely you don't mean to imply T-L-E has a soul?"

Ben watched with fascination as these two giants debated one of the mysteries of the universe across the very first Unified Field Trans-Light-Element Threshold ever devised in recorded history – Gamiel, standing at home in his own laboratory; Ben and Trevor standing in the first T-L-E laboratory in Finland looking across the very first international T-L-E Gateway now known to them as the 'Finnish Connection'.

Gamiel smiled at Ben looking back and forth at them, and said, "Trevor, consider the moment and the implications of what we are saying. The sacred scriptures record the conversation between the earth and God. That may be a literary device to convey the story; but I still hold to the principle that intelligence is a living reality even in the essence of simple elementary substances – much more so in Trans-Light-Element. Now, does it mean that simply because something has intelligence – it has a soul? I am not prepared to answer that, yet – however, when we attended church with Mark and his family yesterday I was introduced to some eye opening concepts – something you and I need to sit down and talk about."

Trevor paused to hear what his friend was saying, recognizing a turning point in his friend's life.

Ben was listening but growing impatient. He asked, "I know all this is really important, but can go find Leslie?

Trevor turned and shook Ben's hand, and said, "Young man, the elements have recorded that you are the first to walk through the Trans-Light-Element Door. God bless you to never forget the moment. Before I return to Colorado, I just have to look outside this old barn so I can really see I am in Finland."

Trevor stepped lightly to the door and stepped outside. He was thrilled. He came back in after minute and walked back across the threshold into Colorado as Gamiel walked back into Finland meeting each other in the middle and shaking hands, again.

Gamiel turned and said, "This moment is recorded. Now let's get to work finding Leslie."

Trevor replied, "My team is already on it. What do you want me to tell Senator Richards?

"Tell her we are moving heaven and earth to find her daughter."

Chapter 23
Finnish Detectives in Action

From the moment Ben knew Leslie was in danger, his entire being wound up tightly into a catapult engine barely able to constrain himself from running out the laboratory door in Colorado and down the street to start his own investigation. Nothing seemed as urgent as the clarion call to find Leslie.

Gamiel noticed Ben seemed withdrawn as they went through the rest of the exercises to complete the certification of the first T-L-E Port. There was much to do and both men were very busy.

At length, Ben paused and asked, "When can we start using the T-L-E port to go back and forth?"

Gamiel answered, "After our two countries agree on protocol for crossing international boundaries."

Ben asked, "How long will that take?"

Gamiel paused as he was recording technical data, and said, "Trevor's lawyers are drawing up the documents even as we speak. We don't plan to go public; but we will file with the State Department and get provisional visa's that cover this new capability."

Ben asked, "Doesn't that involve a lot more people in our secret?"

Gamiel explained; "What we are doing threatens the security of nations. Unless we act prudently, a climate of fear and mistrust will severely limit our options. Trevor has friends in high places we will approach discretely."

Ben asked, "What about people like Dr. Gillespie?"

Gamiel answered, "I was naïve to even talk with Dr. Gillespie. It was before we opened the door and discovered T-L-E. I won't make that mistake again.

Ben worked on in silence.

Gamiel interrupted Ben's thoughts, "I trust Trevor to avoid disclosures to the wrong people. But, whatever happens, always remember this; we own T-L-E and all the processes that make it work."

Ben looked through the open T-L-E Port then looked at his dad, and said, "It is hard. I want to walk home and find her."

Gamiel said, "I know. So do I; but, Trevor's best people are looking for her. They are much better at it than we are. Let reason guide your thoughts and rule your feelings. You must think through each move; try to anticipate your opponent's next move. You choose the time and place of your next move – not your opponent."

Father and son continued working in the lab through the morning. Several times, they traveled back and forth to and from their laboratory in their home backyard.

Around noon Finland time (3am Denver) Mrs. Nibley brought fresh sandwiches she made in the Reuel kitchen. Together, they walked into Finland to join Gamiel and Ben for lunch. They went over their plans for using T-L-E to start searching for Leslie.

Laura Nibley said, "I like Leslie a lot. I am concerned about the danger she is in with every minute that passes.

Ben noticed she looked very tired and realized she had already been up all day before and never had a chance to rest.

Gamiel noticed, too, and asked, "Have either of you had any rest?"

Laura smiled, and answered, "I was nodding off for a good nap when Senator Richards knocked on our door. After that, I could not sleep."

Trevor smiled, and said, "I pity the kidnappers when Senator Richards catches up to them." Finishing his sandwich, he said, "OK, I have to show Laura we really are in Mark's back yard."

They all exited the lakeside door to a pristine vista of Finnish Summer countryside.

Trevor exclaimed, "What a paradise!

Laura agreed, saying, "What an appropriate place to open the first gateway."

Trevor turned around and dropped his jaw at the site of the old barn. "Gamiel, I think you are on to something here. No one would suspect such a rundown old barn is a hub of intergalactic travel."

Ben was amazed. For the first time since his family had left home, he was reminded that T-L-E could be a means of traveling to distant galaxies. He wondered what new vistas awaited them on far-away worlds; would T-L-E help mankind finally understand the universe?"

Trevor said, "Well, enough for now. My blood tingles with the excitement of what we have done. I wish the bad guys would go away and leave us to our fun. That said, I have to catch a plane to speak with the Secretary of State. He has given me an audience concerning Senator Richard's daughter. I will be in touch, Gamiel. Don't do anything rash."

Trevor turned to shake hands with Ben and said, "Pray for Leslie's safety, but wait for my boys to find her. Whoever took her – now has to face the ire of ALL the people of the United States."

Laura gave Ben and Gamiel a hug and followed her husband as he went back into the barn, followed by Ben and Gamiel. The Nibley couple continued walking through the T-L-E gate as if it were just another hallway between the two laboratories.

Gamiel wanted to follow him. He was unaware of the quiet plans formulating in the desperate heart of his young Ben.

A dreadful engine of drastic action was frantically organizing thoughts in ways that were new to Ben. Although Ben did not realize it, love was born in a heart driven to action by feelings of desperation. The conversations he had shared with Leslie were knitting into a bond of friendship now threatened by an unseen enemy he was learning to despise.

The note left behind demanding the containment formula made it clear Ungman had masterminded Leslie's abduction to force his father out of seclusion. Secretly, Ben began forming a desperate plan that would save Leslie and keep his father safe. Emotions began to override some of his routine logic. Reason took a back seat to action.

Ben needed help. He could not do it alone. In his emotional state, he decided his safest choice would be Timo Seppälä. He planned to bring Timo into his confidence after the detective club meeting tonight.

Later that evening after supper, the Lahti Chapter of the Finnish Detective Club met in the basement of the Seppälä residence. Parents had agreed it was a safe enough place. The first order of business was the induction of new members. Timo Seppälä called the meeting to order.

Ben was aware his father had not yet activated the T-L-E roving security monitor due to technical issues that would take another day to resolve. What was said here tonight would be said in complete confidence.

"This meeting will come to order." Timo spoke crisp English with a strong Finnish accent. The others in the room gave him their undivided attention.

"Niina Seppälä, please call the roll and take the minutes."

Niina called the names of club members present; some responded with a verbal 'here', others just raised their hands. "It is noted that other members listed in the club records are either on vacation or absent for other duties. Tonight will be a short business meeting to induct our new members and resolve Dr. Reuel's missing watch."

Timo Seppälä said, "Thank you, Niina. I present the following names to be accepted into our club. Alexi Leppänen, Koira Leppänen, Vanessa Reuel, Benjamin Reuel. All in favor please say yes."

All present echoed in the affirmative.

"All opposed?"

No one spoke.

Timo said, "We have a unanimous vote. Welcome new members of the Lahti Detective Club. Niina, please come forward and induct our new members."

Niina stepped forward and said, "Alexi Leppänen, Koira Leppänen, Vanessa Reuel, Benjamin Reuel, please stand and raise your right hands."

All stood. Niina continued, "Do you promise to keep the by-laws of the Finnish Detective Club, obey the laws of Finland, and keep the confidences that belong to this club?"

Each nodded their heads and said, "Yes."

Niina said, "You are hereby formally accepted as life time members in the Finnish Detective Club as witnessed by all those present. The secretary will enter your names in the register and record your membership."

That done, Timo, got down to business.

"Now we will talk about what has been done so far to find Dr. Reuel's missing watch. Koira and Niina divided up the Leppänen household staff between them and asked each of them what they know about the missing watch. Vanessa and I have examined all the testimonies and prepared a report. I would like to ask if Ben could please read the report and Alexi comment with suggestions."

Ben took the report. It was written in very good English. He was very impressed as he read;

"Only one of the staff, the limousine driver, claims to have seen the missing watch – and that was through the rear view mirror in the limousine where Dr. Reuel laid it in the seat between him and Mrs. Reuel. Alexi's dad was questioned; he never saw the watch in the seat. The driver says it was there when they left the airport. However; he thinks it was not there when he looked again immediately after they left Helsinki. He assumed Dr. Reuel had placed it back on his wrist.

Dr. Reuel was questioned on more than one occasion by both Niina and Koira – who have both stated Dr. Reuel firmly believes he put it in the seat and never returned it to his wrist. Dr. Reuel also mentioned that it was the first time he had removed the watch in over a week."

Something clicked in Ben's mind. He began to mentally rehearse the events of that first week after his father's close call escape from the T-L-E Vortex. His mind was racing on parallel tracks even as he continued reading the report.

"Many of the household staff reported removing all the seats from the limousine, using metal detectors and magnets. The watch simply was not in the car.

Question: Could it have fallen out when everyone got out? Answer: Yes – but the staff scoured the grounds right after the car was emptied and found nothing.

Question: Did Dr. Reuel or a family member leave the car before it arrived at the Leppänen home? Answer: No.

Question: Could the watch have been placed in a handbag absent mindedly by any member of the family? Answer: Yes; however, every bag has been dumped out and searched - no watch.

Question: What are the remaining options? Answer: To be discussed tonight.

Alexi stood up and commented. "We have strong evidence the watch really exists. We have more than one testimony it was laying on the seat by Dr. Reuel in the car. That was the last place the watch was seen."

Timo looked at Vanessa, and asked, "You were in the car. Can you remember anything?"

Vanessa said, "I saw the watch on the seat. There was a point during our ride it was not there anymore. I thought nothing of it until Dad started looking for it when we got out of the car. We all assumed it fell on floorboard."

Timo asked, "Ben did you see anything?"

Ben answered, "I remember seeing the watch on the seat, but thought nothing of it until Dad said he could not find it. He later told me he took it off because it was irritating his skin. I asked him if it had ever done that before and he said no"

Ben felt a tingling in his spine as he reached a strong conclusion there was a connection between Trans-Light-Element and the missing watch. He stood up and said, "Now, I have been thinking – about Dad's comment that it never irritated him before – and his other comment about it being the first time he took it off all week. Dad rarely removes it because it is a valuable family heirloom."

Vanessa nodded her head, and said, "It belonged to his father; and his father's father. It was a classic Swiss Watch. Whenever it needs repairing, he takes it to an old watchmaker downtown. He refuses to get a new digital watch."

Ben continued, "I know something about that watch you don't – and it involves some experiments of my dad's that I can't talk about. I want to ask each of you to be patient and let me go back to Dad and ask him a few more questions."

Alexi looked at Ben and asked, "Are you saying that you think one of your dad's experiments could have something to do with the disappearance of his watch?"

Ben nodded his head. Even as he thought about it, excitement rose up in his mind; together with some fear. He remembered the effect the unstable vortex had had upon his father – how close he came to losing him... *just like the watch*!

Alexi said, "OK, I propose we put this business on hold until Ben can discuss this with his father. What other business do we have?"

Ben raised his hand.

Tim recognized Ben and gave him the floor.

Ben said, "We have something more important to worry about than a missing watch. We now have a missing person."

The immediate concern manifest by all concerned convinced Ben he could not just talk with Timo. He explained, "A very good friend of ours was kidnapped yesterday."

Vanessa asked, "Who, Ben?"

"Leslie."

Vanessa's countenance reflected alarm and consternation. She was sure Ungman was behind it. Her heart skipped a beat.

Alexi noticed her alarm and asked, "Who is Leslie?"

Vanessa answered, "Our neighbor. Her mother is a U. S. Senator. We have known them for many years. They are good friends of the family."

Ben looked around at the members of the club and realized he was faced with a dilemma. Should he tell them about Trans-Light-Element? If so, how much should he discuss? He needed to talk with Dad before sharing secrets, but he needed their help, now. He looked at Vanessa who knew instinctively what he was thinking. She nodded her head in agreement.

Ben asked, "Will each of you raise your hands and repeat after me?"

All stood and raised their hands.

Ben said, "What I am about to tell you is Top Secret. Repeat after me, I, (say your first name), promise to never divulge a word about anything Ben tells me – to keep it to myself until Ben says it is OK to talk about it."

Everyone repeated his words.

Ben said, "My father made a huge scientific discovery that could shake up the entire civilized world. Bad guys tried to steal his work from him. We didn't just come to Finland so Joseph could be cured from cancer. We came here in secret to hide from evil men."

For the he next hour, without disclosing the details of Unified Field or Trans-Light-Element, Ben related the key points of the story of what had happened to the Reuel Family since those world changing events in the last week in May that now seemed so long ago.

Everyone was on the edge of their seats - especially when Ben related his clever escape from Ungman. When Ben was done, all sat in stunned silence.

Ben concluded, "I am almost certain that mysterious diver we saw on Friday was sent to find us since we locked up Juri Tarkonen. We now have a letter demanding ransom for Leslie. Their price; make Dad tell them about his secret experiments! We have friends who are looking for Leslie. Senator Richards has already talked with the FBI. But we don't have a lot of time. Every minute is another moment Leslie could be in mortal danger. Will you help me find her?"

Timo and Niina stood up and hugged their new friends, asking "What can we do to help?"

Koira stood and said, "Well, are we not detectives? We have permission from our own Finnish government to investigate and help where ever possible. I make a motion to ask every Chapter of the Finnish Detective Club to help find anyone who has anything to do with this Imperial Planet or whoever they call themselves."

Timo stood up and called the meeting back to order.

"We have a motion to help Ben and Vanessa find Leslie. We need to be careful because these guys are very clever and we don't want them to know what we are doing. It could be dangerous. Do you want to help?"

All stood and gave a resounding, "Yes."

The meeting adjourned soon after members of the Lahti Detective Club had accepted specific individual assignments. The search for Gamiel's missing watch was put on hold. The name of Leslie Richards was now written on the heart of youthful peers she had never known from the other side of the world.

Timo contacted all the other Finnish Chapters of their club with the names and descriptions of Leslie and her suspected kidnappers with extreme cautions to not disclose their activities or do anything that might tip off the bad guys.

By morning, over a thousand Finnish youth some in High School and some in College throughout the land of Finland were surfing the internet, researching material at public libraries and other public records – all under the cover of students gathering data for a research report. No one suspected any single person or group was part of a larger investigation.

By mid-afternoon of the following day – Alexi and Ben were pouring over the reports streaming in over the internet – via encrypted emails. Ben was in Alexi's bedroom sitting beside him at his computer console.

Alexi said, "Ben, a lot a people are working to find out all we can about Leslie. They are practicing all the disciplines we teach – to be discreet and not disclose any affiliations. Look at what we have learned!"

Ben was amazed. He could not have learned this much in a year on his own. A missing person's report filed with Interpol by the FBI had Leslie's picture, Carl Ungman's picture, and a complete dossier on his entire life. Another report had names and addresses of every person ever employed by Imperial Planet, quarterly earnings over the past 10 years – together with every product, every major transaction, and every news article ever published about the firm was clearly laid out before them.

Ben asked, "How much of this information can I share with Dad?"

Alexi answered, "All of it. But, you will have to tell your dad you told us about your real reason for being here."

Ben felt uncomfortable. He said, "Yes. I don't know what he will say. But I think he needs to know what we are doing."

Alexi smiled. "Ben, your dad will understand. He is a great man."

Ben answered, "You are right. I will tell him this morning."

Alexi smiled and said, "We have contacts in other countries, you know."

Ben smiled. This was going to be good.

Together, Ben and Alexi began contacting international chapters of the Finnish Detective Club. Within one hour – Finnish youth in every nation around the world were all, collectively cooperating over encrypted virtual internet phone, email, blogs and chat rooms – sharing pictures, articles, last known sightings, even as recent as 12 hours ago, of key employees, associates, and top executives of the now highly visible corporation;

– Imperial Planet.

Chapter 24
A Matter of National Security

S ecretary Carlson looked across his highly polished cherry wood desk at his old friend, Trevor Nibley. Trevor had insisted on meeting with him personally – had called his home direct at 10 pm the night before. His voice was still ringing in his ears.

"George, I have to report a matter of highest national urgency. If you don't see me in your office at 7 -o-clock tomorrow morning, I'm going to go over your head and talk to the President myself."

Now it was 7:03 and the Secretary had a busy schedule today. Whatever Trevor had to say had better be good. Secretary Carlson said, "OK, Trevor, we have been in this business too long together to mince words. Give it to me straight."

Trevor grinned in a way George had seen before. It brought back memories of when he and Trevor had served together in the Navy. That grin had always preceded the unexpected – often dramatic presentations. He braced himself for another such adventure.

Trevor touched a lapel pin on his left collar, and, with an air of profound drama, spoke quietly, saying, "Sam, you can send it now."

In two seconds, a round white object with a curious opaque surface appeared on the Secretary's desk. George stared at it in disbelief. "Trevor, what kind of magician's trick are you playing?"

Trevor looked at his old friend. They both came from a very practical no-nonsense background – both Navy Seals, both seasoned by the burdens of command – now retired, hard core businessmen. George had just recently accepted a call to serve on the Cabinet of the Executive Branch as a personal favor to the President – replacing the previous State Department Head who had suddenly resigned for personal reasons. Trevor hoped his old friend would not let him down.

Trevor answered, "This is just the beginning. Allow me to demonstrate."

Trevor spoke into the T-L-E lapel pin phone, and quietly said, "Gamiel, commence Operation Disclosure."

The round orb began lifting into the air above Secretary Carlson's desk in a spiral trajectory as it drifted towards the center of the large spacious office. A vortex appeared in the middle of the room which opened up and swallowed the round orb. A Trans-Light-Element Door opened right in the middle of room; on the other side stood Gamiel Ben Reuel in his newly completed Finnish laboratory.

Trevor said, "Gamiel, would you care to join us?"

Gamiel said, "Certainly, with Secretary Carlson's permission?"

George Carlson was speechless. He stood up and stared at Trevor and then Gamiel, then waved Gamiel into his office. He asked, "I don't know who you are, but where did you just come from?"

Gamiel answered as he entered the room, "Before I answer that Mr. Secretary, do I have your word of honor to never disclose my location?"

George looked at Trevor and back to Gamiel who now stood before him where just seconds before had been his private 'secure' and inaccessible office. He said, "Very well, if that is how you need to play this – then just tell me why you are here."

Gamiel took his cue and began to explain. "First, I will say that room you see through that virtual doorway is in a country on the other side of the Atlantic. Right now, if you desired, you could walk into that laboratory some 6000 miles away in just a few seconds time."

Gamiel paused for effect, and then continued, "This is a live demonstration of my personal discovery which Trevor has partnered with me to share with the world. We are just beginning to understand its power and some of the implications it is already having upon the history of our planet. It is highly technical so please don't ask me to explain how it works."

Gamiel concluded, "At some time in the near future, you are invited on a private tour of our new Intergalactic Space Port now under construction at an undisclosed location. For now, we have a more urgent matter to discuss. I will turn the time back to Trevor."

Trevor relaxed and asked, "George, can we all have seat?"

The three men assembled around the large desk and got comfortable. George brought over refreshments from the wet bar as Trevor wasted no time telling the story. "George, allow me to introduce my colleague, Dr. Gamiel Ben Reuel, an ex-navy seal like ourselves, but perhaps one of the world's most brilliant yet modest scientific minds I have to say rivals or even exceeds Albert Einstein himself."

Gamiel blushed, and said, "Really, Trevor, we shouldn't make such a claim."

Trevor smiled and brushed aside his friend's self-deprecating way, and continued, "Gamiel is a physicist who, up until recently, has been teaching in a less known university in Denver. He tinkers in his backyard laboratory on his own time. His son often works at his side like young men used to do generations ago. About 4 weeks ago, Gamiel first opened the vortex into Unified Field.

Through trial and error, and some help on my part, we opened this vortex again just days later and stabilized it – in so doing, opened a window we discovered could be moved anywhere by typing coordinates on a computer keyboard. The open doorway Gamiel just came through is just like that window – only now it is a two way gate firmly secured between two locations. We have trained technicians standing by ready to open others just like it to remote places on the earth, the space station in orbit, and even the surface of the moon – all in the space of an hour.

George, anyone who attempts to open a Unified Field doorway without our patented process for stabilizing the vortex – runs a great risk of ripping this planet apart!

Trevor paused to let that fact settle then continued, "Nibley Enterprise Security has uncovered a number of competing interests who are on the verge to doing just that. The leading venture in this race is the UK based corporation, Imperial Planet, headquartered in London with offices in most industrialized countries – including the United States. They have proven to be very adept at corporate espionage and willing to break the rules."

Trevor paused to see if the Secretary had a comment. Secretary Carlson let the moment pass in silence as he studied the open door in the middle of his office with concern. He motioned Trevor to continue.

Trevor took the queue, "They have already invaded Gamiel's private residence and threatened his family's safety. That is why the Reuel family is now in seclusion.

Trevor placed a picture of Carl Ungman on the desk in front of Secretary Carlson. A key operator in this industrial espionage ring is a man named Carl Ungman. He is an independent freelance operator with offices in Berlin."

Trevor paused again to see if that name elicited any change of expression. There was none. Either Secretary Carlson didn't know him or he was getting better at controlling his facial cues.

Trevor continued, "Just a few days after Gamiel first opened this door, Mr. Ungman forced his way into the Reuel family backyard laboratory and began pilfering the place searching for Gamiel's proprietary data and processes. When Gamiel's 16 year old son, Ben; (You will really like this young man, George.) when Ben happened upon the intruder, Ungman tied Ben up and threatened him. Fortunately, Ben was clever enough to work his way free and trick Ungman into leaving the laboratory control room long enough for Ben to close the door and lock him out – thus thwarting Ungman's plans."

Trevor continued, "Ungman was arrested but escaped with the help of undercover friends. Nibley Security is looking for him. However, Ungman has vast resources at his disposal and continues to elude us while searching for the Reuel Family. We are certain he may have already located where the Reuel Family is staying. Two weeks ago, there was an attempt to kidnap Gamiel's oldest daughter, Vanessa, in broad daylight."

Secretary Carlson shook his head.

Trevor placed a photograph of Leslie Richards in front of Secretary Carlson and continued, "Fortunately, my Senior Operative in country foiled their plans just in the nick of time. After that attempt failed, Ungman's people expanded their strategy by menacing close friends of the family, namely our own Senator Richards. Her daughter, Leslie, was kidnapped right out of her own home last Sunday evening."

Secretary Carlson looked at Leslie's picture and asked, "What evidence do you have that Ungman did this?"

Trevor presented a report Nibley Security had received from the FBI, and said, "We have an unsigned ransom note left in Senator Richards' home – demanding Gamiel's trade secrets in return for Leslie. The FBI shared this report with me confirming Ungman somehow opened an emergency exit and left the plane he was riding under an assumed name and false passport in Colorado Springs just before it reached the gate. I personally interviewed the Chief Investigating Officer of the Metropolitan Police in Colorado. Based on this and other facts you can read in this report, I am convinced Ungman met with those who had Leslie and took her out of the country before law enforcement could intervene."

Trevor paused to gather his thoughts, and said, "Mr Secretary, we must find Leslie and get her back safe. I appeal to you to put pressure on the German government to expose Mr. Ungman and his accomplices and demand they return Leslie unharmed – and, submit to justice."

Trevor pulled an envelope from his inside coat pocket, and replied, "I have here a complete intelligence report; enclosures include appropriate diplomatic protocols and prepared letters for your signature."

George looked at Trevor and smiled, "Ever ready Trevor... just like in the old days."

Trevor smiled and said, "You wouldn't expect anything less from anyone who works for you, would you?"

George shook his head and began perusing Trevor's documents with intent.

Trevor continued, "…and, Sir, of even more importance – as you have just witnessed for yourself – this new exciting capability Gamiel has discovered cannot fall into criminal hands. If it does, it would spell the end of the civilized world as we know it." Trevor paused.

After familiarizing himself with the contents of Trevor's envelope, Secretary (George) Carlson laid the documents on his desk and stirred the ice in his drink as he contemplated his choice of words. Gazing into the T-L-E Doorway that had miraculously admitted Dr. Reuel into his private secure office, he concluded there was no denying the fact that it did work and that this was a history making, epoch defining, possibly earth-shattering discovery. His mind began to race ahead to all of the domestic and international legal complexities involved with regulating such technology. Then he stopped himself as he realized the two men sitting before him already had the power to avoid any regulation whatsoever – if they were of a mind.

Slowly at first, then like water rushing from a broken dam, his mind began to consider the full impact of the T-L-E door falling into the wrong hands. His face went pale.

Trevor knew their message had just sunk home. Seizing the moment, Trevor said, "Sir, we not only have foreign interests collaborating in this insidious plot to steal Gamiel's discovery; there are also Americans either complicit with or at the very least conspiring to use Ungman to get this knowledge for themselves. One of these personalities is none other than Dr. Gilbert Gillespie."

At the mention of Dr. Gillespie, Secretary Carlson's face turned three shades of red as his eyes narrowed. He said, "I am not surprised. I will arrange to speak with the President, today. He may want a demonstration."

Trevor replied, "That can be arranged."

Secretary Carlson reflected upon the gravity of what he had just witnessed, and asked, "What does Gillespie know about this?"

Gamiel replied, "Only that my son and I have discovered a new substance called Trans-Light-Element. Gillespie may suspect more if Ungman told him about his own experience in my laboratory."

Secretary Carlson said, "I would like to arrange for Dr. Gillespie to be called in for questioning – however; such an action must wait until we have Leslie back. I don't want to tip our hand to Ungman that we are on to a member of his spy network. In fact, Gillespie may be able to unwittingly help us find Ungman. I will authorize surveillance and monitoring. Don't worry; Dr. Gillespie's espionage days are numbered."

Gamiel leaned over the desk, and looking directly into the Secretary's eyes, said, "Sir, All I am asking is the cooperation and protection of the United States Government – and for your help getting Leslie back safe. I must have the guarantee in writing from the President, himself, that the Federal Government will leave me free to pursue my research without hindrance. We voluntarily came to you and disclosed critical trade secrets in the interest of protecting the nation from likes of Carl Ungman. I am a loyal citizen, a veteran, and a family man. I love my wife and children with all my heart. Their safety comes before mine. I fear anyone who has anything to do with me may be vulnerable. It is my hope that our mutual cooperation will help secure all of us from a world controlled by power hungry criminals."

Trevor added, "George, you help us find Leslie, we will pop open another door like this wherever she is and whisk her away to safety."

Gamiel stood up and said, "I need to get back. I have pressing matters with my family. Trevor will keep me posted. Good to meet you." Gamiel shook hands and casually walked back through the T-L-E Door disappearing around the corner of the laboratory control room wall.

Seconds later the doorway collapsed on itself and vaporized into thin air as the floating orb reappeared and returned to Secretary Carlson's desk. The whole process took about 25 seconds. In less than a minute, the only evidence anything out of the ordinary had taken place was the orb sitting on the desk.

Trevor shook his friend's hand, and said, "Keep the Orb. It is made of Trans-Light-Element. It will allow us to reach you without being monitored. It detects and prevents unauthorized surveillance."

Reaching into his coat pocket, Trevor produced another object, and said, "Here is a lapel pin like mine. You can talk to me any time with that pin without paying a dime to Ma Bell. Also, if you will take that orb with you, we can open a new doorway wherever you are. George, mark my words, T-L-E will revolutionize the entire world as we know it."

It is said the machines of government move slowly. However, inside desperate circles of influence – decisive actions can move at the speed of light... in this case, Trans-Light.

As soon as Trevor left Secretary Carlson, the Secretary was on the phone with his personal secretary, "Kendi, please cancel all my appointments for today."

"But, Sir, you were scheduled to meet with Ambassador Bosley at 9 am; and with Under Secretary Pierce at 11 for an early lunch. Also, you have a dinner engagement this evening with Director Billings."

"I know, Kendi. Please call all of them and cancel. Tell them I am very sorry, but a matter of extreme national importance has just come up. I will contact them later to reschedule. Thank you. Please send them a personal invitation to the next state dinner at the White House."

The Secretary then picked up his direct line into the Oval Office. He wondered if it were somehow compromised. The ring was short, and the other end picked up before the 2nd ring.

"What do you need, George?"

"Mr. President, I need to speak with you about a most urgent matter."

"You can't tell me about it on this phone?"

"No Sir, this requires my personal presence."

"Very well, George, you know who to call. Get on my calendar."

"Mr. President, this cannot be a scheduled appointment. No one must know I am seeing you."

There was a pause. Time to consider the years of friendship and trust that had motivated the new President of the United States to personally request George Andrew Jackson Carlson to serve in his most trusted and vulnerable capacity in the President's Cabinet. The concept had always included the possibility where President and Secretary must collaborate. The decision fell in favor of the meeting.

"OK, George, lets meet in the rose garden – say 11:15 this morning before lunch. I will be surrounded by Secret Service, so make it look like a chance meeting."

At eleven-o-twelve, Secretary Carlson concluded an item of business with a member of the White House Staff next to the garden terrace door. He remarked, "I think I will take a breath of fresh air in the Rose Garden," and stepped outside. His GPS watch read 11:14:59 when the President rounded the hedge with the words, "Fancy meeting you here George. I need to talk with you about a simple matter. Will you join me in the war room?"

George shook hands with the Commander-in-Chief and together they entered the Oval office garden door passing through a little used entry to 'the war room'.

Once inside, the President motioned his staff and security to leave as he pushed a button that silenced all communications devices either in or out of the room. Taking his reserved seat, he motioned to his Secretary to have the next one nearby.

Once both were seated, the President asked, "We have five minutes. What's up?"

George wasted no time coming to the point. He laid the Trans-Light-Element Orb on the table in front of them and the envelope Trevor had given him. "Read the enclosures, Sir. Then I will explain."

The President had become accustomed to speed reading and while details remained for further study, he grasped the general situation and laid down the contents of the envelope, saying, "We now have three minutes."

George said, "Trevor, if you are listening, open the door."

The President glanced quickly behind him with a start. When no door opened he looked back at George with some concern to see the Trans-Light-Orb circling in the air. In less than twenty seconds another

T-L-E doorway had opened. This time it was from the Denver Laboratory from whence Trevor Nibley stepped into the war room with George and the President.

The President stood up, speechless.

Trevor wasted no time. "Mr. President; I asked George to meet with you to explain the urgency of our concern. Thank you for your time. If you have read the documents, then you can understand that if Carl Ungman or someone like him gets his hands on this capability – your War Room is toast – so is any place in the White House, or any other secure compound this nation depends upon for national security."

The President gaped at the T-L-E Doorway and asked, "What just happened? How did you get in here? Where does that go?"

George put his hand on the President's shoulder and said, "Sir, that is some sort of controlled space/time warp that allows anyone to walk in anywhere. Trevor just demonstrated it in my office this morning. Now you understand why I needed to see you right away."

The President of the United States shook his head in wonder. "How does it work?"

Trevor said, "Sir, unfortunately, we do not have time to explain. We need your permission to use this capability to find Leslie. Furthermore, we need your express permission to continue researching this capability un-harassed by well-intentioned U.S. lawyers and judges."

"We need an emergency Presidential pardon and Proclamation to the owner and inventor and his family so that no one can come in and sue either of them for damages or anything else arising from the development of this new technology. Also, we need yours and the State Department's sanction to go into foreign nations under diplomatic immunity without passports or visas through these doorways. You can hammer out the legal complexities of future commercial applications and trade agreements, etc. all you want – after we first have your guarantee of Federal protection and limited – very limited – government monitoring of our affairs."

Trevor took a deep breath. He knew he was already imposing on the President's time and needed to get out and close the T-L-E door before someone else came in the War Room just to make sure the President was OK. He gulped and said, "Sir, we need your help to find Leslie, because her life could be in mortal danger."

The President was still recovering from shock; but, looked at his long trusted friend and said, "Gentlemen, when do I meet the man who brought this into our world?"

Trevor answered, "As soon as we get Leslie back."

The President pulled out his pen and began signing documents among the enclosures. Secretary Carlson signed his name where needed. Trevor scooped up the documents and said, "Thank you. This will free our hand and speed up Leslie's rescue. George I will be waiting for your report regarding Mr. Ungman and Dr. Gillespie. My friends, welcome to the new world of Trans-Light-Element – our gateway into the 21st Century – and the Universe."

Trevor exited back through the T-L-E door and around the corner of the laboratory control room. Ten seconds later, the T-L-E orb reappeared through the T-L-E door a split second before the door winked out of sight. The pulsating orb quickly spiraled along its original path to settle quietly back in its original spot on the table between the President and the Secretary of State. Both looked at each other in amazement – scarcely able to contain their excitement.

The President said, "George, this is the breakthrough we've all been praying for."

At that moment, a Secret Service Agent opened the door to inspect the room and admit the White House Chief of Staff who said, "Mr. President, your next appointment is waiting for you in the Oval Office."

Chapter 25
A Matter of Time

It was after 4 pm when Ben left Alexi's room with a fist full of papers he had printed to study and show his Dad. He had decided to tell his Dad about the Finnish Detective Club. As he approached the laboratory he noticed his father working on something outside the barn. He stopped to inquire what it was.

Gamiel looked up at his son, and said, "There you are. A lot has happened. Come inside and I will explain."

Ben asked, "What is this?"

Gamiel smiled and replied, "This is a new Trans-Light-Element application device."

"Really?" asked Ben with immediate interest. "What does it do?"

"Let's go inside and find out. We have no time to waste."

"Did we find Leslie?"

"No, but we got more help." Father and son entered the old barn together. Inside, Gamiel continued his remarks. "Trevor and I spoke with the U.S. Secretary of State a couple of hours ago – he has decided to help us find Leslie – and help us put Ungman behind bars where he belongs."

Ben asked, "How can he help?"

Gamiel said, "He is in a position to speak with the President. He also represents the President in matters of State. We hope he can put pressure on the German government to reel in Carl Ungman and his espionage ring."

Ben asked, "How can he help us find Leslie?"

Gamiel continued, "With government cooperation, we can begin doing things with T-L-E that might have been illegal before. Trevor is working that issue right now. As soon as he gets back, I will show you what I mean. Meanwhile, Trevor's team back in Utah made a few more discoveries we can start using today."

Ben said with excitement, "I can't wait to see them!"

Seated safely in the control room, Gamiel fired up the torsion generators and deployed the sensor array. Then he turned on the video screens so the laboratory appeared on the control room walls as if it were windows. Gamiel began commenting as he worked. Ben sat in the 'co-pilot' chair and listened.

"With the help of Trans-Light-Element, we are now able to enhance all our technological devices by simply making them from T-L-E. Electronics, computer chips, static hard drives – all function more efficiently. T-L-E has limitless memory. Not only that, we have observed T-L-E initiate intuitive program code adjustments that speed up all our processes – sort of like your word processor software prompting you when you misspell a word. T-L-E anticipates executable functions and speeds up processing time at a sub-atomic level."

Ben was soaking it in as fast as he could. He asked, "Does this mean T-L-E is really alive – like some kind of plant?"

"It seems to be a medium of pure intelligence."

"Wow."

Gamiel paused, and pushed the play button, saying, "Watch this, Ben. This is what I wanted to show you."

Ben watched the history screens as they re-enacted the sequence of events that took place earlier that day. He saw his father open the T-L-E door and walk through. The scene changed to follow Gamiel into an office Ben had never seen before."

Ben asked, "Where is that?"

"That is the office of the Secretary of State."

Ben's jaw dropped in amazement.

"How did you go there without making another gateway first to lock in the path?"

Gamiel said, "This is what I wanted to explain. Trevor's engineers found a way to use one of the T-L-E orbs to fix the coordinates and open a door. They first pop an extra orb through a one way T-L-E Port. Then, the orb transmits a true four dimensional coordinate fix which allows us to open a new T-L-E door virtually anywhere – within reason. We don't want to go popping in on people unannounced – and we still don't trust this process to open – say a doorway on another planet where our gravitational time reference is not the same."

Ben became excited, as he remembered the papers in his hand. He said, "Dad, this means we can go get Leslie! Look at these papers. I printed them off the internet this morning. Alexi and I have been on all day long scouring for information about Mr. Ungman!"

Gamiel examined the wealth of intelligence Ben showed him about Ungman. He was fascinated. He asked, "How did you find all this? This alone is enough information to convict every one of his people in court! Look! This is Leslie! Someone caught her on camera going into that building with those guys!"

Gamiel's blood felt like it was starting to boil. He asked again, "Tell me how you and Alexi found all this."

Ben said, "Vanessa and I joined their Detective Club."

Gamiel looked up and asked, "You did what?"

"Timo and Niina belong to the Lahti Chapter of the Finnish Detective Club. Alexi and Koira and Vanessa and I joined."

There was a pause. Gamiel's face reflected concern.

Ben gulped, "I was desperate to find Leslie. So I asked if they could help. We got all this stuff from other people who belong to the club all over the country – and in other countries."

Gamiel sat in silence for a moment taking it all in. Then he calmly asked, "What else did you tell them?"

Ben gulped again, "I didn't say anything about T-L-E or Unified Field. I did tell them we came here to get away from Ungman because he was trying to steal your work. They all took an oath to keep it secret."

Gamiel asked, "And what of your oath, Ben? You took an oath not to disclose it. This should have been a matter we discussed together before you took this decision upon yourself."

Ben gulped. He felt trapped between wanting to do the right thing to find Leslie and his relationship with his Dad.

Gamiel continued, "Ben, I know you felt like it was OK because of the trust you have developed in your new friends; but, that was not enough. You have placed a heavy burden on them. With knowledge comes responsibility and sometimes personal danger."

Gamiel allowed this to soak in, then continued, "Now, they could be in mortal danger, Ben. If you don't consult me before taking this kind of action, how can I trust you to help me with my research?"

Ben sat in silence. He said, "I didn't say anything about your work."

Gamiel got up and paced the floor studying the information Ben had placed in his hands. Then he sat down and asked, "When Alexi was surfing the web to get all this, how did he protect his own identity?"

Ben gulped again, and said, "Alexi said they were using discreet cover as students doing research."

Gamiel pondered the implications of thousands of hits on related webpages showing up in the reports of some of the most advanced scientific minds in the world. He envisioned a counter-intelligence surge of hackers learning the identity of the Finnish Detective Club and possibly the names of all their members along with addresses, etc.

Gamiel sat down with his head in his hands. He felt like the entire situation was getting out of hand. Picking up a T-L-E phone from the Control Console, Gamiel said, "Please get me Trevor Nibley."

In an instant, Trevor was on the view screen in front of them, "Yes, Gamiel. What's up?"

"Trevor, we have a new twist developing. It seems a group of bright, intelligent, would be detectives belonging to an international club have joined our search for Leslie without my knowledge. I am going to send you copies of documents Ben just gave me so your security people can analyze and respond. I also need a complete risk evaluation of the danger in which members of this detective club may have placed themselves. Please let me know as soon as possible."

"That's a tall order my friend. Send me the documents and we will put our new T-L-E Intelligence Analysis device to work."

"Your what?"

"It should come as no surprise to you with as many people I have diverted to this project that we are coming up with new applications almost every hour. My intelligence resource analyst developmental group just demonstrated T-L-E's astounding capacity for gathering intelligence – and, analyzing it on the spot."

Gamiel smiled and said, "I see. Well we may need it sooner than we expected. Ben and I will be here when you call back."

Ben was absorbing the comments through layers of guilt mixed with anxiety for Leslie.

Gamiel smiled at his son. He said, "Ben, lets speak of other things for now. However, I cannot be more emphatic when I remind you about the power of an oath and the destruction that comes from breaking it."

Ben nodded.

Gamiel explained, "The device I planted outside in the flower bed by the barn door serves the same function as an orb, only it does not move. It opens a virtual T-L-E doorway – indiscernible to the naked eye. However, at the command of my voice – either standing nearby or via any T-L-E transmission device such as this lapel pin I am going to give you – it becomes a communications device that will transmit video and voice signals through a T-L-E port just as easily as this port we just opened earlier allowed me to walk right into Secretary Carlson's office."

Ben took the lapel pin and studied it. It was clearly made of Trans-Light-Element. He asked, "How does it work?"

Gamiel answered, "It is a two way communicator. It is also a mini-coordinate transmitter which will allow us to open a T-L-E door wherever you are. All you have to do is give it this command – Activate Port. Try it."

Ben said, "Activate Port."

Instantly, the lapel pin began spiraling to a point in the control room where it paused. Gamiel explained, "It is waiting for the signal from a Torsion Generator Array Control Console to begin transmitting fixed coordinates. It won't do so unless I give it the encrypted algorithm I assigned when the pin was forged in Trevor's Trans-Light-Element production foundry this morning."

Ben said, "Wow. Does this pin also let you know where I am at all times?"

Gamiel nodded and continued, "…and, allows me to see you on this screen by the use of the T-L-E transmitter I planted in the garden outside the barn. The way that works is by the voice command – Activate Transmitter. Tell the pin to Deactivate."

Ben said, "Deactivate Port."

The lapel pin returned to Ben's hand.

Gamiel said, "Now say – Activate Transmitter."

Ben did so and immediately, he saw himself sitting next to his Dad on the big screen.

Gamiel said, "Now that you understand how the pin works, tell it to deactivate then put it in your pocket or pin it to your lapel."

Ben did so and put it in his pocket.

Gamiel then said, "Look at the big screen."

Ben looked up and saw Trevor and others working feverishly over a console in some facility he did not recognize. He asked, "Is that a lapel pin on Trevor's shirt just like mine?"

"Yes. The reality is this – it doesn't have to be a lapel pin. It could be a key chain in your pocket or a button on your shirt. It could be anything formed out of Trans-Light-Element; a baseball hat, a pair of shoes, or even your underwear. We decided to use lapel pins because they are easier to carry around a lot of them and hand them out to others. I now have one, as does Trevor – and you will notice everyone surrounding him is wearing one."

Ben smirked and asked, "How can you make underwear out of Trans-Light-Element?"

Gamiel answered, "Very easily. T-L-E can be instructed to take any shape. It is the most comfortable clothing I have ever worn. Trevor brought me a set of T-L-E underwear just this morning. It keeps my body at the right operating temperature and protects me from harm. This shirt is made of T-L-E."

Ben got up to examine the plaid colored shirt his dad was wearing and said, I can't even tell. How does it wear?"

"I can barely tell I have it on. It seems to adjust to my torso size and movements. T-L-E clothes don't have to be washed; they are self-cleaning. This shirt also protects. It is programmed to stop a bullet. So is my underwear. Trevor is bringing my pants next."

Ben laughed, and said, "Unbelievable!"

Gamiel smiled and said, "Son, this is just the beginning. If we were not bothered by the likes of Carl Ungman right now, we would already have men in space wearing T-L-E spacesuits impervious to space junk collisions – suits that transport breathable air, water, and food directly from the planet as needed – suits that also transmit carbon dioxide and other bio waste products back to the planet. Ben, the possibilities are endless. We are just beginning to tap the proverbial tip of the iceberg with Trans-Light-Element!"

Ben watched Trevor on the screen. Trevor paused and picked up his T-L-E phone and called, "Gamiel are you there?"

Gamiel laughed and said, "Turn on your view screen."

Trevor smiled at them through his view screen, "I see you have been spying on us while we worked. Here are the results – they are coming in on the auxiliary screen."

Gamiel flipped another switch so he and Ben could see the information streaming across the screen – images and data almost too fast to discern.

Trevor continued talking, "We are amazed at what a handful of amateur detectives discovered by using brilliant tactics and strategies practiced by professionals for years. There was some exposure to a few young people but not as bad as you might have imagined. My security team is putting together a protection package for the whole group. You will be pleased to note that nothing traces any of this back to Lahti – not even Finland. They covered their tracks very well."

Gamiel breathed a sigh of relief. Ben finally realized why his father was so concerned.

Gamiel said, "When you come through the door this time, you need to stick around. It may be necessary to call in some of these young people and give them a security briefing. I am debating on whether to bring in their parents as well."

Trevor asked, "Gamiel, did someone spill the beans?"

Ben looked down at his feet.

Gamiel simply said, "I will tell you more when you get here. Did the President sign the papers?"

"Yes. We released a diplomatic pouch in both the German and British Ambassadors offices just moments ago. The President was very impressed. He can't wait to meet you."

Gamiel shook his head, and said, "I was afraid of that. He and I don't belong to the same party."

Trevor smiled and nodded his head, saying, "At this point, I wonder if the President himself is thinking of changing parties after what he saw today."

That comment put a bright smile on Gamiel's face. Gamiel asked, "Trevor, when are you coming. We don't have any time to waste."

"Give me fifteen more minutes please, Gamiel. My staff needs more time to position our forces before we pop open the door. If we don't do this right someone could get hurt, including Leslie."

Gamiel continued, "Understood. I need you here for other reasons. We need to go over some of our latest findings before we try sending a whole squad through one of these doors. I also want to get Mark in on a council of war and make sure his people are ready, too. By the way, where is Leslie?"

Trevor was consulting with his Chief Security Director. After a second he faced the screen and said, "I have just been informed they are moving Leslie. She was in a downtown Berlin office building. She is being moved to a taxi which our sources say is now en-route to the airport. I wonder if some of our diplomatic saber rattling has had impact. ...just a second, Gamiel."

Ben and Gamiel watched as Trevor stepped into another room. Gamiel made an adjustment to the monitor and followed Trevor into the private chamber. Gamiel made another adjustment and the conversation became as clear as if they were standing in the same room.

"Mr. Nibley, the German government has demanded Carl Ungman return the girl. Our sources say Ungman may be putting on the appearance of compliance but really plans to move her out of the country and claim ignorance."

Trevor said, "Where are our teams now. Can they get to her?"

"Not without risking harm to the girl. We are following in cooperation with local police."

Trevor nodded and said, "Alright. Keep me informed."

Trevor left the chamber and headed to the Torsion Generator Array where a new T-L-E Port was being opened. He spoke out loud, "OK, Gamiel, if you were following, I am sure you know as much as I do right now. I need to head to the men's room, then grab a quick bite to eat before I join you. I am turning off my lapel pin now. Deactivate."

The view screen went blank. Gamiel turned off the video. Both sat in silence contemplating Leslie's feelings.

Ben asked, "Dad, what is keeping us from opening our own doorway right into the taxi and pulling Leslie back here?"

"A moving vehicle."

"I don't understand?"

"We can monitor and keep up with moving vehicles, but we don't have this science perfected and refined enough to move human beings between moving vehicles relative to the earth's surface. That includes popping up to the Space Station – as well as over to another planetary body such as the moon. It all has to do with a single gravitation center. Objects at rest on the earth share the same simultaneous gravitational center. Objects in motion have different epoch events – in short – simultaneity does not exist between masses of independent inertia."

Ben felt lost again. He asked, "What does all that mean?"

Gamiel smiled and apologized. "I am sorry, let's get a few things in order while I explain."

Father and son set about cleaning up and closing down the control room. As they did, Gamiel talked. "To put it another way, if I weigh 200 lbs. and move around in my own rhythm while you weigh 140 lbs.

and move about in your own rhythm – the chances of you and I ever moving in the same direction at the same rate of speed in the same rhythm are practically zero. We are completely out of sync. We have the same chance of snatching Leslie from a speeding automobile – much less an aircraft in flight. We have to catch her when she is walking in a clear area – perhaps on the tarmac between the taxi and the aircraft."

"That could be any minute now."

"Yes, but we are not prepared. We have to watch for such an opportunity. It will be when the aircraft lands."

They carried the copies of diplomatic documents Trevor had transmitted to the table in the middle of the laboratory and sat down to go through them together – each signature block in original digitally T-L-E enhanced clarity.

Gamiel examined them and exclaimed, "The President gave me authority to carry out my experiments without delay with NO Federal intervention whatsoever!?!"

Ben asked, "What does that mean we can do?"

Gamiel did not answer right away, but continued to peruse other documents, pausing to exclaim, "Look at this – we have diplomatic immunity to open a door anywhere on or off the planet we choose! Wow! Son, we are in business now!"

They both continued to study each document – including the demands by the United States to Germany and Great Britain that Carl Ungman release his captive hostage immediately to authorities.

Ben was a little overwhelmed by all the legal templates and diplomatic protocol involved in the packages submitted. He was impressed with the broad sweeping liberties his father had been granted to carry out Trans-Light-Element research.

Gamiel looked up at his son, and said, "To answer your question; we can do anything a normal citizen can do with full diplomatic immunity in any country – provided we don't do anything really stupid – like sneak into a bank vault with our little magic door and steal things that don't belong to us. I have a feeling that if we ever started misusing this gift our God has given us, He would take it away from us – in a heartbeat. Do you understand?"

Ben nodded and asked, "Dad, have you found your watch?"

"No, why?"

"The Detective Club investigated – asking every member of the house staff about the watch. Not a one of them had ever even seen it. Something else; did you say you had not removed the watch in over a week?

"That's right. I just got too busy."

Ben said, "So you never removed it after I pulled you from the vortex until you were riding in the limo?"

"Yes."

"Then you took it off because it started irritating your skin? Can you tell me what that irritation felt like?

Gamiel thought a minute, then he said, "It was more than an itch. It was actually painful."

Ben felt a strange excitement as he started connecting the evidence. He said, "I was thinking of the orbs that pass through T-L-E doors and disappear – only to return again when the door is closed. Did you ever have your watch examined after you came back through the vortex that first time?"

"No. I never thought about it. Everything was happening too quickly."

Gamiel stood up, suddenly understanding his son's line of questioning. As he did so, he felt a little strange and weak. He said, "Why was it irritating? Where did it go? What happened to it when was drawn into the vortex? Did it become Trans-Light-Element, too?"

Gamiel began to feel heavy mental and physical stress, but he forced himself to think. Then he added, "What if my watch was changed? What if it somehow became Trans-Light-Element? If so, what did that mean? Is it possible my watch is wherever those orbs go when the doors are opened?"

Ben asked, "Dad, I know this may sound a little weird, but what happened to you when you went through that vortex. You were just as exposed to Unified Field as your watch. Have you seen a doctor since then?"

At that moment, Ben noticed a strange glow around his father. Ben stood up and asked, "Dad, look in the mirror! Are you OK?"

Gamiel looked and said, "No. Something isn't right. Hurry out to the garden and bring me that transmitter I buried out there. It will only answer to my voice command. If I go out I will be seen like this. And if I start moving towards it, who knows what will happen. I think something is sending a sympathetic signal to that transmitter and opening a virtual transmission channel to my T-L-E clothes. I am going to start taking them off while you get the transmitter."

Ben said, "But, Dad, where is it? What if something happens before I get back with it?"

"Just do it. Hurry!"

Ben rushed out to find the transmitter. Where was it? He dug and dug and finally found it, another orb.

He ran back inside just as Gamiel was putting on other clothes. His body stopped glowing, but the transmitter was humming.

Ben asked, "What do you think was going on?

Gamiel sat down to think. Then he said, "My watch."

Ben said, "Huh?"

Gamiel said, "My watch. It must have been changed to T-L-E. It must be getting a signal from my clothing, wherever it is, and replying back – my T-L-E clothes and my watch are communicating… at least while I am wearing them. I wonder…"

Gamiel struck his thoughtful pose, hand under his chin, and began taking notes.

Ben was worried, and asked, "What if this transmitter tries to send you somewhere – wherever the watch is? What if the watch is somewhere outside earth's current position – what if it went back into the place where the earth was when the vortex took you the first time?"

Gamiel said, "I don't think the watch is outside the earth's gravitational field. I am not even sure it is in another time – just perhaps sitting out of sync with our view. I don't know Ben. We are just guessing on this. I need more time to work with Trevor and make solid findings. If my watch became T-L-E; it probably returned to the relative time phase in which it was reformed. Something must have triggered a change. We need to try to understand; find it and reset it."

"I thought you did reset it?"

"I did, mechanically; – electrically, it may have developed a new space time reference." Gamiel shrugged and said, "There are too many variables to say right now."

Ben went over to his Dad and gave him the transmitter... and said, "Until we know for sure where it is – shouldn't we turn this off."

Gamiel said, "Transmitter Deactivate."

The humming stopped.

Gamiel looked over at his T-L-E clothes. His old clothes felt so uncomfortable after getting used to the new intelligent clothing.

Ben watched his father with grave concern – taking care to observe his every feature. He thought what he had noticed before was just his imagination – but now, in the light of what they had just discussed – Gamiel Ben Reuel's physical body seemed to be somehow different – his eyes, even his hair seemed to reflect the same translucent properties of Trans-Light-Element.

Chapter 26
Where is Gamiel?

Both Reuel and Leppänen families were gathered in the Laboratory in the middle of the big old barn; along with the entire Security Staff. Despite the size of the barn, it was filled to capacity. Timo and his sister, Niina, together with other local members of the Lahti Detective Club were also assembled.

Trevor had transported chairs through the T-L-E port for everyone. They were made from Trans-Light-Element and designed to conform to the shape and size of the occupant. Ben could not remember sitting in a more comfortable chair.

Trevor stood before the entire group, briefing them upon the security risks and responsibilities of knowing about Trans-Light-Element and Unified Field. Even Joseph was there, sitting next to his mother and sister. Ben noticed Kaila Leppänen seemed to be most disturbed by what she was hearing. Mark was trying to comfort her – but it wasn't taking. It was too much too fast.

Trevor stopped and looked at Kaila – and spoke in Finnish.

Ben wondered what he said; wishing he fully understood the Finnish language. Whatever it was, he noticed her countenance relax – and felt his own heart burn within him. He felt Trevor was speaking words of truth.

Ben turned his view to his own father and mother. They seemed such a happy endearing couple. Their happiness and strength gave him confidence to face an uncertain future. He watched his dad's features closely. They seemed normal now; yet, somehow – like Trans-Light-Element. He made a mental note to talk to Mother. Ben turned his attention back to Trevor as he began to speak English again. Ben wondered why at that moment Trevor had been watching Ben curiously.

Looking at the group, Trevor said, "The important thing to remember – is this; don't talk about it – even between yourselves. If you do, someone sometime will hear you. Keep it to yourself. If you want to learn more about it – come to the lab and visit with Gamiel." Trevor paused, then added, looking straight at Ben, "… or Ben."

Ben blushed.

Trevor added, "From now on, you will see many new things made of T-L-E, and, many new capabilities never before imagined possible. We need your help to protect it."

Alexi raised his hand, and asked, "What can we do to help?"

Trevor smiled and said, "I am glad you asked." Then he began passing out lapel pins to everyone, saying, "Wear these, or keep them in your pockets. They will monitor your surroundings and transmit to this laboratory via T-L-E sub-transmission side-bands. It will enable whoever is sitting in that ops control room to see you wherever you are."

"Wow!" said young Joseph. "That is way cool."

Ben noticed his little brother had been picking up some new phrases from his new friends in the treatment center.

Mark stood beside Trevor and spoke. "I want to also speak on behalf of the Finnish government. Diplomatic agreements have already been drawn up between our country and the United States. T-L-E is now an official Finnish Government Secret as well.

We must not speak of it outside this barn. To anyone else, or to anyone sitting here now – after we go outside, it simply does not exist. Do we understand?

Heads nodded in agreement.

Gamiel stood up, and spoke. "I am sorry we have to take such precautions. However, we live in a dangerous time in history. Until we have secured our bases and understand exactly how T-L-E and Unified Field theory really works – we must proceed with caution."

Gamiel gestured towards Trevor, and continued, "Trevor and his research team back in Ogden, Utah, have prepared a little demonstration. We will walk through a Trans-Light-Element Unified Field Door Way to first visit my laboratory in Denver, Colorado. Then, we will take a quick tour of Nibley Enterprises Laboratories. After that, we will all walk right into the Great Hall in the Leppänen mansion. We will do this in about twenty minutes passing through three different T-L-E doorways. Trevor, you have the stand."

Trevor motioned everyone to stand. As they did so, an orb appeared from nowhere – suspended in space for a moment. Almost immediately, a round port the size of a bus appeared just in front of where the orb had been suspended. The orb itself disappeared – but the new opening into Gamiel's home laboratory remained open and inviting.

Trevor said, "Please, everyone, follow Dr. Reuel. It is just like a door into another room – perfectly safe. That is how I got here. This will become our new way to travel. I just hope we all don't get too lazy and get out of shape."

Everyone laughed as they walked into the 'next room' literally thousands of miles away through a curious round doorway that seemed to appear out of thin air. Trevor walked through last. As he did so, the door winked out of sight.

Everyone gasped except Trevor and Gamiel who had planned this down to the second. Trevor continued, "Follow Dr. Reuel as he shows you where he first opened the door into Unified Field and with the help of his brilliant son – Benjamin, went on to discover Trans-Light-Element."

The group walked around the laboratory, in and out of the control center, pausing in front of 'the wall' to listen as Ben described what it was like to pull his father out of the vortex.

Trevor said, "I am sorry we don't have time to linger. Follow me now as we take a short walk over to Nibley Laboratories in Utah."

At that instant, another orb appeared just like the last only to be swallowed up at the opening of the second door way to Nibley Laboratories. The entire group followed Gamiel and Trevor without hesitation into 'another room' hundreds of miles to the west next to the shores of the Great Salt Lake.

Trevor said, "Ladies and Gentlemen, welcome to Nibley Enterprises. Here we do everything from the mundane to the outrageous. The facility you are now seeing was just finished yesterday – built entirely out of Trans-Light-Element using Dr. Reuel's patented Unified Field process. This is where we made those cool chairs you were sitting in."

Trevor gestured to large plate-glass windows and said, "You ladies will like this. Here we are beginning to develop the latest Trans-Light-Element Textiles; smart clothing for the smart woman looking for the perfect fit. These are clothes that truly one size fits anyone because Trans-Light-Element not only adjusts to fit you, it will adjust to any cut, trim, or color you specify verbally. It also protects the body from heat, cold, and get this – it stops knives, bullets, and even protects you from collisions – setting up some kind of force field not only around the part of your body that appears to be covered – but your entire body is protected in an invisible force field. When you wear Trans-Light-Element clothes, they self-clean continuously, change color and styles at your command, and protect you from harm."

There were oohs and awes amongst excited conversation. Ben was impressed. He had not realized how far Nibley Enterprises had carried on their fast paced research while he and his father had been hiding from world. Ben looked forward to getting back into the laboratory with his Dad like they used to.

At this point, an employee rolled a large cart into the area and began handing out coats to each guest. Trevor explained, "These are gifts from Dr. Reuel. He had these made special for each of you. They are Trans-Light-Element coats. They will keep you warm no matter how cold it gets; and – will also keep you cool, no matter how hot it gets. In addition, your coat will protect you from falls, collisions, bullets, knives, and explosions. It will also change to whatever size and shape you desire. Just tell it. It will assume the look of a sports coat or a parka. Tell it what color you prefer, what tint or shade, dark or bright according to your desire. What is more, each coat knows you, the owner – your weight, your height, your size – as well as your name. It also knows your heart rate, your blood pressure, etc. Your coat will not work for anyone but you. Try putting on your neighbor's coat."

Everyone tried. Ben was tickled as he watched the coats slip out of the hands of those who did not own them; but, when the true owner picked up his own coat, it seemed to put itself on almost without effort.

Everyone put on their coats; each experimented with instructions about fit, color, and style. Gamiel even put on a coat that was made for him as did Rachel, Vanessa, and Joseph. Ben was excited. Finally their hard work and worry was paying off in a big way.

Trevor looked at his watch, and whispered into a lab-tech's ear who left quickly through a side door. Trevor spoke to the tour group, "Ladies and gentlemen, if you please; follow me."

The Reuel Family and their Finnish tour group left the research laboratory wearing their new 'comfort coats' following Trevor into a large room. Ben could hardly tell he was wearing a coat. It did not bind or bulk; it was almost as if he were not wearing a coat, at all.

The new spacious room was more like a sports stadium; featuring a geodesic dome roof that covered an open space large enough to enclose a football field. The lab-tech reappeared from another side door and gave a sign to Trevor. He then left the same way he came as Trevor stopped in the middle of the room to turn and speak to his guests.

"This is a special room. Constructed entirely of Trans-Light-Element; rooms like this will soon appear all over the country – indeed all over the world. You now think of airports as places where we come can and go – ports of entry from places all over face of this planet. Well, this is a Unified Field Trans-Light-Element Port; or, 'Uni-Trans-Port' – UTP for short."

Trevor looked at Gamiel and said, "Gamiel, would you mind explaining how your new Trans-Light-Element Space Port works? This room is built according to your specifications."

Gamiel began to explain, "Unified Field is a theory that holds all energy fields in the known universe are really a part of each other; Electromagnetic, Nuclear, and Gravitational fields actually inter-react as one with ebbs and flows, checks and balances between each. Whenever we do something with one energy field, we unknowingly affect the other two in ways heretofore un-measured – so we have not been able to discern the impact."

Gamiel licked his lips, and continued, "To put all this into terms you can clearly see and understand – think of the air molecules we breathe in this room. They are made up of oxygen, carbon-dioxide, nitrogen, argon, and several other trace elements. They also carry dust particles consisting of escaped fragments from our clothes, skin cells, particles from construction materials, fine silicon from the dirt outside that blew in when a door was open, etc. These trace elements and particles affect you and me differently."

Gamiel sneezed, and everyone laughed. He continued, "Some of us may be allergic to one of these particle types. In every case – every molecule is obeying the law of gravity, the law of electromagnetic fields, and nuclear fields within each."

Gamiel pointed to the roof, and said, "This entire building is made of Trans-Light-Element; a new substance formed out of the effect of a Unified Field Vortex upon the elements that surround us. There is no dust in this room except what we brought with us on our clothes or in our hair. Trans-Light-Element monitors sample and control this air supply at recommended ratios and air pressure. The walls do not emit gasses and do not fragment into molecular or dust particles. In short, the new substance formed from the old is contained within a Unified Force Field. The material is somehow intelligent in that it can store digital information within its sub-atomic frame work and communicate that information across a type of sub-space-time network no longer bound by gravitational time references as we know it. How does all this work? Allow me to simply demonstrate."

Gamiel looked at Trevor and asked, "Is that lab-tech ready?"

Trevor nodded.

Gamiel snapped his fingers – and, immediately there appeared a Trans-Light-Element orb in front of him. It floated ten feet away from the group where instantly appeared another T-L-E doorway – large enough to drive a jet through it. Gamiel spoke over the excited comments of his family and friends, "This is a space port. It will take you back home, or to Helsinki or anywhere on the earth you wish. It will also take you to the Space Station." He paused for affect as everyone – except Ben – gasped. Then he continued.

"It will also take you to the moon." There was stunned silence as Gamiel continued.

"It will also take you to Mars, or any place in deep space to any star system we know about. The problem we are working to solve now is one of pure mathematics – and, time. We will not go to Mars today – even though we could make space suits and space habitats that would protect you and give you plenty of oxygen. What we are not yet certain about is the synchronized time insertion and departure points. While we may go, we might never return to this space time continuum. You cannot accept that risk and I certainly cannot – and therefore will not risk it."

Gamiel looked at his wife, and said, "I once took a short journey into this vortex before it was stabilized. It was not fun. Were it not for Ben, I would not be here to tell you about it."

Everyone looked at Ben, remembering his account in Colorado about how he saved his dad.

Gamiel continued, "This is the model for future spaceports we can build anywhere on the face of this planet. It is secret for now. Someday, it will be common knowledge in a society mature enough to responsibly use this knowledge."

Gamiel held out his hand and asked, "May I have a glass of water?"

There appeared in his hand a glass full of water, as if some unseen hand had simply given it to him. He took a sip, and said, "Thank you!" Then, he gave it back to the unseen hand as the audience watched it disappear again.

Gamiel explained, "In addition to this large port, Trans-Light-Element is capable of very small ports especially in a facility like Mr. Nibley's. Someone actually just handed me a glass of water through one of these mini-ports."

Gamiel looked at Joseph and smiled as he continued, "We have also been using microscopic-port technology to assist medical practice to cure patients of heretofore incurable diseases."

Joseph nodded and said, "That is what is helping me get well."

The group smiled with sounds of awe and approval.

Gamiel continued, "This space port allows us to now move about the planet with relative ease and comfort at very low risk because this earth is contained within the same gravitational time reference. Without going into a lot of physics, let me simply state time is a function of gravity. It speeds up or slows down depending on our relative speed and distance from our common gravitational reference at the center of the earth."

Gamiel paused to let that soak in before continuing, "Other planetary bodies have gravitational time reference standards we have not yet determined. For this reason, for now, we need to restrict our T-L-E travel to this planet's gravitational reference. This includes the Moon as well as the Space Station."

The tour group clapped energetically.

Gamiel turned the time back over to Trevor.

Trevor smiled and said, now – we are going to demonstrate this large doorway and show you a view of Mark's home. Suddenly before them appeared the Leppänen family estate. Everyone felt as if they could simply walk back home.

Trevor said, "Before we return to the Finland, we have prepared one last demonstration."

There suddenly appeared a large bus through an unseen T-L-E port. Trevor motioned everyone to get on the bus. After they were seated, he explained, "This is no ordinary bus. This conveyance is made entirely of Trans-Light-Element. It is, in many respects, a time capsule as well as a space ship. It will shield you from the effects of any force outside. It has no wheels and no engine – and no driver." There was a gasp.

Trevor continued, "Think of a train propelled by magnetic fields through an underground tube. This bus is propelled through a Unified Field controlled by Trans-Light-Element devices engineered into the infrastructure of this space port. We will now demonstrate the use of the large portal in front of us."

The scene on the other side of the portal changed to the surface of the moon. Gamiel leaned over to Trevor and asked, "Are your tests conclusive? Should we expect any problems with this?"

Ben who was sitting closest to Trevor overheard his quietly whispered answer, "We have been to the Moon and the Space Station several times in the past two days. This is about as easy as it will ever get."

Gamiel turned and asked, "If there is anyone here who feels uncomfortable, you can disembark if you wish. We are about to go to the moon and back."

Some gasped. No one got off.

Gamiel turned to Trevor and said, "Please proceed."

The bus suddenly moved soundlessly and swiftly through the Trans-Light-Element Space Port and rested on the surface of the moon.

Trevor spoke clearly for all to hear, "Notice you are still breathing normal air at normal cabin pressure. Also notice you are not weightless. Trans-Light-Element generates a gravitational field using the principles of Unified Field. Also, the coats we gave you a moment ago will become spacesuits should the atmospheric pressure drop below safe levels. Ladies and gentlemen, you are among the first people to visit the surface of the moon since 1978. Unfortunately, for the time being, you cannot brag about it to your friends and family members. For now, please keep this to yourselves."

Ben asked, "So, if we opened that door, these coats will provide oxygen and warmth as well as air pressure?"

Trevor said, "Yes, we have already tested them. Our lab-techs have been back and forth to this spot several times."

There was a sigh of relief among most.

Gamiel said, "The purpose of this demonstration is to help you understand the magnitude of Unified Field and Trans-Light-Element; to understand why it is such an important secret right now – to imagine what it would be like if the wrong people gained control of this technology."

Somber silence filled the bus.

Trevor's new Trans-Light-Element cell phone rang. He answered, "Yes?"

All ears listened as Trevor said, "OK, bring us back immediately."

The bus lifted from the moon and moved swiftly over the surface suddenly appearing in the Space Port at Nibley Laboratories again settling softly on the floor. Ben noticed he could not detect any feelings of motion even though his visual reference indicated they were traveling very fast. He could not feel the stopping motion either; proof that Trans-Light-Element was using Unified Field to alter the gravitational forces upon their bodies such that their ride was quiet and comfortable.

Passengers filed out of the bus. Ben was talking with Trevor, and asked, "Mr. Nibley, was that phone call news about Leslie? Trevor said, "Yes it was; her plane is landing at a secluded airport in Algiers. We must move quickly to rescue her while she is walking on the tarmac. Gamiel, we will need..." Trevor's voice drifted into disturbed silence.

Ben turned to look at his father – but could not see him. The last of the tour group left the bus as Ben ran back inside expecting to see him waiting politely for his guests to disembark. No one was there. In mounting desperation, Ben called out, "Dad, where are you?"

Chapter 27
Miraculous Rescue

Mrs. Reuel looked up to watch her children milling aimlessly about the office where she was talking to Nibley Security. She checked her watch. It had been an hour since Gamiel's mysterious disappearance. The security team had searched the entire complex. It was incredible. Gamiel had been there one instant – and the next he was nowhere.

Most of the tour group had returned to Finland – except for Mark. He refused to go home until they found Gamiel. He was standing next to Detective Grand, who had been invited to witness Leslie's rescue and help find Gamiel. Trevor was absent. He was personally leading the ops team assigned to rescue Leslie.

Rachel was talking to Detective Grand, who was asking a lot of questions. She said, "I saw him as we left the moon's surface. I know I did. I got off the bus with the Leppänen family thinking he had left before me."

Detective Grand simply shook his head in utter amazement. Despite the fact he himself had just stepped through a T-L-E door into this complex, he still found it hard to believe Mrs. Reuel and her children had just returned from the moon. He asked, "Did you see him inside the spaceport?"

"No. I don't ever remember seeing him after we re-appeared in the spaceport. It all happened so quickly. One second he was there, and the next..." Her voice trailed off in despair. She wondered if she would ever see her beloved husband again.

Ben was staring into space out the large office window. From their location just West of East Skyline Drive and Highway 89, Ben could see the air traffic departures at Hill Air Force Base to the south west of his current position. He wondered what the Air Force would think if they knew about Trans-Light-Element. His mind was drifting in and out of emotional shock.

Vanessa was talking with Joseph.

Joseph looked up at his big sister and asked, "But, where did Daddy go?"

Vanessa looked troubled, then changed her countenance to reflect a false cherry temperament to say – "Daddy is OK. He will be back very soon. He just went through a T-L-E door without telling anyone."

"Why did he do that?"

Vanessa answered truthfully, "I don't know."

Ben was half listening to the conversation, half thinking to himself... "Dad was wearing that T-L-E Coat. When we came back through the T-L-E port from the Moon, his watch must have locked on to his coordinates and diverted him ... But, where?"

His mind racing to stay abreast of everything that was happening, Ben also monitored the huge T-L-E observation screen that covered the entire East wall of the Operations Center. A jet was just landing at what must be the airport in Algiers. Ben felt he was supposed to be there, but now, with his father gone, he did not know where he was supposed to be.

Ben left Joseph and Vanessa talking and went over to the console where the Security Operations Officer was controlling the coordinated rescue. He could hear Trevor's voice on the speaker.

"Jack, our Swat Team is in place. Launch the orb through the portal on my command and wait to open the doors."

The T-L-E screen showed the tarmac in Algiers where Leslie's captors had just landed. It almost felt like they were standing there.

"Launch Orb."

Ben watched in fascination as an arrow flashed on-screen pointing to the location where an orb appeared from nowhere undetected behind the aircraft that had just parked. Suddenly from behind the parked plane through an invisible T-L-E port, Ben saw a ladder car emerge looking just like the one that was barely exiting the hanger a half-mile away. The driver rolled up and secured the mobile staircase to the aircraft passenger door. The door opened and passengers started down the ladder.

Ben heard the Operations Officer comment, "Trevor, the ladder is in place and the passengers are disembarking. Target is spotted."

"That's good Jack, wait until Leslie is on the Tarmac to open all the doors.

Once Leslie was walking on flat ground, several T-L-E doors opened at once all around the captors – one right next to Leslie. From the perspective of the people on the ground, they were suddenly surrounded by armored personnel carriers emerging out of nowhere. Ben noticed they did not have any wheels. He deduced these were made of T-L-E. Without so much as a struggle, Leslie suddenly vanished. Ben knew someone had reached through an invisible T-L-E doorway and snatched her from her captors.

The whole thing was over in seconds. Everyone else on the ground was encased in a T-L-E force field and loaded into the armored personnel carriers. Ben suddenly recognized Trevor leading a group of armed men wearing T-L-E uniforms as they rushed up the stairs into the jet. In minutes everyone on the plane was removed, placed in T-L-E containment fields, and loaded in the personnel carriers. In another instant all the vehicles including the ladder car drove through their invisible T-L-E ports and vanished from site.

Then Ben watched as the jet itself was taxied by a pilot on the Nibley Security Team through another invisible T-L-E portal the size of a hanger door and vanished from sight! The people from the airport hangar were only half way to the parking site when they noticed everyone and everything including the full-sized passenger jet that had just landed – had simply disappeared. They scratched their heads in fear and wonder – and made a hasty retreat to the hanger.

Meanwhile, the monitor screen showed the original orb leaving the area then switched scenes to armored personnel carriers arriving back at the Nibley Security Complex in Ogden, Utah. Ben was amazed as the jet that had just taxied into a T-L-E port in Algiers suddenly appeared behind the returning personnel carriers inside the very space port they had just used to go to the moon. By now, Mrs. Reuel, Vanessa, and Joseph had joined Ben to watch the history making events unfold before their eyes. Gamiel Ben Reuel's discovery that had put the family at such peril was now the means of rescuing their dear friend, Leslie, and capturing the bad guys.

The whole thing was not lost on Detective Grand who stood in utter amazement – even admiration. He sensed the world and the business of law enforcement had suddenly changed. Only time would tell how men used this newly discovered power. A new fear burdened an already heavy heart. "What would happen if bad men got control of this?" "What will keep the good guys from going bad?"

Suddenly, Leslie appeared in the control center where the Reuel family greeted her with great joy. Ben stood by trembling with emotion. Tears flowed freely. Ben and Leslie hugged each other with renewed gratitude.

Ben asked, "Did they hurt you?"

Leslie said, "Only once when I tried to get away. I am OK. They didn't do anything to me. I am not sure what happened. Everything was changing so fast. One minute, I was walking outside at some strange airport – and the next thing I knew, this guy dressed in the strangest looking uniform I ever saw was escorting me down this long white corridor – and here I am."

The family turned to watch the big screen as Trevor stepped out of the captured plane and walked down the stairs to go through a door close by.

Within minutes, Trevor entered the room where they now stood. Mark and Detective Grand joined Trevor as they walked quickly to where Leslie was visiting with the Reuels.

Ben looked at Trevor and exclaimed, "That was amazing!"

Trevor replied, "Even with the best equipment and T-L-E, it still could never happen without these people sitting in this operations center – and a bunch of special guys you didn't see driving the cars and operating the new T-L-E doors."

Trevor looked at Leslie and asked, "Are you OK, Leslie?"

"Yes, thanks to you. That was a wild ride."

"We are so glad you are back safe, young lady. You must know it took a Presidential Executive Order to rescue you. Now, if you are feeling well enough, your mother should be arriving any minute."

~ 265 ~

Everyone turned to look at the T-L-E observation screen as a new scene appeared near the Capitol Building in Washington, D.C. The scene followed FBI Agents as they escorted Senator Richards from the Capitol Grounds into a Nibley Security Services limousine.

The limo moved quickly down the main streets suddenly turning into a back alley to drive through an invisible T-L-E portal. The scene shifted as the limo suddenly appeared out the other side next to the captured aircraft inside the new Spaceport. The driver pulled the limo past the personnel carriers and stopped next to the doors leading to their room.

Leslie looked on with astonishment, then looked at Ben as Ben smiled back at her.

Ben said, "Watch that door."

Leslie gazed at the door Ben indicated. In another minute, Senator Richards came through the door looking anxiously around; spotting her daughter, Denise ran to embrace her.

The End

Don't miss the next Trans-Light-Element episode entitled:

The Search for Gamiel